A Vintage of Regret

THE SECRETS OF STONE BRIDGE
BOOK ONE

JEN TALTY

Book Description

Wine isn't the only thing aging in Stone Bridge—secrets are, too.

After nearly a decade of chasing adventure across the globe, Riley Callahan never expected to return to Stone Bridge, California. But when her father dies under suspicious circumstances, she has no choice but to face the ghosts of her past—both the family she left behind and the man who broke her heart.

Her homecoming is anything but welcoming. Tension with her siblings runs high, old wounds refuse to heal, and the town she once longed to escape still holds its secrets close. None more so than Bryson Boone, the boy she once loved who is now the successful owner of Stone Bridge Winery. He's built a life rooted deep in the land she abandoned—one that's now tangled in the mystery of her father's death.

As Riley searches for answers, she unearths long-buried truths about her family and the town itself, uncovering a past darker than she ever imagined. And the more she digs, the clearer it becomes—someone doesn't want her to find the truth.

With danger closing in and old passions reigniting, Riley must decide if she's still the girl who runs... or if it's finally time to stand her ground, fight for the truth, and maybe even risk her heart.

For Kris Norris. Thanks for always listening. For Chris Allen-Riley. Thanks for helping with cowbell!

A special shout out to Bradley Brown, the founder and owner of Big Basin Vineyard in Santa Cruz, California. I can't thank you enough for answering all my crazy writerly questions.

One

The morning mist still clung to the vines like a secret not ready to be told.

Tendrils of fog snaked toward Bryson Boone as he stepped off the ATV and walked the last few yards into the rows of Syrah grapes, boots crunching softly over the dewy ground, a cold cup of coffee in one hand. In his haste to hurry out the door, he hadn't bothered to pour it into one of those fancy mugs that kept it hot. In the other hand, his cell with the pruning schedule open. He scanned the trellises with a practiced eye. It was early, but this morning seemed quieter than usual.

The vineyard was never loud, not really, but there was usually a hum. Birds rustling. Clippers snipping. Maybe a low whistle from Sean, always a tune Bryson couldn't name. Today, there was nothing. Just the mist and the smell of dirt and growing things. Bryson swiped the screen on his cell, pulling up the text from Sean, making sure he'd gotten the time right. Perhaps Sean had overslept. It wasn't like Sean to be late, but it happened.

Bryson took a moment, like he always did, to soak in the morning. To soak in his family's growing legacy. His grandfather had started this winery on a whim and a dream. It hadn't been much back then. His granddad had barely gotten the vines to take root, but it was a start. It had been his father who turned it into a business.

And now, it was Bryson's turn to make it into a household name. He was still working on that. So many things had changed in the wine-making business. Seltzers, low-calorie wines, and his all-time favorite peeve... all-natural wines, which were utter nonsense. His father had worked hard to create a fully organic vineyard, and in today's world, most people didn't understand what that meant, and Bryson had grown tired of explaining it.

Though, his generation barely kicked back and enjoyed a good glass of vino these days. It was all about these damn vodka-infused drinks. Or even wine in a can. Made it nearly impossible for him to grow because he couldn't compete with the big names, and he honestly didn't want to.

Sure, he wanted to stand out—be seen over the clutter. But no way in hell would he ever become a mass-produced factory. He liked to feel the earth under his feet. Smell the flavors in the air as the grapes ripened in anticipation of each harvest. It had been his dream since he'd sat on his father's shoulders when he'd been a child and stared over the vineyard at the beauty of it all.

He scanned the rows of vines as the sun peeked over the horizon. He'd always loved the mornings. Full of promise, the dawning of a new day had always drawn him outside. There'd only been one time in his life when his early sunrise routine had been tainted.

He sighed as old memories crept into his brain. When they'd been little, he and Riley would race through this very patch of land, giggling, chasing each other, until they were breathless. When they'd become teenagers, they'd come out here for stolen kisses.

And then she'd walked away... taking a piece of him with her.

But that seemed like a lifetime ago. A haunting tale he couldn't forget—but didn't want to remember. For the last twelve years, no matter how hard he tried to shake her from his daily thoughts, he couldn't. And today was no different. She was a quiet, yet constant thought. Someone he could never regret, yet he regretted everything about how things ended.

However, there wasn't a damn thing he could do about it. He'd tried to move on with his life, but he'd failed miserably.

This winery—this town—was a living tribute to what he'd lost—and what he'd never find again. Though he tried not to dwell on the past, seeing Sean every day made it impossible to banish it from his mind entirely.

It wasn't odd that her father had retired from his long-standing career as an electrician for the local power company one day, and the next, he'd come knocking on Bryson's door in search of a job. Sean had grown up around the vines—worked them as a teenager. And Bryson had learned a lot from the man. From a young age, Bryson had always looked up to him and even though Sean worked for Bryson, the older man had been a mentor, a close friend, and a father figure. Even when Riley had taken off and broken Bryson's heart.

Though, Bryson had to take some ownership of that heartache. It hadn't all been her fault. Nor had it been all his.

He tucked away those thoughts in that box, like he did every day, and moved on about the business of living. Or maybe it was existing. What else could he do? Riley was gone. A faint murmur of regret whispered through the vines.

He stuffed his cell in his pocket, as well as his memories, and went looking for Sean. He had no idea what the man wanted to discuss, but whatever it was, it seemed important.

Sean was a reliable man. Solid. The kind of man who worked hard, made everyone laugh, and always had a story in his back pocket. The kind you were lucky to have on your crew. For eight years, he'd walked these rows like he owned the place—not with ego, but with care. However, something had changed in him during the last couple of months. He'd grown distant and almost secretive. That bothered Bryson, and he wanted to make sure the old man was okay. Things in the Callahan family were always a little bit off. Not Riley, or Sean—but the rest of them—well, years of history had taught Bryson to keep his distance.

Back then, Bryson had been too young—too immature —to put a finger on it. Hell, he still didn't know exactly what it was. But he did have a better understanding of the dynamics. He knew that Elizabeth, Riley's mother, had always wanted more.

More money. More respect. More everything. Certainly, more than Sean's modest blue-collar paycheck brought in. She'd had an affair, and she and Sean divorced when Riley was fourteen. It had been a difficult time in her life, and her mother's infidelity was one of the things that had sparked their big family feud.

Bryson checked his phone and frowned. Not only was it past the early meeting time Sean had requested, but it was also well past the time he'd normally walked the vines —a ritual Sean had started from the day he'd begun at The Stone Bridge Winery. Dread dragged its fingernails across the nape of Bryson's neck, and he started searching the rows— slowly at first, then his steps became urgent. Near the edge of Block Seven, he spotted the hat first— sun-faded straw, lying crooked in the dirt. Then he saw Sean.

"Sean?" Bryson dropped his coffee and jogged the last few steps. "Hey—Sean, you okay?"

The older man slumped awkwardly against a support post, one gloved hand still curled near his chest, the other limp in the grass. His face was pale. His chest wasn't moving.

Bryson dropped to his knees and grabbed Sean's wrist. No pulse. Bryson's breath lodged in his throat like tar. Fumbling for his phone, he hit nine-one-one.

"Nine-one-one, what's your emergency?"

"This is Bryson Boone. I'm at Stone Bridge Winery— west vineyard. I think one of my crew, Sean Callahan—he's —he's not breathing. He's not responsive."

"Sir, does he have a pulse?"

With his breath caught in his throat, Bryson firmly pressed his fingers against Sean's neck to check again. He waited for a few seconds. Nothing. He pressed harder. Still... nothing. "No."

"I'm dispatching emergency medical services now. I need you to begin CPR immediately. Can you do that?"

"Yeah. Yeah, I can," Bryson's voice cracked.

"Lay him flat on his back if he isn't already. Place your hands in the center of his chest—one on top of the other," the man on the other end said.

Bryson positioned himself, hands trembling. He'd taken CPR. Got recertified every year.

But damn, he'd never had to do this for real.

"Push hard and fast, two inches deep. I'll count with you—ready?"

"Yes," he whispered.

"One, two, three…"

He pressed, over and over, feeling the weight of every beat. Sweat gathered at his temple. His knees dug into the damp earth. The dispatcher's voice continued, calm but urgent, guiding him through it.

But Sean didn't move.

Didn't cough. Didn't blink. Didn't breathe.

Bryson kept going, even as hope started to fade. The sun hurled its face over the horizon—the field growing brighter and brighter. Time ticked by. His pulse beat disturbingly fast, but every movement proved slow and painful. The distant wail of a siren cut through the silence, drawing closer.

"They're almost there," the dispatcher said. "You're doing everything right."

A few minutes later, the EMTs arrived, rushing across the rows, gear in hand. Bryson stumbled back, giving them space as they dropped beside Sean, one checking his vitals while the other began chest compressions without missing a beat.

They didn't speak much. Just quick, efficient commands to each other.

"O2 in."

"Starting bag."

"Charging pads—clear."

Bryson stood frozen, hands clenched at his sides as they worked. He could still hear the dispatcher's voice faintly buzzing from the phone in the grass. A third medic rolled the gurney in.

Even after the defibrillator fired, there was no response.

"Pulse?"

"Still nothing. Continue CPR."

"Copy."

Minutes passed—five, maybe more. Then one of them finally looked up. Not with finality. Just with grim resolve.

"We're transporting him now," the medic said, glancing over his shoulder. "Are you family?"

Bryson released a slow, shaky breath. "His boss. His friend," he said faintly. At one time, he thought he would have been his son-in-law, but that ship sailed away years ago.

"Can you contact his family? Let them know we're taking him to Stone Bridge Medical?"

"Yes," was all Bryson could manage.

They worked quickly, lifting Sean onto the gurney and strapping him down with practiced care. One of the medics climbed in beside him, still performing compressions while a second hopped into the back, adjusting equipment. The third medic quickly closed the ambulance doors and raced around the vehicle.

The siren wailed again as it pulled away down the gravel road toward the main drag.

Bryson stood in the clearing, Sean's hat still lying in the dirt beside his feet. A chill settled in Bryson's chest that had nothing to do with the fog. Sean had been a constant in Bryson's life. Through losing Riley, through every triumph and failure in the vineyard. The older man had offered guidance without judgment, love without condition.

Bending down, he picked up his phone from where it had landed in the grass, the screen still smudged with dirt and sweat. His fingers hovered over the contact list for a second before he clenched his jaw, turned, and made his way back toward the ATV, picking up his discarded mug along the way.

The engine still ticked softly in the cool morning air as he climbed in. He didn't want to make the next call—not because he couldn't handle grief or shock. He'd dealt with more than his share of both. It was who he had to call.

Grant Callahan.

Bryson didn't hate the man—but he wasn't sure he liked him either. As small boys, they got along well enough. Ran through the yards playing cops and robbers. But as the years gave way to adolescence, something shifted in Grant. An unwarranted arrogance fed by his mother's need to be the most important and influential person in town.

Then, when Bryson and Riley went from being friends to being something more, things turned explosive. That had been when the boys were all of sixteen and fourteen. Grant made it crystal clear that some kid with grape juice under his nails wasn't the right person for Riley. But what

Bryson's family did for a living had nothing to do with why Grant didn't like Bryson, and everything to do with his mother and her need for power, prestige, and money.

Well, that and the fact that as a freshman, Bryson was the starting quarterback, and Grant, a junior, sat on the bench.

But that had been a lifetime ago. However, the tension had never faded. Especially not after Riley left. Especially not after Bryson stayed.

Still, none of that mattered right now.

He tapped Grant's name and lifted the phone to his ear. It rang twice before it connected.

"Bryson?" Grant's voice came in sharp and alert. "Why are you calling me?"

Bryson exhaled. "It's your dad."

A pause. "What about him? Is he okay?"

"I found him out in the vineyard. He collapsed. EMTs just left with him."

"Jesus," Grant breathed. "Is he—"

"I started CPR. They worked on him all the way to the ambulance. But it didn't look good." Bryson stared at the empty space where Sean had been. "It didn't feel right."

"What do you mean?"

"I don't know. No obvious injuries that I could tell. No sign of a fall or anything like that. Just—I don't know what happened." He paused. "They took him to Stone Bridge Medical."

"I'll call Erin and have her meet me there," Grant said. "Thanks for the call."

Bryson hesitated, then said what had been pressing at

the back of his mind since the moment he saw Sean's still body. "What about Riley?"

There was another pause—longer this time. "I believe she's still in Patagonia, but she was looking to move again. Not sure. We haven't exactly been best friends since she took off right after graduation...no thanks to you." Grant always had to get that one dig in.

Bryson pinched the bridge of his nose. That wasn't what happened, but that's what Grant, Erin, and their mother liked to believe. Why? Bryson honestly had no idea. He didn't think Riley had given them that impression. Or maybe she had, Bryson didn't know. A lot had happened in the weeks leading up to her departure. Some his fault. Some hers. And some had to do with other people.

But mostly, because of what had happened *to* them... and that was something only a few people knew about.

"Would you like me to call her for you?" Byson asked.

"Why would I want you to do that?"

"I'm just trying to help out." Bryson's voice sharpened.

"I don't need it," Grant said.

Of course, he didn't. Grant had never been the kind of man to ask for help. No matter the situation. He'd always been proud and stubborn.

"My little sister left years ago. Breaks my mama's heart. Riley doesn't understand that her actions have consequences. The only person she thinks about is herself. Regardless, this is my family, I'll handle it."

Bryson wasn't about to argue with him. "I'm heading to the hospital. If you need anything, please let me know."

The call ended.

Bryson sat back, gripping the steering wheel with both

hands, and stared out at the mist curling low over the vines. Riley Callahan had left Stone Bridge for reasons no one understood, except him. Their loss had been the final straw. They'd loved each other. He didn't care that others believed two dumb teenage kids weren't capable of such a thing. They'd been all in. But things... and people... happened. It changed them both. It hardened her.

And nearly destroyed him.

When she left, she had no intention of ever coming back.

But Bryson had a feeling that was about to change.

———

The hospital waiting room felt like it hadn't been updated since the early nineties—scratchy blue chairs, scuffed tile, and a vending machine humming just loud enough to be irritating. Bryson stood near the window, arms crossed, watching as the ambulance that had brought Sean in pulled away, empty.

Bryson scratched the center of his chest, which tightened with each beat of his heart. It had become difficult to suck in a deep breath, and he couldn't form a coherent thought.

"Here." Devon, Bryson's older brother, handed him a cup of coffee.

"Thanks." Bryson lifted the paper cup to his lips. The brew was lukewarm and tasted like cardboard. Jesus, he had shit luck with coffee today. "You didn't have to come."

"I wasn't going to leave you standing in this place alone after what you just went through." Devon leaned against the windowsill and ran his hand across his mouth. His gaze shifted past Byson and toward the double doors that led to the emergency department doors. "How ya holding up?"

Bryson stared into his coffee. "I'm numb."

He'd known from the moment Sean hadn't responded to CPR that he was gone. But being in this antiseptic-filled space, waiting for the doctor to confirm it, left an emptiness expanding in his chest.

"Have you heard anything from the doctors? From the family?"

"Nothing from either front." Bryson turned and paced. He'd never been good at being patient. He paused, staring at the doors leading to the outside world. Every time someone pushed them open, he expected to see Grant, Erin, or their mother race into the room, and Bryson wasn't mentally prepared to deal with them. He glanced at his watch and did his best to keep his emotions in check. The last thing he wanted to do was break down in front of Grant.

Bryson didn't understand Grant and his dad's relationship, other than knowing it was strained and had been for years. It had started before the divorce and intensified when Grant publicly scolded his father for leaving his mom, despite knowing full well that hadn't been the case. It quieted when Grant went to college. Got better when he married his wife, Kelly and had a family. But things had gotten worse after his mother invested in Wilkerson's Ponzi scheme.

When Bryson brought the tensions up to Sean, all he'd get in response was, "Why'd you let her leave?"

As if Bryson'd had a say in the matter.

So, he'd stopped asking.

But he did know that Sean had been hurt by his two older children when they'd been younger. How they'd taken to Elizabeth's new husband and were angrier with Sean than her—which Bryson found strange because it had been Elizabeth who'd stepped out on the marriage.

Grant and Erin had also been upset with Riley for choosing to live with her dad, and not with them and their mom.

Bryson had never been so grateful for his family. They were all a little different, but in a normal way. They often got up in his face about things. But they also respected his privacy.

"I'm surprised I beat Grant here."

"If he was anywhere near his mother when you called, I'm sure he had to *console* her before heading out the door." Devon shook his head. "She's a piece of work."

"True, but Grant plays into that," Bryson said. "And often, he's no better."

"Did you hear he's opening a second spa?" Devon asked. "Callahan's Hot Springs Resort is doing quite well. Grant might be a pain in the ass, but he's smart as hell, especially when it comes to numbers."

"Gotta give him credit for that." Bryson sipped the shitty, cold coffee. His stomach churned, but it wasn't from the beverage. As the seconds ticked by, so did the pressure in his chest. He tossed the mug into the trash. A plaque with the name Robert Wilkerson burned a path across his vision. "I can't believe that thing is still hanging." He pointed "You'd think after everything that went down with

Robert and the Ponzi scheme, the hospital would've removed it."

Devon rubbed his eyes, as if to remove the sight of it from his vision. "I'm sure they'll get around to taking it down."

"I hope so. That man hurt a lot of people.

Another ten minutes ticked by in thick silence before Grant and Erin came stomping down the hallway, both tense and composed in their own unique, uncomfortable way.

Bryson swallowed, hard. He had no idea what to say. "They took your dad into a room. We haven't heard anything."

Erin let out an exasperated sigh before sitting slowly in one of the chairs, her expression filled with worry—and anger. "I told him working in those fields was going to be the death of him. When he retired, he should have stayed retired, but that stubborn old coot wouldn't listen to me. He doesn't listen to anyone."

Bryson thought that was harsh. Sean wasn't any older than his dad, who'd just turned sixty. Besides, Sean didn't do heavy labor. They didn't have him on large machinery or ladders. He didn't work long, hard hours. He came and went as he pleased, working more in the tasting room in town, or the one on property, or giving tours.

God, people loved that man. He knew the wines, and he could tell one hell of a story.

"While I didn't like him working out in the vineyard anymore, he did love his job at the tasting room." Grant sat down next to his sister, looping an arm around her and squeezing her gently. He glanced up. "However, I can't help but blame you for this, Boone."

Before Bryson could even catch his breath to respond to Grant's comment, a doctor strolled through the emergency doors. "I'm looking for Bryson Boone."

"That's me." Bryson turned, stepping closer, his brother right at his side.

"I'm sorry to—"

"If this is about Sean Callahan," Grant bolted to his feet, jumping in front of Bryson and Devon, "I'm Sean's son. Talk to me."

"All right." The doctor gave Bryson a slow nod before lifting his gaze to Grant.

Byson took a step back but stayed in earshot. Devon practically bolted toward the side wall.

"I'm sorry. There wasn't anything we could do. Your father was gone when he arrived." The doctor reached out and squeezed Grant's forearm.

Erin gasped, shaking her head, covering her eyes, letting out a guttural sob. "No," she whispered.

Bryson moved closer to his brother. The ache in his chest only deepened. He couldn't believe it. Sean was gone. Bryon's eyes welled. The finality of it hit Bryson like a brick. There would be no more morning conversations over coffee, no more quiet wisdom shared while walking the rows. Sean's infectious laugh, his amazing jokes, his unwavering optimism—all of it silenced forever.

The man had been so full of life. So full of energy and love. No matter what had come his way, he lifted his chin, put on a smile, and went about making the world a little brighter.

"What did he die of?" Grant asked with an undeniable tightness in his voice. Something Bryson wasn't used to. At least, not from Grant.

"We don't know," the doctor said. "We'd need to do an autopsy."

"My father was a private man. He wouldn't want that. He wouldn't want people poking and prodding into him like a science experiment," Grant waved his hands wildly before swiping at his cheeks.

"Considering the way your dad died, I'm not sure the medical examiner will sign off on that," the doctor said.

"I understand. But I'm sure his ticker gave out," Grant said, lowering his head and rubbing the back of his neck. "Heart disease runs in our family. My grandma died at seventy-three of heart failure. Grandfather shortly after that —same thing." He let out a short breath. "My dad's a stubborn man. He wasn't overly fond of doctors and had an aversion to being cut open. We'd like that to be respected."

Bryson knew all about Sean's idiosyncrasies but if he were in Grant's shoes, he'd want to know what happened. However, it wasn't his business. And people dealt with grief in strange ways.

A flash of pain smacked him right between the eyes. The pregnancy. The miscarriage. He'd barely been able to process it all. He'd handled it horribly. He'd done and said some stupid things in his life, but that had to have been the worst. Talk about regrets.

"I'll discuss the situation with the ME," the doctor said softly. "If you'd like a moment with your dad, we can make that happen. We'll need about twenty minutes to prepare a viewing room."

"My sister and I would like to see our father, thank you." Grant shook the doctor's hand before the doctor disappeared through the emergency room doors. Grant turned. His face hard. His eyes full of fury—tears mixed with sadness and anger—directed at Bryson. He blew out a puff of air. "My father died at your winery." He pointed his finger at Bryson's chest. "You gave an old man a job. A man who wasn't fit for that kind of hard work. I blame you for his death."

Stunned, Bryson took a step back. He'd never understood Grant. But he did understand grief. "I'm so very sorry for your loss," was about all he could manage. "Can I call anyone for you?"

"No," Grant said. "You and your family have done enough."

Bryson stole a glance toward his brother, who'd taken a seat, elbows on his knees, hands on his cheeks, sorrow in his eyes. "What about Riley? Have you called her?"

"You've got to be kidding me." Grant eased back into the chair next to Erin, looping his arm around her, tugging her close as she continued to cry into her hands. "Is that all you care about? Finding your long-lost love? The one you drove out of town?"

Devon stood. "That's not fair."

"Could you please leave us alone?" Erin asked. "This doesn't concern either of you."

Bryson drew in a breath and released it slowly. "If there's anything we can do, please, don't hesitate to reach out."

Neither Grant, nor Erin, responded.

"Come on." Devon motioned toward the emergency bay doors. "Let's go."

Bryson followed his older brother. Once outside, he paused near the parking lot, where he'd illegally parked, grateful he hadn't been ticketed. "I can't believe he's gone," he whispered. "Just yesterday, he was telling customers at the tasting bar stories about dad when they were kids."

"He'll be missed." Devon looped an arm over Bryson's shoulder and tugged him close for a much needed brotherly hug. "Do you think they'll reach out to Riley?"

"I'm sure they will. I just worry about how that will go." Bryson ran his fingers through his hair. "Sean and I discussed dozens of things on our walks through the vines. Riley was one of those topics. But we always kept it to her different jobs. All the places she'd been. He didn't like discussing the problems between his children." The unspoken family tensions had always hung in the air between them, thick as mud. "Not only did I respect that, but I also honestly didn't want to hear about it. Not to mention, I didn't want to dig too deep into the Riley conversation outside of hearing about her wild adventures."

Devon glanced toward the parking lot. "Do you have any idea where Riley is right now?"

Knowing where Riley was and doing anything about it were two entirely different things. "After Monica and I divorced, I tried looking her up on the Internet. I just wanted to see what she'd been up to. She has no online presence. A few years ago, I asked Sean about that, and he told me that she's never opened any kind of social media account. Nothing. But he's kept me up on where she's been, always teasing me about contacting her. She's currently in Patagonia."

"Are you gonna to reach out?" Devon stepped in front of him, giving him that older brother arched brow. "Because you're still hung up on that girl."

"I'm not hung up. I'm worried she won't have a single friendly face in this town." Bryson pushed past his brother and marched toward his truck, waving his hand over his head. "I'll see you later."

"I can't stand Grant. But even I have faith he'll do the right thing when it comes to this," Devon called.

"That depends on your definition of right." As soon as Bryson slipped behind the steering wheel of his truck, he called his little sister, Hasley.

She picked up on the second ring.

"Hey. Dad told me what happened. Is Sean okay?"

"No." Bryson dropped his head back and sighed. "He passed." More tears filled his eyes. He wasn't sure he'd be able to stop them now.

"Jesus. That sucks."

"It does," he said. "I need a favor."

"Name it."

"Could you call Dad's lawyer and find the name of the private investigator he uses. I need to contact him," Bryson said.

"I'm headed to see him right now. Do you want me to ask him to call you?"

"That works."

"I just left yoga class. Shouldn't be more than ten minutes," Hasley said.

"I've got a few errands to run, and then I'll be home."

Bryson ended the call and dropped his head to the steering wheel and let out a soul-crushing moan. Growing up, Bryson had never been considered sensitive. Quite the opposite. He'd been an all-star football player and went on to play in college. He'd been brains and bravado. If he couldn't charm his way out of something... he muscled through it. Sometimes literally. Showing his emotions hadn't come easily to him. However, like a good wine, he'd grown into them—giving them the legs they deserved.

But damn, this hurt like fucking hell.

Two

The Patagonian peaks stretched endlessly before Riley Callahan. Their jagged silhouettes carved against a sky so vast it seemed to swallow sound. Here, at the edge of the world, the silence should have been absolute. Broken only by the whistle of wind through granite and the distant cry of a condor riding the thermals. But even in this cathedral of stone and sky, the past had found her.

The wind coming off the ridge still carried the bite of late-season snow, but Riley barely noticed. Instead, her cell tormented with the voice message from her brother had left an hour ago that she hadn't listened to yet. Grant generally called on holidays, birthdays, or when he wanted to argue. Though, last time they spoke, it had been random. They'd been trying to make things better. Trying to have a relationship that didn't consist of insults and accusations. It had started off well enough. Grant talked about his kids. Their activities. How his daughter was turning out to be an angsty pre-teen. But then the conversation shifted—toward their parents—and landed firmly in the past.

Never a good thing. Riley and Grant didn't shout, or even hang-up, but it didn't make their relationship any easier.

She'd deal with her brother and the rest of her family later. If it were truly urgent, her father would've reached out. For now, she'd enjoy the moment. She'd earned it.

She sat cross-legged on a flat rock overlooking the river, a thermos of instant coffee steaming in her lap, boots kicked off beside her. Below, the last of their group picked their way back toward basecamp, laughter echoing faintly through the trees. Another successful hike. No sprained ankles. No altitude sickness. No couples fighting over who packed the wrong gear.

A win by Patagonian standards.

"You actually smiled," Mateo said, flopping down beside her. He passed her a protein bar and cracked open his Coke, which he'd somehow managed to keep cold without the use of an icepack or even a small cooler. "Should I be concerned?"

"I always smile," she said dryly, took the bar, and ripped open the package. But it wasn't the first time someone had made a comment like that over the years. She'd been called quiet and a loner, and those two statements weren't false. She never stayed in one place too long, always searching for the next big adventure in a new country. She'd lived in all sorts of places over the last twelve years. Spain, Italy, Africa, Madagascar, Iceland, you name it, she'd probably spent time there. The longest she'd lived anywhere had been

Alaska... nearly a year. But that had been when she'd first left home.

"No, you smirk. Or grin. Or tip the corners of your mouth upward in a lame attempt to be human." Mateo tilted his head and did his best to demonstrate.

Oddly, it wasn't too far off the mark, and it reminded her of her sister, Erin. When they'd been younger and Erin would babysit Riley, before all the bickering began, Erin would try to mimic the way others talked, or walked, or used hand gestures as a way to entertain Riley.

"That's pathetic." She took another bite of her bar and stared off at the mountains.

It had been a long time since she'd actually thought of Stone Bridge as home, but lately, that town—and her father —had been oddly tugging at her heart. She sipped her coffee and let her mind drift to the last conversation with her dad, only a week ago. Her father had sounded a little off —tired and frustrated—and that wasn't him. Even when his world was torn apart, he'd always viewed his life as a glass of water that was never quite full, but always full enough. Life hadn't been easy for him. When her mom had cheated, he took the high road. He quietly left, letting the town believe he'd been the one to call it quits on his marriage.

The good people of Stone Bridge concluded he'd abandoned his wife. Just walked out of their life together for no real good reason, except maybe he was bored. A year later, her mother remarried the man she'd had an affair with. It killed Riley that there'd been no whispers about that. No chatter at the water cooler. That no one even questioned it. That no one knew, or if they had, they'd never openly discussed it.

Then again, Stone Bridge had been built on secrets, and people there knew how to keep them. They also knew how to spread lies.

"Yeah, well, I liked the smile. It was refreshing, unlike your usual grin. This one was more like 'maybe the world's not entirely terrible'. Very rare. Very endangered," Mateo said with a wink.

God, she loved Mateo. The longer she spent time with him, the more he'd become a true friend, and that was even rarer than her smile. She sucked in a deep breath, letting the cool air fill her lungs, leaned back, and soaked in the sky, the quiet, the sense of purpose she always felt at the end of a trip. Out here, she could just be. She didn't have to explain anything to anyone. She didn't have to feel anything. She didn't have to relive the guilt, the grief, the pain of what she'd believed had been betrayal... but hadn't... until it was.

And she sure as shit didn't have to deal with her fucking family. At least her dad had stopped bringing up her siblings. Stopped asking her to make things right with Grant and Erin... and her mother. To come home. The only thing he constantly did was talk about the flipping winery... and freaking Bryson. Somehow, that was worse. Every time, the memories flooded her brain like an old silent movie, all fuzzy and faded, but they were there, rolling across her mind. And they wouldn't go away.

In the past, she pushed them aside when she'd been awake, only having to deal with them late at night when she struggled to fall asleep. She'd hike, canoe, white-water raft, zipline, or whatever other activity she was into that season, and not deal with the past, because it was in the rearview.

Only, that mirror was always there, taunting her like a bad horror movie that played on a loop and wouldn't stop.

But none of it mattered.

She was doing the thing that would have destroyed her and Bryson, anyway. He was born to be one with the earth. To have his fingers in it. To grow wine. It was all he'd ever wanted to do. He'd never leave Stone Bridge, except to attend college, and he hadn't gone far.

She'd wanted out. She didn't care how it happened, but staying in that town was going to suffocate her. Destroy the very essence of who she was and who she wanted to become. She could feel the town suck the life right out of her, and that was the one thing Bryson hadn't understood —even if he said he had.

The last few months they were together, they fought about it all the time. She'd planned on taking a gap year before college. She wanted to travel. To see the world.

He wanted her to go to college. To be with him.

And then it happened. It changed everything. She hadn't been ready for it. Neither had he, but it was there, and then it wasn't. She hadn't been prepared for the emotions of either thing. It fundamentally changed her... forever.

"That's very poetic," she mused. "I'm simply contemplating my next move."

"Already? You just got here, and we've been having so much fun." He shook his head. "You Americans," he said with a laugh. "Where do you think you'll be off to, next?"

"I'm looking into doing Sea Kayak tours in New Zealand. Overnight ones, camping, and hiking trips. I hear it's beautiful there. I'd like to spend a few months on the

South Island and possibly a few more on the North Island. I've got a few feelers out. Want to come?"

"Oh, you could twist my arm. I'd travel the ends of the world with... you." He blew her a kiss. "I've never been, but I did spend two years in Australia. Ayers Rock and Cains. It was amazing."

"I loved Ayers Rock." Her phone buzzed beside her.

She almost ignored it. The signal was spotty at best and rarely worth chasing. But the caller ID blinked across the screen—Stone Bridge, California—and everything in her stilled, including her pulse, until she sucked in a cold breath and her heartbeat went wild. It was just a number. No name. Not her siblings. Not her parents. No one she knew.

Mateo leaned over to glance at the screen. "Who's calling you from the States? Family? You never talk about them."

She gave a noncommittal shrug. "It's not a number I recognize." Even if it were, she wouldn't answer. Dealing with her family always needed to be done in private—with a nice shot of tequila.

"You gonna answer it?"

Riley let it buzz a few more times, then hit the decline button. "It's probably a scam or telemarketer. If not, and if it's important, they'll leave a message."

Mateo leaned back on the rock. "I don't mind if you take it."

"I don't take calls from people I don't know."

"What if it's some ex-boyfriend or that best girlfriend from high school trying to get a hold of you for old times' sake?" He gave her that look—the one that said he was fishing for gossip and loving every second of it. "That's always so much fun. I recently reconnected with this girl I used to know way back in the day. We have some of the wickedest conversations."

"I can only imagine." She smirked. "But, I don't have either of those, and I have no desire to reconnect with anyone I once knew."

"You're no fun," he said with a chuckle. "I often take calls from telemarketers just to mess with them.

"Of course you do."

"It's so much fun to let them get right to the end of the sales pitch and then tell them no."

"That would just annoy me, and then we'd be back to that funky smile of mine you hate so much."

"Ah, we don't want that.".

Riley took a sip of coffee as she scanned the horizon... thinking about that number. And Stone Bridge. And everything she once held dear.

Mateo leaned back on his elbows. "Stone Bridge is in wine country, right?"

"It is. Some of the best wines in California are made there. I actually lived right next to one." She looked at the screen again. "They left a message."

"Intriguing." He watched her a moment, then gave her one of those perfect Mateo smiles—encouraging without being pushy, interested without being intrusive. She'd never had a friend who understood the art of being present without being suffocating. "Are you going to be daring and listen to it?"

"I am." She tapped the voicemail, hit play with her pulse pounding in her throat, and pressed the phone to her cheek.

"Hey... Riley, umm, it's Bryson," he said with a clear crack in his typically confidant tone. At least, that was how she remembered him. "So... yeah.... this is out of the blue—and I wouldn't be calling if it weren't serious." A long pause. "There's been an emergency. You may have already heard. It's about your dad. So, um, well, can you call me back?"

She didn't breathe for the whole message. Bryson's rich, deep voice washed over her like a tidal wave. It rushed over her skin like the fog rolling down from the mountains. When it ended, she stared at the screen as if it the message might destroy itself in seconds.

Mateo sat up straighter. "You okay?"

"You were right. That was... someone I used to know." Riley's voice was quiet.

"Who was it?"

"Doesn't matter. But I need to call him back." She stood. "Excuse me."

On shaky legs, Riley walked a few paces down the rocky slope, away from camp and the sound of Mateo cracking open another soda. The wind tugged at her braid as she pulled out her phone again, staring at the number and thinking about that damn message from her brother. She should probably listen to it before she called Bryson back. But fear snaked through her veins. Whatever it was, something told her it was better to hear the news from her ex-boyfriend than her brother, as cold as that felt.

She hadn't spoken to Bryson Boone in twelve years. Not since the day she packed her things, walked out of his life, and swore she'd never come back. She had her reasons, and at the time, she'd believed they were good ones—albeit good ones wrapped in tragedy.

A tragedy she hadn't been prepared for, but who is? Thing was, she hadn't realized how much she'd wanted that baby until it was gone. But out of pain and anger, she'd told Bryson she didn't want it. That she didn't want him. That she'd been glad she miscarried. The look on his face when she'd said those words still broke her heart.

But words can't be taken back.

Her fingers hesitated over the screen.

Then she tapped "Call."

It rang once.

"Riley?" His voice hit her like a gust of wind—familiar, low, steady. The years hadn't changed it much.

"Hi, Bryson." She cleared her throat. "I got your message. What's going on?"

A pause. "It's your dad."

Her chest tightened. "What happened? Is he okay? I just spoke to him last week." She squeezed her eyes tight, fighting the tears. Praying it wasn't the news that she knew deep down was coming, because Bryson wouldn't call if it wasn't the worst possible thing in the world.

"He died this morning." Another pause. "They think it was a heart attack. He was out in the vineyard. I found him. I'm so sorry, Riley."

Riley went still, gaze locked on the distant snowcapped peaks, a couple of tears dripping down her cold cheeks. "My brother called earlier. He left a message, but I haven't listened to it or called him back yet," she managed as the tears dribbled unchecked down her neck. She sat down hard on a nearby boulder, the phone pressed tight to her ear. "He was healthy. He worked every day. He was—"

"I know," Bryson said gently. "I keep telling myself the same thing."

Silence stretched between them. She wiped the dampness on her face as she continued to stare at the mountains. She'd always loved being outdoors. She didn't care where it was, as long as it was outside. She'd shared that passion with her father and with Bryson. They were all in love with the earth. The land. But she wanted the world. And Byson wanted the vines.

The irony wasn't lost on her—here she was, surrounded by some of the most beautiful wilderness she'd ever seen, and all she could think about was how her father would never see another sunrise over a mountain peak. He'd taught her to appreciate the way the light played across granite and snow. She'd spent twelve years chasing the same light in foreign places, thinking there'd always be time to share new discoveries with him. Now there was nothing but silence where his voice should've been.

"Riley? Are you there?"

She blinked, realizing she'd been lost in her thoughts. "Yeah, sorry," she managed.

"You okay?"

"I was just thinking about Dad. About how he used to take me hiking in Santa Cruz." The memory hit her with an unexpected force—his patient voice explaining which peaks were which, how he'd let her set the pace even when her sort legs meant they'd barely made it a mile. "I can't believe he's gone. I can't believe…"

"What can I do for you?" Bryson asked.

"I need to call my brother, but before I do that, is there anything else you can tell me?"

"I honestly don't know much," Bryson said. "The medical examiner hasn't released the body yet. I think they're deciding whether there's a need for an autopsy."

"Dad never did like doctors much." She swiped at her cheek. "Always said that surgeons and medical examiners had to be sociopaths because it's not normal to want to cut into the human body."

Bryson chuckled. "That certainly sounds like something Sean would say."

"Has my family started on any funeral planning yet?" Riley asked.

"I think so," Bryson said. "But Grant and I still can't stand the sight of each other, so I'm not really sure. I'm happy to ask, though. That is, if you want me to."

She sighed. "I need to call him back anyway." Riley closed her eyes. "I'll book a flight back as soon as I get off the phone."

"I can pick you up at the airport if you text me your plans," Bryson offered. "And—if you don't want to stay with your family—you can stay at the winery. The guesthouse has been remodeled. Plenty of room."

"I appreciate it," she said quickly, "but I'll book a room at Stone Bridge Inn on Main Street."

"Of course," he said, though his voice sounded faintly disappointed. "Just figured I'd offer, and that offer stands if you change your mind. Just say the word."

Riley rubbed a hand over her face. Speaking to him

again made her ache in places she thought had long since gone numb.

"I wasn't sure I should call you," Bryson admitted after a beat. "But... well, your brother and I had words. I knew things between the two of you were still strained, just wasn't sure how bad it was."

"I've never gone home, and they hold that against me. I suppose I can't blame them for that," she said. The familiar burn of being the family outsider settled in her chest like an old wound. "We just can't ever get past hello without a fight happening. Thanks for calling me."

"You're welcome." His voice softened. "It was good hearing your voice again, Ry."

She flinched at the nickname. Not many people used it. Her mother hated it. Forbid the family from using it. Said it made her sound like a boy, and God forbid Riley be a tomboy, which she'd been her entire life. Her dad almost always called her Ry, and so had Bryson—he'd grown up using it. It wasn't until they'd become teenagers that he started using her full name.

"Ry?" Bryson hesitated. "Can I ask you something a little awkward and perhaps uncomfortable?"

She braced herself. In her experience, questions that came with disclaimers were never actually questions at all—they were something else entirely wrapped in politeness. "Okay," she said.

"The last few weeks or so, your dad seemed quiet and distant. We didn't have as many morning coffees or even glasses of wine. But the night before he died, he reached out and asked if we could meet in the vineyard early the next morning. He said he needed to speak to me about something important." There was a hitch in his voice. "Was there something going on with him? Did I miss something?"

The question slipped through her like a blade.

Riley stood, heart pounding now for a different reason. She had to agree that her dad had been a little off during their last few conversations. When they had the opportunity to FaceTime, he looked tired. Worn. Or maybe worried. "I don't know. Are you concerned about something? Is there something you're not telling me?"

"No. No. It's nothing like that. It's just that I spent a lot of time with Sean since he started working for me. He loved being out in the vineyard in the early morning, and we'd often walk through the vines, chatting about this or that. Lately, I felt like he was somewhere else. Preoccupied. And while he was still working a lot, he'd shifted his focus. Worked different hours. Came in later. I thought, because he'd left the Stone Bridge Revitalization Committee, that either he'd work more or retire altogether. But neither of those things happened. I don't know, but something just felt... off."

"He was distant with me too, and if I asked him about it, he told me it was nothing." She looked out at the endless stretch of sky. Her chest tightened. "I just don't have a clue as to what might have been bothering him, and that makes me feel...like..."

"Hey. Don't worry about that now. It's okay," he said, almost too easily. But then again, Bryson had always been the type to give space—until he didn't. "We can talk about it later—when I pick you up at the airport."

She weighed the offer. Calling her siblings was an option. Grant would absolutely do it. Erin would say yes, but somehow her husband would be the one showing up at the airport. She'd have to see them all at some point, but she'd rather have a moment to breathe before that happened. Bryson seemed like the least painful choice. "I'll text you my flight details," she said.

"Safe travels, Ry."

She ended the call.

For a moment, she just stood there, the wind pulling at her jacket, the ache behind her ribs growing sharper with every breath. She'd just opened a door she'd nailed shut years ago—and on the other side, the past was waiting like it hadn't missed her at all.

Bryson entered the study. It smelled like old leather, cedar, and the kind of wine that had aged better than most men. It was the kind of scent that typically made Bryson feel right at home. Tonight, it put him on edge.

He paused for a moment, staring at his father, who sat in one of the leather chairs, wine glass in hand, staring into it as if it had all the answers in life. He lifted his free hand and swiped at his cheek.

His dad turned. "Come in," he said with a scratchy tone. "I poured you a glass."

Bryson sat in one of the deep chairs by the fireplace, a half-full glass of cabernet resting in his hand. Across from him, his father, Walter Boone, poured himself a splash more and didn't bother hiding the tear that rolled down his weathered face.

Bryson had to remember that his dad lost a dear friend too.

As a small boy, Bryson used to love to follow his father and grandpa, and sometimes Sean, around the vineyard and listen to them talk about the grapes. About the vines. About the land and everything that went into making Stone Bridge Winery come to life. It began with a simple passion for fine wine and a family legacy. To build a place where people came together to share stories, love, and life.

Bryson glanced across the fire at his father—the man's broad shoulders still square despite the years, silver at the temples now, hands strong and steady from a lifetime working both vines and deals. Talking to his dad was like looking into a mirror set years in the future. Same build. Same eyes. Same stubborn jaw. But it wasn't just the resemblance that Bryson respected. It was the way his father carried himself—with quiet conviction and the kind of loyalty that never wavered. He was a good man. A better husband. And the type of father Bryson thought he could have been, had he been given the chance.

His chest tightened, as it often did when he allowed himself to think about that time all those years ago—which was more often than he cared to admit—even to himself. The swirling emotions. The confusion. The shock. Followed by joy. Then anger. Resentment. And then, of course, came the grief. That crushing, gut-wrenching pain that he'd buried into one massive mistake that he still carried.

"They believe it was a heart attack?" his dad asked,

swirling the wine but not drinking yet. He stared at the rich liquid as it hugged the side of the glass as if it held all the world's answers.

"That's the unofficial word," Bryson replied. "No autopsy scheduled, yet. Erin asked me if they could hold a reception at the winery, and I, of course, said yes. But Grant—and Elizabeth—are still telling me and anyone who will listen that it's all my fault Sean's dead. I understand they're hurting and need to blame someone, but it's hard enough when I blame myself."

"It's not your fault." His father lowered his chin. "But are you really surprised that they're putting all the responsibility on your shoulders? Even if you hadn't been the one to find Sean, Elizabeth has never liked you—and she pitted Grant against you."

"Grant still holds me to the fire about Riley and why she's never returned."

"You're not at fault for that, either. Riley made that decision on her own. And frankly, it's no one's business but Riley's," his dad said. "But Grant has always been reactive and quick to judgment. Remember when his stepfather was first diagnosed with cancer? Grant, and even his mom and sister, blamed you when Riley didn't come home when Parker started treatments."

Bryson let out a long breath before lifting his glass to his lips. The wine went down so smooth. One of the better vintages, but it didn't help ease the tension gnawing in his gut. " Grant and Parker have always been weirdly close. It always surprised me that it didn't bother Sean more."

"Not sure close is the right word. More like Elizabeth used her son as a prop, and Grant just stood like a trophy.

And let's not forget, Sean never wanted his children to resent him and chose to stay out of the kids' relationship with their stepfather. He always wished all three of his kids would get along. It just never happened."

"I wish I could say that was all on Grant and Erin, but Riley can be as stubborn as they are," Bryson said. "But from where I sit, Grant and Erin never made it easy."

"It's a difficult dynamic, and those kids were put in the middle of it by their mother."

Bryson cocked his head. "It always struck me as odd that Grant and Erin, being older, couldn't see that, where Riley did."

"She's always been a bit of an old soul, like her dad," his father said. "But she has an impulsive streak, one that drove Sean crazy." His father chuckled. "When we were kids, I used to tease him because he was the type of kid to make a pro and con list before making a decision. And he'd worst-case scenario everything. Where I just jumped in with both feet."

"That's funny coming from you. You always made us kids look at both sides of the coin."

"I learned that from Sean." His dad rubbed the center of his chest as if he were having sympathy pains. "When I decided to expand this baby winery my dad started, because he just enjoyed making it for his family and friends, into something bigger, Sean sat me down and told me I needed to take a page from his playbook. That I needed to ponder things, and that man was right."

"Sean was one of the smartest and kindest people I've ever known." Bryson leaned back and stared into the fire. "I can't believe he's gone. That he just up and died of a heart attack. Sean was in better shape than most guys half his age. I know Sean wasn't overly keen on doctors, but Grant's words still shocked me. If it were you, I'd be demanding an autopsy. I'd want to know why. I'd need the answer if only to give me closure."

"You and Grant are two very different people. Grant was raised by a mother who told him he was better than everyone else, and she demanded he be the best. I remember when you were named the starting quarterback. Elizabeth was furious, and she accused us of paying off the coach. Of using our influence and wealth to make sure you had that spot because you weren't that good, and her son was better. She even insinuated that your mother had sexual—"

"I don't need to be reminded of that one." Bryson stuck his finger in his ear and wiggled. "That was a rough year for me. Besides, it has nothing to do with what we're discussing."

"True," his dad said. "But you have that furrowed brow your mother says I get when I'm either questioning something, or don't believe something. What's really bothering you?"

"I don't know." Bryson shook his head. "Whatever Sean wanted to discuss, he said it was personal, and it felt urgent. And now, it's bugging me."

His dad finally took a long, slow sip, then set his glass down. "You're hurting. He was your friend, and you once cared a great deal for his daughter." His dad lowered his chin. "You carried a torch for that girl since you were in grade school, and I don't think you ever got over her."

"I have, but Riley was always going to leave," Bryson said without a drop of bitterness. He'd released that a long time ago. But the ache in his heart still pulsed. She was the one that got away. The one he'd always remember. The regrets still lingered in the vines. The one that he couldn't quite stop comparing everyone else to, which was why he was still single, and his marriage had blown up. Though, that relationship was doomed from the get-go. "That first year I was at college, while she still had one more year of high school, we could barely have a conversation without arguing. We broke up and got back together a couple of times."

"I remember." His dad leaned forward. His tone soft. Kind. It was almost as if he'd wanted to spare Bryson past pains. "It was quite the rollercoaster ride for everyone. However, we always figured the two of you would work it out."

Bryson groaned. It was rare for him to talk about that time in his life. When Riley had left, his parents begged him to open up about what had transpired, but he'd closed himself off and focused on two things... his studies... and freaking Monica. What a mistake. The nail in the coffin. Poor taste, but fitting.

"It was a long time ago," Bryson said softly.

"Maybe, but you're still holding onto it like some battle scar, and don't try to tell me you're not." His father raised his hand. "You married the wrong woman right out of college. The rebound girl. Not to mention, she used to be Riley's—"

"I'm well aware of who Monica was and what happened to our marriage. I'm reminded of it every time I see her or even run into some of her friends that used to be our friends, like Kim, Stephanie, and Mae. But we don't need to rehash that, and it's not what's bothering me."

His dad arched a brow. "Yeah, well, you haven't had a girlfriend since your divorce."

"Not entirely true." But it wasn't false. He dated and had one girlfriend who'd lasted two years, but she complained that she was competing with a ghost—and it hadn't been his ex-wife. He'd had another one that lasted a year. She bitched that he lived at home with his parents, and he didn't want to move out. In the end, all she'd wanted was the family name.

Since then, he hadn't bothered much, and he still lived at home with his parents. But he had an entire wing to himself. Not to mention they lived in a freaking mansion. People got lost in his parents' house.

His two sisters lived there. And Devon, the oldest, lived just down the street.

"Are you going to get to the root of the problem?" his father asked.

The fire cracked softly in the hearth, casting flickers of light over the built-in shelves and wine-soaked history lining the walls.

Not that Bryson wanted to continue with this dangerous topic, but he did want his father's insight.

"I called Riley," Bryson said, holding his father's unwavering gaze. "She's coming back."

That got a longer pause. His dad raised his glass to his lips as if he were trying to hide a smile. But he couldn't disguise the crinkling around his eyes that suddenly glinted with amusement. He sat forward slightly. "You two haven't spoken since she left town. How'd that go?"

"It was interesting. Weird. But good." Bryson took a slow, long sip. Liquid courage. The familiar warmth spread through him, steadying his nerves. It worked. "I didn't think I'd ever hear her voice again."

"And how did that feel?" Sometimes, his father enjoyed treating conversations as if he were peeling an onion.

The question hit deeper than Bryson expected. He'd been trying not to analyze the phone call, not to pick apart every inflection in Riley's voice or the way his heart had hammered against his ribs when she'd said his name. "Like someone split my chest open and poured twelve years right back in." He hadn't meant to be that honest, but there it was—the truth he'd been avoiding.

"I've never understood what happened between the two of you." His dad waved his hand. "I know. She wanted to travel and see the world, but you'd never leave this winery or give up any time at school. You had a goal, and nothing was going to get in the way. You were both so stubborn." His father's words weren't judgmental or harsh. If anything, they were laced with a tinge of regret. "You both made decisions, dug your heels in... and well, the rest is history."

"It was bigger than that, Dad."

"Most parents worry about teenage love. Kids getting in too deep, too young. Your mother and I never worried... until you went off to college and you started to have problems. Your sisters did tell us some of the gossip that was going around school."

"Most of it was just that."

"But you ended up with Monica anyway," his father said, voice softer now.

Bryson stared into his glass. That time in his life had

been filled with confusion, anger, and a need to move past the deep hole loss had created. "We loved each other, but it wasn't enough. It was never going to be... enough. In the end, the only way for us to survive was if I left Stone Bridge. If I did that, I doubt we still would've made it, because I would have wound up resenting her. And that's a truth I know deep in my bones, or I would have chased her years ago." Bryson raised his glass. "This winery is part of me. The dirt, the grapes... It's always been my future. Letting her go was one of the hardest things I've ever done, but it was right for both of us."

His father's eyes softened. "Sometimes, we have to let things go to allow them to come back."

Bryson snorted. "Sometimes, that's just cowardice dressed up as wisdom."

"Interesting hearing my words repeated back to me," his father whispered. "Sounds like you made my point about still being hung up on that girl."

They fell silent again while Bryson collected his thoughts. Sorted his feelings. He'd been pushing them down for twelve years. But a volcano was brewing in his gut, and eventually, it was going to blow.

"It's not that. It's just that with Sean's passing and her coming back, it's brought so much to the surface." Bryson gave his wine a good swirl before taking a nice, satisfying mouthful. "She's staying at the inn," Bryson added after a moment. "Didn't even consider staying with family. I understand that. Things are still tense with them."

"She's been gone a long time." His dad lowered his chin. "Riley does have to take some accountability for her relationships with her family."

"I won't argue with that," Bryson said. "But they didn't make returning easy. They judged her for every decision she made. It started with her wanting to live with Sean. Dating me. Wanting to travel. I know I also made that one difficult, but once she left, they wrote her off."

"And how do you know this?"

"Because Grant, Erin, Elizabeth, my ex-wife, and even some of Riley's old friends—like Stephanie—enjoyed letting me know that if it weren't for me, she might have returned." Bryson rose and made his way to the fireplace. He set his glass on the mantel and stared at the fire.

"I would think Monica was glad about that."

Bryson snorted. "Oh, she was... mostly. I mean, Erin didn't like Monica back then, because she blamed her for Riley taking off. But once things went sideways with my marriage, Monica liked to poke me about it. As if I were the reason she'd lost one of her best friends." He ran a hand over his mouth. "I suppose, in a way, I was."

"Again, not your fault."

"I'm partly to blame." Bryson lifted his glass and took a nice, long draw. "So many people act like Riley abandoned them when she left. But it's Riley who felt that way her entire life."

"Are we talking about her parents' divorce?" his father asked. "Because you're all over the place right now." His dad held up his hand. "I get it. Sean just died. We're all emotional. But I have no idea where you're going with this conversation."

Bryson knew exactly what he wanted to discuss, but he wasn't quite sure how to get there. Perhaps it was best to start at the beginning. "Riley was so deeply affected by her mother's affair and how no one in this town seemed to know about it. Or how they all treated her dad as if he was the one who ended the marriage."

"While Sean is the one who walked away and filed for divorce, this entire town knows about Elizabeth's affair. The only reason no one whispers about it is because of Sean. He didn't want that for his kids." His father's voice dropped lower, as if the walls might be listening. "I shouldn't tell you this, but Sean always planned on leaving Elizabeth."

Bryson blinked, gripping his gobbler a little too tightly. "Excuse me?"

"He didn't want to do that until Riley was out of high school and on her own. His children were more important to him than his own happiness, something I think he deeply regretted in the end."

"I had no idea." Bryson made his way back to the chair, collapsing into it.

"I know that Riley caught her mother and Parker together while her parents were still married."

"Did you also know that Elizabeth expected Riley to keep that information to herself? To perpetuate the lie that Parker and her mom didn't start dating until after Sean moved out?"

"I did. The entire thing was a lot for a child, and she felt alone and betrayed." His father waved his hand. "However, she ran from this town and left a lot of heartache in her wake. I'm not saying she didn't have her reasons, I'm just saying she made what appeared to be rash decisions."

Bryson gulped down a few more sips. "I offered Riley the guesthouse, but she wouldn't take it. I hate that she'll be in a hotel... alone. This town can be so damn unforgiving. She'll need people she can lean on." Mentally, he kicked himself for being such a coward and not telling his father what was really on his mind.

"I understand your concern. Even so, would you consider staying with your ex-girlfriend in a situation like this? Under these circumstances?"

Bryson managed a faint smile. "I suppose not."

His dad reached for the bottle and refilled both their glasses.

Bryson downed half his glass in record time, barely enjoying the richness of his own blend. He couldn't carry this burden a second longer.

"When she gets here, let her find her footing. Let her grieve. The rest... it'll come when it's time." His father's tone gentled, the way it always did when he was trying to plant seeds of possibility. "Twelve years is a lot of space. Maybe you two can spend a moment and heal."

Bryson turned toward his father, his pulse thundered, it radiated—everywhere. "There's something I never told anyone," he said quietly, fingers tightening around his glass. "Not you. Not Mom. Not even Devon. Sean knew, but outside of that, it's probably the best-kept secret in Stone Bridge. And I need to unload it before I face Riley again."

His father set his wine glass aside. "I'm listening."

"It happened about a month before Riley's graduation. Right before she changed her mind again about staying." Bryson swallowed. Hard. "Right before me and Monica happened."

"Don't beat around the bush, son. Just spit it out."

"Riley was pregnant, but she had a miscarriage." Bryson

couldn't believe he'd spoken the words aloud. The words that had haunted him for so many years. The pain... the guilt... the anger. It had hung over him like a dense cloud ready to dump a storm.

The words spun in the space between them, raw and heavy.

Outside, the wind picked up, rattling the windows as if even the vineyard could sense the weight of what had been revealed.

His father's expression didn't shift at first, but Bryson saw the shock in his eyes. The sadness for his child etched in his parted lips. "My God, son. I... we... your mother and I had no idea."

"Riley didn't want anyone to know. Said it was hers to carry. Plus, she was so angry at me over Monica. Over that kiss. We were kids... scared and stupid. I was just finishing up my first year of college. Things had been so up and down. We fought all the time about the future, and it wasn't looking bright for us."

His dad flopped back, arms dangling on the sides of the chair... stunned.

"The whispers about me and Monica had been swirling. It was frustrating, and it was even harder for Riley because she and Monica were friends. Everything was compounded by the fact that Monica and I went to the same university. We did see each other, and while I tried to avoid her, it was impossible." Bryson ran a hand over his mouth. "Right around the time Riley learned she was pregnant, Monica came at me hard. She made her move, next thing I knew, we were in a lip lock. I ended it quickly, but not quickly enough because someone took a picture, and the rumors spread even faster."

"That's a lot for an eighteen-year-old to deal with. And I mean both you and Riley."

"Riley, she was already spinning out of control." Bryson stared into the fire, his voice low. "The thing with Monica just pushed her further away, and I couldn't leave school. There was this baby, and yet we were on the brink of being over, and then the baby was gone, and then so was Riley. No way to fix that."

Walter pushed himself out of his chair. Quickly, he closed the gap in two strides. Before Bryson could react, his father wrapped his arms around him—not the awkward, obligatory embrace of holidays or goodbyes, but the fierce, protective hold of a parent who just realized his child had been carrying an unbearable weight. "I'm so sorry that you had to go through all that alone," his father said, his voice thick with emotion. "All these years, and I never knew. I should have seen it. Should have been there for you.

Bryson's chest split open—not the sharp kind of break of fresh pain, but the slow, inevitable crumbling of the walls he'd built to hide this secret. He'd forgotten what it was like to have someone else carry even a fraction of what he'd been shouldering.

When his father finally pulled back, tears welled in his eyes. "I love you. I know I can't make this better, or right. But I will always be here for you."

"I know." Bryson's jaw worked as he struggled to keep his composure. The relief of finally telling someone warred with the guilt that had become his constant companion. He pressed the heels of his palms against his eyes, trying to stem the tide of emotion threatening to overwhelm him." I don't know how to face her. What to say to her or how to act. Her father just died, and I'm also reeling over that."

The fire popped softly, as if exhaling the last of the secret that had finally been set free.

"All I can say is, be a safe place for her to land. Twelve years is a long time. Fundamentally, you're the same man, but people grow, and they do change."

"And she won't stay," Bryson said softly.

Three

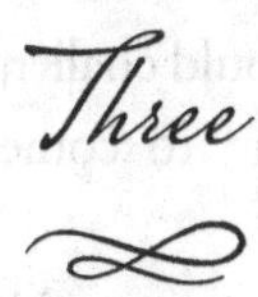

The airport doors slid open, and Riley stepped into the thick California air, the weight of her duffel bag tugging on her shoulder, though it was nothing compared to the heaviness sitting squarely in her chest.

It had been a long flight—longer still, given what waited on the other side. Grief clung to her like humidity, making every breath feel dense. But it wasn't just the ache of her father's death that made her stomach churn.

It was also knowing who she was about to see.

Bryson Boone.

There hadn't been a single day in the last twelve years that she hadn't thought about Bryson. She'd never had to wonder what he'd been doing because her father had always filled her in with those details. All of them. The marriage. The divorce. The few short relationships he'd had over the years. And of course, Bryson's one true love... Stone Bridge Winery.

The man had been born to that single patch of land.

And almost literally, as his mother had gone into labor while taking a morning stroll through the property with his dad. All the Boone children were connected to it, but Bryson had a unique bond with the vines that couldn't be broken. Not even love could challenge it.

Something she'd had to come to terms with a long time ago.

Quickly, she shot a text to Mateo, letting him know she'd landed safely. It was strange how their friendship had morphed from tour guides, to buddies, to besties at warp speed and all because she hadn't been able to keep it together yesterday when Bryson had called.

Thank God for Mateo. He'd saved her from sitting on that rock, crying into the dark night, alone.

Tucking her cell in her pocket, she scanned the area, spotting Bryson before he saw her. Standing by the passenger side of a dark blue truck, one arm resting casually against the doorframe, his head turned slightly as he scanned the crowd.

He looked older.

Not aged—just more solid, more sure of himself. His jawline was more defined, and silver threaded lightly through the dark strands at his temples. His posture was still relaxed, but something in it—something in him— seemed taut, coiled.

When his gaze landed on her, the rest of the world stilled.

Their eyes locked, and for a beat, neither of them moved—they just stared at each other as if they weren't sure what to do next.

Then his mouth twitched into something that wasn't quite a smile, but not quite neutral either.

"Riley," he said as she approached, her boots crunching against the concrete.

"Hey," she replied, the word catching in her throat. She couldn't form any more of a response.

They stood awkwardly, memories swarming between them like ghosts. There had been a time when they wouldn't have hesitated—when she would've flung her arms around him without thinking, when he would've pulled her in close and whispered something to make her laugh.

Her father would've hated this—seeing them like strangers when they'd once been everything to each other. Her dad had always believed they'd eventually find their way back to one another. But now, her dad was gone, and she was standing here drowning in grief while the one person who might've been able to comfort her felt like a memory from another life.

"Your flight was early," he said, stepping forward to take her bag. Their fingers brushed, and the contact sent a jolt up her arm.

"I had to fly out of Santiago at the crack of dawn but had no real problems." She tried a smile. It didn't quite hold. "Thanks for picking me up."

"You're welcome." He glanced at her again. "You look... different."

"Twelve years will do that to a person."

Bryson chuckled and opened the passenger door. She climbed in, the familiar scent of leather and cedarwood hit her hard—he'd always smelled like that. A sudden, sharp ache flared in her chest. God, she wasn't ready for this. Not for how easily twelve years could collapse into nothing with just a scent, a sound, the simple act of him opening the door. Quickly, she faced forward and stared out the windshield as he walked around to the driver's side.

They pulled away from the curb, and the silence inside the truck cab stretched between them like a thick fog. When they'd been kids, sitting in quiet spaces with him had been easy. Back then, they hadn't needed words. They could just be.

As adults, it was uncomfortable as hell.

The hum of the engine was the only sound between them for miles. Riley kept her hands folded in her lap, watching the scenery shift from the outskirts of the city into the rolling golds and greens of Northern California wine country. The hills were the same. The roads hadn't changed.

But she had.

"How was Patagonia?" he asked, finally breaking the quiet. Thank God it was a question she could answer. A question about the present. Something simple. Nothing that would bring up all the ugliness that she'd left behind.

"Cold. Rugged. Beautiful." She glanced sideways. "Unforgiving, but in the best ways. I loved it there. But honestly, I was getting ready to move on to the next spot." She sputtered, as she often did when discussing her travels, but her usual excitement over it all had somehow vanished. It was as if she'd left it on the plane. As if coming back had taken that away.

Or maybe she was just tired.

"Sounds like you."

She smiled faintly. "That sounds like a compliment."

"It is."

Silence again, but this time it wasn't so stifling. As if the small talk had cut through some of the invisible barrier that years of absence had built.

"I heard you've made a real name for yourself," he added. "Guiding climbs, trekking remote places. Living the dream."

"I've done exactly what I've always said I wanted to do," she said, allowing herself a slight smile. She was proud of her life. She'd lived and seen more than most. But if she was being honest, being a nomad had become less of a thrill and more of a challenge, and not necessarily in a good way. The last time she'd been back in the States, she'd met her father in Denver and confessed that she'd been thinking about settling down somewhere—maybe not permanently—but at least having a home base. He'd listened without judgment, the way he always had, and told her that growing tired of wandering didn't mean she was giving up on her dreams, just that her dreams were evolving. She wished she could have that conversation with him now. "Most nights I sleep in a tent or a hammock. Shower when I find a spring. It's not a life for everyone. It's certainly not always easy."

Bryson chuckled softly. "Yeah. Still sounds like you."

She looked over at him, her voice gentler. "You haven't changed that much, either. Or at least that was the report I got back from my dad."

His hands tightened slightly on the wheel. "Some things don't change. Others..." He shrugged.

They fell into silence again. Not quite comfortable but not entirely strained either. It was like trying to wear clothes you'd outgrown—still familiar, still recognizable, but loose in some places and tight in others. Misaligned.

"Your dad used to come by the vineyard in the mornings before either going to the tasting bar or working in the office," Bryson said after a while. "He'd wander the rows like he was looking for something he'd lost."

Riley's throat tightened. "He was probably just clearing his head. He always loved being there. I remember when he called me to tell me he'd taken the job. How much it felt like going home. I was genuinely happy for him."

"He was an asset to the business. But lately, I'd find him talking to himself. Swearing at the grapes about nothing. Sometimes, he'd sit out by the fermentation shed and eat those god-awful peanut butter crackers he kept stashed in his glove box."

A laugh slipped out, surprising her. She hadn't expected to feel anything but sadness today, yet here was this small spark of joy her father's memory had lit. "He hoarded those things. Said they were the perfect snack."

"They were cardboard."

"I know." She smiled, even as her eyes stung. "But he used to share them with me when I went hiking as a kid. He'd pack them in my little fanny pack, along with a note. I think he believed they were magic."

"I found myself buying an entire carton earlier." Bryson's smile faded slightly. "He was a good man, and he will be missed."

She swallowed, hard. "He was the only one who kept in touch when I left, even though he was mad at me for never wanting to come home to visit and even though I saw him when we took short trips together, that's something I..."

Bryson glanced over at her. "Your dad... he loved you, and he was proud of you. Don't you ever forget that."

Riley looked away, focusing on the familiar curve of the road as it led into town. "Both Grant and Erin are being pretty passive-aggressive with me. They say they're grateful that I agreed to return, but everything's coming out sideways. Everything feels like a dig. Of course, I've only spoken to them once since my dad died. Everything else has been in text. Erin is a little nicer about things, but God, her husband. I heard him in the background dictating what she should say to me." She shivered. "It's gross."

"Everyone calls them 'the Chaos Couple'. I don't believe your sister is very happy." Bryson exhaled. "But after what Chad did, I can still barely look at him."

"I'm not sure how I'm going to," she said quietly. "And I don't want to be at odds with my sister the entire time. Things are strained enough as it is."

"I'm always around if you need an ear."

"Thanks, but I'm sure we'll manage." She stared out the window as the highway turned into small-town roads. "So, what's new with things in Stone Bridge? Anything exciting with the old gang? I haven't heard from Kim, Stephanie, or Mae in forever."

"Same, but different," Bryson said. "I see them, but don't spend much time with them anymore. My focus is on work and family."

"And how are your sisters? Devon?" she asked. "My dad mentioned they're all still single."

"Sure are." He chuckled. "Devon's still playing the field, like always. And my sisters, well, their standards are pretty high. Going to take someone special to sweep them off their feet."

Riley fiddled with a few loose strands of hair. The conversation almost felt natural. Almost.

They reached the Stone Bridge Inn just as dusk crept over the hills. Bryson pulled up in front, shifted the truck into park, and turned to face her. The light from the overhead streetlamp cut across his face, throwing shadows beneath his eyes.

"You sure you want to stay here?" he asked. "We've got space at the guesthouse. You wouldn't be imposing, and I'm worried about you here all alone. My folks and sisters would all love to see you."

She hesitated, then shook her head. "Thank you. But I'm good here, and I'm sure I'll see them all around town and at the funeral."

He didn't push. Just like the Bryson she used to know —stubborn but respectful. Quiet but always watching. She'd loved that about him, then. Right now, she wanted to hate him for it, but she couldn't.

"I'll carry your bag in," he said, already climbing out.

She met him at the entrance, where he handed it off and lingered a moment.

"I, uh... I'm really sorry, Riley," he managed.

She met his eyes. "Me too."

Another long silence. Then she said, "I'll see you around."

He gave her a half-smile. "Call if you need anything."

She watched him drive off, the red taillights disappearing around the corner.

Then she turned, walked into the quiet lobby, and

checked in with a woman who looked vaguely familiar but didn't ask questions.

It wasn't until she was upstairs, alone in her room, sitting on the edge of the bed that she let herself finally breathe.

But even that was hard.

She was back in the one place she'd sworn she'd never return.

And everything hurt.

The weight of it all crashed down on her at once—her father's death, being home after twelve years, seeing Bryson. The perfect storm of everything she'd been running from. Her chest tightened, and suddenly she couldn't get enough air. The grief, the guilt, the overwhelming familiarity of a place that held too many memories—it was suffocating.

She fell back on the bed and grabbed her phone with shaking hands. Quickly, she found Mateo's contact information.

"Riley?" his voice was on instant alert. "Did you get in okay? Is everything alright?"

"I can't—" The words came out broken. "I can't do this. I thought I could, but I don't know how. Dad's gone, and he was always the one who I talked to about stuff like this. And I saw Bryson. I don't know what I was thinking. As if time was going to make that wound go away."

"Breathe. Just breathe. In and out. Nice and easy," Mateo said. His voice was calm. Soothing. It was a side of him she didn't often see but so needed.

She closed her eyes, focusing on anything but being in Stone Bridge.

"Better?" Mateo asked.

"I'm not jumping out of my skin."

"Just remember you're there for your dad. Because you loved him and he loved you, and that's bigger and more important than anything else. You're not the same person who left. You're stronger. You've built a life, traveled the world, you've become exactly who you were meant to be."

"But seeing Bryson? It shook me."

"Of course it did, and that's okay. But you don't have to be anything other than yourself. You don't owe anyone explanations or apologies."

She blinked open her eyes and stared at the ceiling. "What if I fall apart?"

"There are worse things in the world," Mateo said. "You've got this. And if you don't, you've got me to remind you to smile."

She chuckled. "You're obsessed."

"Damn right I am. Now get some sleep. No need to let exhaustion make things worse."

"Thanks for everything. I owe you." She ended the call feeling more centered. Mateo was right—she wasn't the same person. She could do this.

She had to.

Bryson tiptoed down the hallway toward the security office before pausing at his father's open office door. He poked his head in. "Dad? What are you still doing awake?"

His father sighed. and dropped his pen. "Looking over some shit for the revitalization committee." Snagging his reading glasses off the bridge of his nose, he tossed them on his desk. "I should've never volunteered when Sean stepped down."

Bryson leaned against the doorjamb. "I asked Sean why he'd walked away, because it seemed strange to me. He loves this town and has always enjoyed giving back. He said he didn't completely give it up. That he was still on the Wine and Tourism committee. But that it was time he stepped down from the board. That he'd served for years and he wanted to spend his time doing other things—like traveling with Riley."

"They were always so close, even after she left." Bryson's father leaned back in his chair. He ran a hand over his mouth and down his chin, as if he could wipe the grief away. "Sean and I used to sit out at the fire pit, and he'd tell me about the trips he'd take when she'd come back to the States."

Bryson felt that old, familiar ache settle in his chest. He'd treasured every detail Sean had shared regarding Riley's adventures, hungry for any connection to the life she was living. Hearing about them had been both a comfort and a torment—proof she was thriving, but also a reminder of how far away she'd chosen to be. "Sean certainly lit up with pride when he talked about Riley and everything she's accomplished." Not wanting to continue the conversation, he pointed to the mounds of paperwork. "That doesn't look like fun."

"Can't say that it is. This committee is filled with lots of big personalities, chest pounding, and gossip. Most meetings, my leg is rattling, and my eyes are glued to the time."

"So, why are you spending extra time at home on committee work?"

"There's a lot going on with efforts to increase tourism and boost profitability. We've filed for state and federal grants and conducted private fundraising over the past two years to revitalize the old buildings on the west side of town. We've sunk some money into that project." Bryson's dad waved his hand over the stack of papers on his desk. "Only, I'm not so sure these numbers are adding up. I mean, they do, but they don't. There's a mistake in here somewhere, and while Grant actually agreed, he was adamant he'd be one to find it and fix it."

"You're going through the books?" The question came out sharper than Bryson intended. "I'm sure that's gonna piss off Grant."

Bryson's dad chuckled. "Grant doesn't know. Only two of us do, and honestly, I don't have all the information, making this even harder."

"Why are you doing it if not everyone knows?"

"Mayor Jessip's paranoid. He wanted someone he trusted to look at the books."

"Paranoid about what?"

"Possible missing money, though he didn't come out and say that. So far, all I see is that most likely a couple of numbers were transposed. It happens. But I'm no accountant. That's Grant's expertise. But ever since Robert Wilkerson was arrested for that Ponzi scheme that the mayor invested in, he believes almost everyone is a liar and a thief."

"That's almost funny considering Jessip's a politician and hasn't followed through with some of his campaign promises," Bryson said. "Grant was friends with Wilkerson, but he was smart not to invest with him."

"Grant can be an arrogant ass, but stupid he's not. Too

bad he couldn't prevent his mother from investing in that scheme, but I guess she did that without anyone's advice." His dad shook his head. "And, Jessip? Well, he's a decent man... for a politician." He leaned forward, clasping his hands together. "What are you doing up at this hour?"

Bryson lifted his cell. "The motion detector went off on the corner of the property closest to town. I did a quick look on my cell. I think it's Riley, which isn't shocking, all things considered. I'm heading to the security office to double-check."

"I'm not surprised that girl hopped the fence." His dad let out a long breath. "How is she?"

"She looks good. Tired. But that's to be expected. But honestly, I don't really know," Bryson said.

"Twelve years is a long time," his father said quietly. "All you can do is be there for her."

"I'd better go check the cameras. Don't stay up too late, or Mom will have your head."

"I'll be going up shortly." His dad lifted his glasses and pushed them back up on his face.

Bryson made his way down the hall and into the security office. He sat down in the big chair and stared at the glow of the security monitors, rubbing the back of his neck. It was nearly midnight, and he'd been tossing and turning for the last hour.

He leaned closer, staring at the grainy image. A familiar shape. Slender. Purposeful. Still too far from the sensor for the spotlight to catch. But even before she stepped into the faint halo of moonlight, Bryson knew.

Riley.

He wasn't going to let her be out there alone. Not in

the place where her father had died. Not when grief had a way of swallowing people whole. Shutting off the light, he headed out into the night with memories of the past. His heart hammered in his chest like a teenage boy sneaking out of the house to meet his girlfriend, like he'd done so many times.

The cool air wrapped around him, sharp with the scent of grape skins, wet soil, and the faint trace of sulfur from the last barrel clean. The vines stood like silent sentinels in the dark, their heavy leaves rustling softly as he walked the path. His boots crunched over loose gravel as he spotted her, standing with her hands in her jacket pockets, looking out over the rows.

He paused for a moment and just stared at her under the glow of the moon.

With her long dark hair pulled up on top of her head in a wild bun, stray strands cascading down her back, she was still the most beautiful woman he'd ever laid eyes on. Her jeans hugged her curves, showing off the soft lines of her body.

Seeing her here was like taking a trip back in time. He was lost to his youth. He couldn't rectify his mistakes because there was always one decision that would never change. One choice he'd never do differently, even if every other thing that led up to that moment, he'd do over.

It was an impossible situation.

"You always did like this spot," he said, his voice low, not wanting to startle her.

She turned slowly. The moon cast a silver sheen over her face, highlighting the curve of her jaw, the set of her shoulders. Tired. Guarded. Beautiful in a way that punched him straight in the chest.

"I didn't think you'd see me," she said softly.

"I see almost everything out here," he replied, then added, "New cameras."

"Can you see the whole vineyard?"

"No." He shook his head. "Just certain access points. Like the fences near town. Or up by the hills."

"Did you see my dad on the cameras that morning?"

"He would have come in through the access road from the house. But I didn't look," he admitted.

A pause.

"I couldn't sleep," she said, glancing back at the vines. "I thought maybe... I don't know. I just wanted to be near him. Near where he took his last breath, as if that would somehow connect me to him."

Something in Bryson's heart cracked at the vulnerability in her admission. He understood that hollow feeling, the way loss made you grasp for any thread that might still tie you to the person who was gone. It was the same reason he still used his grandfather's pruning shears, still followed the same path through the vineyard that two generations of Boones had walked before him. "That makes perfect sense."

"I don't have too many regrets, but I always wanted to spend more time with my dad. These last five years, we did get together more, but now, it doesn't feel like enough." Her hands trembled as she brushed a few strands of hair from her face. The words were barely a whisper, but they hit hard. He felt the weight behind them—the grief embedded into every syllable.

"He was so proud of you," Bryson said gently. "He told

me once he didn't blame you for leaving. That sometimes love means letting someone go, even when it guts you. And your relationship with him was always solid. Distance never changed that."

She turned sharply. "Did he really say that?"

"He did." But Byson also knew some of those words were meant for him as much as they were to ease the pain in Sean's heart that he didn't get the chance to see his daughter on a daily basis like he saw his other children.

Silence settled again, broken only by the sound of a breeze rattling the vines. She stuffed her hands into her pockets and stared at the rows of grapes. "Where did you find him?"

"Riley, you—"

"Please. I need to know."

He wished she hadn't asked. The image of Sean slumped against that post was something Bryson would carry forever, and he hated the thought of passing that burden to her. But he could hear the desperation in her voice, the way she needed to piece together her father's final moments, and he couldn't deny her that. "Right over there." He pointed. "Against that post."

Slowly, she inched closer to where Bryson had first spotted Sean. The moonlight followed her as if she was guiding it on a journey. She paused just shy of where Bryson had laid him down on the ground, her arms dropping to her sides, her shoulders slumping. "Did you know right away that... he was gone."

"I suspected when I began CPR," he whispered, keeping his distance, unsure of whether he should wrap his arms around her or let her grieve alone. A sense of dread and helplessness washed over him, snaking through his body like the vines growing from the dirt. "I didn't stop trying until the paramedics arrived."

She covered her mouth, lowered her head, and sobbed.

He inched closer, but she shot her hand up, stopping him abruptly. His heart dropped to his toes. "The last thing he said to me was that he loved me."

"Those are good words to have."

She shifted, turning her head. Her tear-filled eyes glowed under the sky. Nothing but sadness and regret etched in their blue depths.

All he wanted to do was shoulder that for her. Be the rock she needed. But he didn't know how to do that for her. More importantly, he had no idea if she'd even want that from him.

"He knew about the baby, you know," she said, abruptly shifting topics to their shared past hanging over them like a storm. "About the miscarriage. He heard me crying the day it happened. I begged him not to tell anyone."

The words hit him like a physical blow, stalling what little breath he had left. He'd never planned to tell her about Sean's visit—about the things Sean had said in pain and anger. But she deserved to know that her father hadn't just kept her secret—he'd also made sure Bryson understood the weight of what had been lost. "He kept that promise, except for letting me know that he knew."

She looked up at him. "What?"

"He wasn't too happy with me." His voice dropped. "He showed up here when I'd come home that weekend because you'd called and told me what happened. He was a little tipsy and a little pissed off. Said that it was my fault because I loved the winery more than I loved you."

Her lips parted in shock. "He said that?"

"He did." He swallowed hard. "And the worst part was, I couldn't argue. Not then. Not with the way things ended... with what you'd said that weekend."

"I didn't mean it," she whispered. "About not wanting the baby. About being glad I'd lost it."

"I can't say those words didn't cut right through my heart. Or that you leaving didn't drive those words deep into my soul," he said, wanting to take her into his arms, but he held back. "However, considering everything, I know you didn't mean them. And I certainly didn't mean what I said in return. It was cruel, and I'm sorry."

"I know." She pressed the heels of her palms into her eyes, rubbed, and then dropped her arms to her sides. "Does anyone else know? Did you tell your family?"

Byson thought about lying, but he couldn't—not to her. "Just my dad and only recently."

"Wow," she said softly. "This isn't a secret I want let out of the bag. And not because I'm ashamed or would care what others think anymore. It's not about them. It's private, and I can't stand gossip. This town can be relentless with it."

He could hear the exhaustion in her voice, the same bone-deep weariness he'd been carrying all these years. They'd both been prisoners of this secret, just in different cells. "It sure can. And my dad's not going to say anything. It's just that I'd held it in for so long, and I needed to do something with it."

"I can understand that."

Something shifted in him. He'd braced himself for anger, for accusations, for all the blame he'd heaped on himself over the years. Instead, she gave him what appeared to be absolution, and he wasn't sure he knew how to accept it.

The silence between them shifted—thicker now. He took another step forward, close enough to see her eyes.

"I'm sorry you went through that alone. That I was away at school when it happened and wasn't here to hold your hand. I've always hated myself for that."

The pain etched in her eyes gave way to a different kind of hurt. She swiped at her cheeks and took a tentative step forward. "You can't control Mother Nature, and there was nothing you could've done. I don't blame you for that." Her shoulders squared, and her resolve hardened in her features. "I do blame you for Monica."

Bryson flinched. "She wasn't—"

"You kissed her," Riley said, voice rising slightly. "You kissed her right after I told you about the pregnancy. I was scared and confused and not sure I was ready to be a mom. I was terrified and you kissed her. And it was all made worse by my friends showing it to me. Not to mention you started dating her right after I left." She stuffed her hands in her hoodie pocket. "And then you married her. How do you think that made me feel?"

"It wasn't what it looked like." His tone hardened, jaw clenched. "First off, she came on to me. I didn't stop it fast enough, and I have to live with that. But I wasn't with her until after you left. Until after you refused to take my calls."

"That's supposed to make me feel better?"

"No." He let out a long breath. "I'm just saying you

weren't here for me to even argue with or explain my side." He threaded his fingers through his hair. "I didn't betray you."

Riley held his gaze. Something between fire and understanding stared back. "That's not how I see it—especially when you simply let me walk away. But it doesn't matter. Not anymore."

"It matters to me," he said, voice raw. "And you think I didn't want to chase after you? I stood on your porch with your dad blocking the door, telling me to give you space. And I did. I gave you space for twelve goddamn years."

She pressed her fingers to her mouth, like she was holding something in—or holding something back.

"I couldn't stay," she said finally, her voice breaking. "And not for all the reasons you're thinking. I would've hated you. And myself. And this place. And in a weird way, because I love Stone Bridge, I couldn't let that happen. Not to mention, you couldn't leave. Wouldn't leave. So, really, this conversation is a bit absurd because we both did exactly what we were meant to do."

A long silence stretched between them. The air was heavy with things unsaid—years of regret, love, anger, heartbreak.

But in the most fundamental way, she was right, and he couldn't argue that point if he tried.

Bryson exhaled and looked toward the vines. This was his home. His heart. He'd always belonged here—but he never expected she wouldn't be a part of it. "Sometimes I walk out here and think I hear you laughing. That stupid, wild laugh you had when you were sixteen and trying to teach me how to dance in the crush pad."

"I remember," she whispered. "You stepped on my foot three times."

"More like six," he corrected. "You just stopped counting."

She smiled, and the sight of it undid something in his chest. For a moment, she wasn't the woman who'd left. She was Riley—the girl he'd loved, the woman he'd never stopped loving. It was an odd sensation... that love... old and familiar, yet new and unsettling because it was still there. It was real. And it was fucking raw as hell, and he had no idea how to deal with it.

He reached out, gently brushing a strand of hair from her cheek. "I've always wanted to see you again. I've always thought about you."

Her eyes shimmered. "I never thought I'd be back. Never thought I'd have the strength to return, much less have that conversation with you."

"You're the strongest person I know," he said. "Even if you've never believed you were."

The wind stirred around them, warm and soft. The vineyard was quiet. Still. Expectant.

He desperately wanted to feel her again. To know what it was like to hold her. To kiss her. He leaned in slowly, watching her eyes, giving her every chance to pull away. But she didn't.

Their lips met—soft, tentative at first, then deeper, more certain. It wasn't desperate. It wasn't fiery. It was the kind of kiss that came after twelve years of silence. After pain, and heartbreak, and the kind of longing that never quite died.

When they pulled apart, her forehead rested gently against his.

"What was that?" she whispered.

"I have no idea," he said. "Maybe it's twelve years of not saying what we've needed to and our way of letting go of the pain."

Riley sighed. "I don't know how I'm going to get through this. Burying my father. Seeing my family. Being back here. It's all too much."

"You don't have to do it alone, Ry. I'm right here. I'm sorry I hurt you. I truly am. I've always regretted how things ended with us. But we can't change the past. Let me be the person you lean on now. I'm not going anywhere."

She lifted her gaze and laughed softly. "No, I'm the one who goes places, and I'll be leaving after the funeral."

"I know," he said softly. "Did you walk from the Inn?"

"I did, and I realized I didn't really think this through. I'm gonna need a car to get around."

"Lucky for you, I've got a second vehicle. You can use that." He placed his hand on the small of her back. "We can get it now, or you can get it in the morning."

"Tomorrow is fine. Thank you."

"I'll walk you back to the Inn."

"You don't—"

"I insist," he said.

They walked back toward Stone Bridge Inn, side by side in the dark, their hands brushed—then twined.

And for the first time since she'd come home, the ache in his chest eased.

Just a little.

Four

The morning sun spilled low over the hills, stretching light across the rows of vines like a familiar hand reaching out to Riley.

She stepped from the Stone Bridge Inn and wished she'd taken Bryson's vehicle last night. But she'd needed the fresh air, the walk, and a few more moments alone with him. She had to admit it felt good to finally have the conversation she'd repeatedly had in her head for years. It had certainly gone better in person than in her imagination.

As she inched along the sidewalk, her heart hammered in her chest. Not over Bryson, or their past, but over something just as traumatizing. She yanked her cell from her back pocket. She pulled up Mateo's contact information and took a chance he'd be available.

Two rings. That was all it took.

"Hello, love," Mateo said. "How are you holding up?"

"Better, but I haven't seen my family yet. That will happen shortly."

"Calling for a little pep talk?"

"Something like that," she said as she picked up the pace. "I'm on my way to Bryson's and I have to walk right past my old home. Like they're next to each other. The one where I caught my mother cheating with my stepdad before my parents divorced. I don't want to see it. I know that seems weird. And I'm gonna have to face it before I leave. But it always brings up a million questions and regrets. Like, why didn't I scream from the rooftops about my mom's dirty little secret?"

"Because it was your father's, too," Mateo said.

Before she'd left Patagonia, she'd broken down, cried like a fool on Mateo's shoulder, and given him a crash course on her life—every freaking detail. Mateo had become the closest thing she had to a best friend.

"My dad told me once that he didn't want his children to have to deal with the rumors flying around school. When I moved in with him, he figured I'd eventually forgive my mom, and he encouraged me to do so, but he never pushed. He was angry that she expected me to keep the lie, because he didn't. He set up therapy sessions. He was always there for me to talk to, where my mom just went on like my dad walked out on her and took me with him."

"Parents do some strange things," Mateo said. "I know mine sure have. But that was all a lifetime ago. Your family's dysfunctional. Maybe a little more than most. But none of us are getting out of here alive. Your dad just reminded you of that. Don't you think it's time to heal these wounds?"

"I think I liked you better when you were full of sarcasm and dares."

Mateo laughed.

Breathless, she stopped at the edge of the gravel driveway of the sprawling house sitting on the edge of the winery—the Boone family home. It was a converted old farmhouse, expanded into a mansion without losing the country feel. She'd meant to be in and out of Bryson's before anyone noticed—but the Boones were already on the porch.

Every last one of them.

"Thanks for getting me past the family home and the memories. I've got to go."

"Call me if you need me. If I'm free, I'll pick up. If not, I'll call as soon as I can."

"Thanks, Mateo. You're a gem."

"See you when you get back."

She ended the call, stuffed her cell back in her pocket, and continued down the driveway.

Bryson stood on the front porch with a coffee mug in one hand, leaning against the railing, looking like he was as much a part of the vineyard as it was of him. His mother, Brea, sat in a rocking chair, her silver-streaked hair twisted into a loose knot and her gaze fixed fondly on Bryson as he spoke.

Walter—tall and trim in a worn flannel shirt—sat beside her with a newspaper folded across his knee, smiling that broad, proud grin of his.

Ashley and Hasley were barefoot, one in jeans and the other in a long, flowing skirt, curled up on the steps with a shared bowl of cut fruit, while Devon, the oldest child, stood near Bryson, tablet in one hand, mug in the other, nodding at whatever Bryson had been discussing.

It was the kind of scene she'd spent her whole childhood aching for, then twelve more years pretending she didn't miss.

Bryson saw her first. He straightened, a smile tugging at the corners of his mouth as he lifted a hand. "Good morning."

"Sorry to interrupt." Riley scurried closer.

"You're not interrupting," Brea called, standing now, arms already open.

Riley hesitated—just a second—then stepped into the hug. It felt both strange and natural at the same time.

"Oh, honey," Brea whispered, pulling back to cup her face. "I'm so sorry about your father. He was such a kind and gentle man. If you need anything at all, please don't hesitate to call us."

"Thank you," Riley said, voice rough.

Walter's expression was sober but kind. "It's good to see you again, Riley, though I'm sad it's under these circumstances."

"It's good to see you as well, Mr. Boone." She let out a slow breath, desperately trying to keep the swell of emotion from unraveling.

"Walter," he corrected. "You stopped needing permission for first names a long time ago."

Ashley jumped to her feet and didn't hesitate before wrapping her arms around Riley. "Welcome back," she whispered. "We're all so devastated about your dad. He was so sweet, and we adored him. If you ever want to talk, we're always here."

"What she said." Hasley inched closer—her turn for a hug.

It was all so overwhelming, certainly not what Riley was used to anymore, and yet, exactly what she needed.

"Words can't express how deeply saddened we all are over your dad's passing." Devon rested his tablet on the railing, kissed her cheek, and squeezed her shoulder.

Tears stung her eyes. She wasn't sure what she'd expected when she set foot in this town, but this wasn't it. She knew the Boones wouldn't have been anything other than kind. But their loving attitude wrapped around her like a protective blanket, all warm and soft, and it was all more than she could bear.

Ashley grinned. "We were just about to head inside for breakfast."

"You should join us, dear," Brea said.

"And we won't take no for an answer," Walter added.

"I've got to get going." Riley swallowed the thick lump that formed in the center of her throat. As a kid, it felt like she'd spent more time in this house than at home. The Boones had been like a second family.

"Have you eaten?" Bryson asked.

"I can grab a bagel in town or something," she said.

"Elsa has cooked a huge spread." Her mother rose with the grace of a princess. She'd always had a certain flair and style but was so down-to-earth. "Bryson, Devon, and their father have already made their morning rounds through the vineyard, and breakfast is about to be put on the table. It'll take less time than stopping at the bakery."

"Come on." Hasley looped her arm through hers. "Coffee's fresh. So are the waffles."

Reluctantly—though it didn't quite feel like reluctance, not really—Riley followed the family inside.

She meandered through the massive foyer, down the hallway that seemed to stretch on for the full length of a football field, and into the big kitchen, trying not to let the ghosts of the past fill her brain, no matter how magical some of those memories could be.

She sat down at the big butcher block island and took the cup Bryson handed her. The warmth seeped into her hands as the smells of maple syrup, butter, and dark roast coffee surrounded her.

It felt like home, and that was something she hadn't experienced in a very long time. Every country, every town, was merely a place she passed through on her way to the next one. It was as if the moment her feet connected with the earth, the itch to see something new settled against her skin. A scratchy sensation that danced around her body that she couldn't quite satisfy.

"Well, my, my." Elsa turned from the kitchen stove. "I heard you were back in town." She plopped a plate of bacon on the center of the island and tugged Riley to her chest. "I'm so sorry about your dad. I always loved listening to that man tell stories. He was the best."

"That he was." Riley hugged the older woman who the Boones had employed for as long as she could remember. She was more than a cook and a housekeeper. To the Boones, she was family. Or as Brea called her, *the heart of the house.*

Elsa cupped Riley's face. "Sean loved to talk about you. He'd come strolling in some mornings with postcards from wherever in the world you'd landed. I feel like I've lived another lifetime through you." She pinched Riley's cheeks like she'd done so many times. "I best get going on making beds. You all enjoy your breakfast."

"Elsa," Walter said softly. "You don't have to go rushing off. Eat something first."

"Already did." Elsa lowered her chin. "Had two cups of coffee too. But I really want to get a head start on things so I can spend some time with those grandbabies of mine before I come back."

"You don't have to cook dinner tonight," Brea said. "I'm perfectly capable, so if you want the evening off, feel—"

"I'm taking tomorrow off, so I'll be back this afternoon." Else set a plate of steaming waffles on the counter and disappeared up the back stairs.

"My darling children, you'd better have made your beds and cleaned up your bathrooms this morning." Brea eased into one of the stools and waved her fork in the air. "That was the deal about living here as adults."

"Please, Mother." Ashley laughed. "Elsa hasn't had to lift a finger for us in years."

"I'm surprised she's still working," Riley said. "I would've thought she'd retired by now."

"Because she doesn't want to leave." Walter laughed. "We've tried to let her go, but she wants to work. It gives her purpose. So, she cooks, she does a little light housework— with the cleaning service that does the heavy lifting—and maybe some grocery shopping with Mom. I think it makes Elsa feel like she's needed, and we can afford to pay her. Besides, she's family. She has a job here for as long as she wants it. Let's eat." Walter dug a fork into a waffle, set it on a plate, added some bacon, and pushed it in front of Riley. "As I recall, this was always one of your favorite meals."

"Still is." She lathered up the waffle with butter and syrup, making sure to hit the bacon strips with a few drops of the sticky stuff. She smiled at Walter. "Nothing beats Elsa's cooking." She took a bite, letting it melt in her mouth, and savored not only the flavor, but the good memories that came out of this kitchen

And there were plenty. She'd practically grown up right on the very stool she'd planted her ass. She'd come over during her elementary school days, eat this very breakfast, and watch Saturday morning cartoons with Bryson and his siblings because of the tension in her own home. Back then, she hadn't known that her parents weren't happy. But she'd felt it.

Then there was Grant.

And Erin.

Riley was the baby of the family, and for whatever reason, she and her siblings had never gotten along very well. Grant and Erin had always been close. They had a bond forged out of the simple fact that they were only a year apart, while Riley had been three years younger than Grant—four years younger than Erin.

Riley had been the interloper. As if those two were part of a private club and she didn't know the secret handshake to get in.

Her mother used to tell her that if she'd stop being so bratty all the time, Grant and Erin would be nicer. Kinder. Her father told her that, given time, they'd all grow out of it. However, that had never happened—but she supposed it was because she'd left. According to her mother, she'd never given her siblings a chance to become friends as adults.

Well, they'd been trying.

But that didn't change the fact that for her entire childhood, they'd constantly reminded her that she'd been a mistake. An accident. The one unplanned child. Looking back, it hadn't really been their fault. That idea had been planted in their brains by their mother.

Grant and Erin were following cues, which they always took from their mom. Whenever Riley acted out, their mother would dramatically sigh, wave her hand, and make a comment about how Riley wasn't even a surprise, but an utter shock. Once, her mom had even told her that she'd contemplated her *options*.

Her dad never once called her a mistake or even suggested he'd never wanted her in any way. He'd always... just loved her.

God, how she missed him.

"You're still on Patagonia time?" Devon asked. If he'd sensed where her mind had wandered, she had no idea, but she was grateful to shift to a lighter conversation.

"Sort of. Time difference isn't too horrible. But my body's confused, and I'm pretending I'm not." She lifted a piece of bacon and stuffed it in her mouth. It tasted like a little piece of home.

"Classic Callahan stubbornness," Bryson teased gently.

She shot him a look, but it was half-hearted. The truth was, this felt... nice. Safer than she expected. And for a few minutes, the conversation flowed around her like a current she could drift in. Ashley updated everyone on her latest mishap with a raccoon the other morning when she'd gone to get the paper. Hasley bemoaned the awful date she'd had last week. Devon listened but constantly checked his phone. Bryson laughed easily. Riley finished her breakfast and let herself forget for one rare moment that everything inside her was cracked.

Until Walter pushed his plate aside, rested his elbows against the counter, and said, "I've been thinking about your dad, Riley. His passing has left an emptiness in all of us."

The air moved slightly. Not dramatically—just subtle enough that everyone shifted their gaze toward Walter.

"Grant told me that he worried about Dad. He was always tired. Erin agreed and also said that our mom mentioned that my father had complained of shortness of breath lately," Riley said carefully. "But my dad never said anything to me."

"He didn't say anything to us, either." Walter shook his head. "Sean was private. Always had been. However, he and I have been friends since grade school, and we've shared a lot over the years. I'd like to believe that if he'd been ill, he would've confided in me. But, I'll admit he'd been acting a little strange the last few weeks."

"I've learned that my dad often kept a lot of things to himself, like knowing about my mother's affair," she said quietly, even though she'd always been able to speak freely in the Boone residence.

"Walter told us about the problems he'd been having with your mom long before they got divorced," Brea added softly. "We've been friends a long time. He stood up for us at our wedding."

"I'm really not surprised my father would confide in

you." Riley palmed her mug. "Over the years, he did fill me in on the issues. It's not like I didn't sense they were unhappy. But I also didn't know the details."

"I've known your mom a long time." Brea smiled. "She often forgets we grew up on the same side of town. I don't mean to speak badly of her, but she wanted Sean to be something he wasn't, and money, prestige, and power have long been things she desired. Things Parker has been able to provide—and he's a good and kind man."

"I do like Parker. He's always been nice to me." Riley let out a dry chuckle. "But my mother and I have always struggled. She wanted me to be some sweet little girl who wore cute pink dresses, patent leather shoes, and pretty clips in her curly hair, like my sister. Not some wild tomboy who preferred to crush grapes with my bare feet during harvest with this guy." She jerked her thumb at Bryson. "She'd always complain my feet were purple for weeks."

"And she'd call us, griping about it, telling us you weren't allowed to play with Bryson anymore." Walter sighed. "It was always a delicate dance, and I'm sorry if we caused you any grief at home."

"You never did. It was just always that way," Riley said.

"But something was going on with Sean," Bryson said, setting down his mug. "I don't think it was his health. He'd been distracted lately, but he was still sharp. And the day before he died..." He looked over at Riley. "Well, we never did get the chance to have that chat. I have no idea what it was about, but he mentioned it was personal."

Riley's stomach tightened. "Personal? Did he say anything else?"

"No, but it felt urgent." Bryson hesitated. "Now, I can't stop wondering what he didn't get the chance to say."

Brea reached out and placed her hand over Riley's. "None of this is to upset you, sweetheart. We all cared about Sean. He was a good man. If he had something to share, I believe it mattered."

Riley's throat grew dry. "Thank you. I... I've had this feeling. That something was unfinished as well. During our last few phone conversations, I heard a tension in his voice. I asked him, and he said it was nothing for me to worry about. I actually called my sister to see if she knew. We got into one of our usual fights about me abandoning the family. About turning my back on everyone. I suppose she's not wrong in some ways."

"I'm certainly not going to sit here in judgment of your decisions. You did what you needed to do for yourself. No one can fault you for that," Walter said gently. "This will be a difficult time for you and your family. But know that we're always here if you need us."

The fact that Bryson had told his father about the baby—their baby—sent an unexpected pang of guilt, sorrow, and regret through her. She'd carried that loss alone for so long, she'd almost forgotten it belonged to both of them.

There was a long silence, broken only by the soft buzz of Devon's cell phone. He jumped right out of his chair. "Sorry," he muttered, tapping his screen. "Excuse me. I need to take this." He stepped from the kitchen.

"Dad," Bryson said behind clenched teeth. "He's not talking to Emery Tate, is he?

"Not the time or place. We'll talk about it later." Walter

arched brow. "Sorry about that, Riley. Were you going to say something else?"

She glanced between the two men, wondering what that was all about, but it wasn't her business. "I'm concerned about the whole autopsy thing," she managed. "When I last spoke to Grant about it, he said they were still waiting for the ME to make a decision. I could hear my mother in the background whispering about it, and Grant feeding off that. The thing is, my dad really did have an aversion to being cut open. But I'm still confused as to why it's just not being done."

"I don't know a lot about how these things work, but I suppose when a family member, or the deceased doesn't want one, I would think, unless there's a specific reason for it, the ME could honor that," Walter said, leaning back, crossing his arms over his chest. "And even though Grant tossed a ridiculous accusation at Bryson, I don't believe the police are taking that seriously." Walter's gaze steadied on her, something understanding in his eyes. "But everyone handles grief differently, and there's no right or wrong way to deal with the death of a loved one. They're hurting same as you."

"If he voiced his suspicion, I suspect they'd have to look into it," Bryson said.

Riley snapped her gaze back to Bryson. "What? Grant blamed you? Why?"

"He's upset that your father died on our vineyard. He snapped at me because he didn't like your father doing what he thought of as manual labor." Bryson gave her what she suspected was meant to be a reassuring smile, but it fell flat, especially since Bryson and Grant hadn't ever really been friends. "But it happened on our property. I'm the one who found him and couldn't save him."

"Still, my brother shouldn't have said that." Riley lifted her mug but only stared at the liquid.

Bryson shrugged. "Your brother and I have always had our issues, and that's no secret."

"I overheard some ladies gossiping in the lobby of the hotel. They mentioned the police came out here. Is that because of what Grant said?"

"Sandy Kane, you might remember her from school. She's the police chief. She came out here late yesterday, asked a few questions, walked the property," Walter said.

"Sandy's a cop?" Wow. Not that it was that far of a stretch. She had a weird obsession with true crime shows throughout high school.

"She went to the academy right after college. Worked her way up the ranks and became chief last year," Bryson said. "She wanted to speak to me. Get a picture of what happened. It's standard procedure when someone dies alone. I don't think it had anything to do with Grant's remark in the heat of the moment."

"So strange for you to be giving my brother so much grace."

"We co-exist well enough in this town and considering the circumstances, I can be empathetic," Bryson said. "And when I ran into the ME yesterday, I asked some questions."

"What?" Riley glared. "Why would you speak to Doctor Gavin?" Stone Bridge was a small town in the Napa

Valley area. Everyone knew everyone, and worse, they knew each other's business.

Bryson grimaced. "I was picking up a prescription for my mom yesterday, and I ran into him. I thought I might be able to get some information for you. But he wouldn't say a thing except for a long lecture on patient confidentiality."

"You shouldn't have said anything at all," Riley said.

"I agree with her on that one," his mother said before lifting her coffee mug to her lips.

"I didn't mean to overstep. I was only trying to help," Bryson said. "Or at least understand the situation."

"Well, that wasn't for you to do." Riley pursed her lips, stood, and brushed off her jeans. Her dad had always said when it was his time, he wanted to go peacefully, and it sounded like he'd gotten his wish. Who was she to go demanding someone cut open his body when no one questioned the reason for his death, other than the untimeliness of it? "Thank you for breakfast. All of you. I should head out. My family is gathering at my mother's place, and they're expecting me."

Brea stepped forward and gave her one more hug. "Don't be a stranger. Byson told us you insisted on staying at Stone Bridge Inn. Just remember, if the walls there seem too tight, or you just get lonely, you can stay in the guesthouse. Or we have plenty of bedrooms here. You're always welcome."

Walter nodded in agreement. "We're here if you need anything."

"Thanks." She hesitated again. "For... everything. This meant more than I expected."

"I'll walk you out." Bryson stood and grabbed a set of

keys from the hook by the door. "I parked the truck in the side yard. It's a little dusty, but it will get you where you need to go, and it's got a full tank." He took her by the elbow and guided her through the house, out the door, and down the porch steps.

"Can I ask you a question?"

"Of course."

They rounded the corner of the house. On the access road leading toward the vineyard sat a pick-up truck with the words: *Stone Bridge Winery* displayed proudly on the side.

Wonderful. The entire town would see her coming and make a judgment about her and her connection to the Boones. But she couldn't really complain. Money was tight. More than tight. She'd always lived paycheck to paycheck, and she'd been fine with that, but the airfare alone to get home had put her back, and renting a car would've made it impossible to get to wherever she was going next.

Now all she had to do was decide if she wanted to call the ME herself and see if she could push the issue—and time was running out. Part of her needed to know if there was something more to her father's death, something that might explain why he'd seemed so tired lately. But another part of her was terrified of what they might find—or worse, what they might not find, leaving her with nothing but more questions and guilt.

"Do you think if I asked the ME to do an autopsy, even against the rest of my family's wishes, he'd do it?" she asked. "I mean, there doesn't seem to be a reason to press it, and I don't need to cause more waves with my family, but I feel like if I don't know what my dad died of, I'll always wonder."

"All I can say is, if it were my dad, I'd be begging for one," Bryson said. "As far as your family goes, I honestly believe Grant and Erin were simply trying to be respectful of your dad. I bet if you spoke with them, they'd hear you." He rubbed his jaw, much like the day Grant had punched him in the chin back in high school. As if he were afraid it was about to happen again any second.

"You don't sound very convincing."

"One thing I know about Grant and Erin is they're fiercely loyal to your mom. And Elizabeth, well, she can run hot and cold with your dad."

"What is—"

"Can I finish please?" Byson asked.

"Sure."

"The last five years or so, your mom's been different when it comes to Sean, and that's weird all by itself."

"I need you to explain that."

"I'm only guessing, because I try to spend as little time as possible with your mom. But your dad was in his glory working in the tasting room. Locals came in just to hear him talk about the good old days when he and my grandfather planted the first block."

"That would get under my mother's skin." Riley could picture her mother's face, tight with disapproval. "But not enough for her to change her tune about my dad."

"I'm not saying she did. I'm just saying she didn't consistently badmouth him." Bryson reached out and tucked some hair behind Riley's ear. "I can see the pain in your eyes, Ry. I can feel the uncertainty radiating off your skin, and it's not just about being back in Stone Bridge. He was your dad. You loved him. You want to know what happened, and I know you and your relationship with the truth."

"It's been twelve years. You don't know anything about me anymore."

"It has been a long time." He took her hand and pressed it against his chest. "But, history doesn't simply disappear."

She shifted her gaze between their hands and his eyes, before dropping her arm to her side and letting out a long, slow breath. "You're right. It doesn't. But I don't want to make things harder with my family. And making that call to the ME won't help. It'll bring up every wrong, every mistake, I've ever made and slap it right across my family's face."

"I can't believe I'm going to say this, but Grant isn't the worst person in the world. He's gotten... softer. His wife is an amazing woman. Talk to him. What's the worst that can happen?"

She snorted. "Maybe things are that way for you, but our conversations derail pretty quickly and can get ugly."

"Your brother might surprise you."

She glanced toward the sky. "Oftentimes, conversations with Grant start out fine and end in a brawl. Same with Erin. It's like we don't know how to let go of the hurt. All the horrible things we've said and done. It's all right there like bubbles at the surface of boiling water."

"We had some issues, and look at us?"

"We're not family, and give it time, I'll find a reason to be mad at you." She gave him a weak smile. Her attempt at humor had fallen flat. He didn't even crack a grin.

"Do you want me to come with you today?"

"God, no. That would just add fuel to a fire I don't need burning wildly out of control. I'm not that same eighteen-year-old kid who tended to shoot off her mouth on a whim. I've got this."

"I'm sure you do." Bryson pulled open the driver's side door. "Promise me something?"

"What's that?"

"Call me after you meet with your family." He leaned in and kissed her cheek. "I just need to know you're okay."

"I can do that." She climbed behind the steering wheel and burst out laughing.

"What?"

"I can't reach the pedals." She adjusted the seat. "I remember running with you in the mornings and yelling, 'Wait for me, I've got little legs.'"

"Only during sprints. You always beat me to the top of a mountain, or anything over three miles." He smiled, then looked away for a moment, before meeting her gaze again. "Listen. I can't imagine how hard this is for you, but I was there through all the bullshit with Grant and Erin. The jealousy. The fights. How they treated you when you chose to live with your dad."

He stepped closer, his voice becoming more earnest. "And I know how they are now. They still aren't making things easy for you, while you're bending over backward to please them." He let out a long breath. "Just protect yourself... emotionally. I know how resilient you are, but it doesn't change the fact that they know exactly how to hurt you." He closed the door.

Drawing a shuddering breath, she stuck the key in the

ignition and turned it. His words hit deeper than she expected. He'd always been able to see through her defenses. The tough exterior she'd perfected over the years meant nothing when Bryson looked at her like that—like he could see every vulnerable spot she thought she'd armored over.

She caught Bryson's eye in the rearview as he waved. The space between them crowded with everything that hadn't been said. But this morning—this moment—wasn't about the past.

It was about the questions beginning to root inside her... that had nothing to do with her family.

All the what-ifs regarding her life choices. The ones she'd never allowed herself to ponder because they hurt too damn much. It meant admitting she'd been wrong.

Five

About five miles out of town, a stately two-story home sat nestled among manicured hedges and blooming hydrangeas, the front porch painted a pristine white that made Riley's skin itch. Everything about it screamed carefully curated perfection—more like fake perfection, just like her mother.

It wasn't that Riley didn't love her mom, because she did. When Riley had chosen to live with her dad, she'd been heartbroken over the divorce. Over the harsh words between her and her mother. Over the expectation that Riley should accept her mom's decision because her mother deserved to be happy.

And over the lie. The one that Riley's mom so desperately needed her children to keep.

It all seemed so pointless. As if clinging to that part of her past had been for nothing.

Riley stood on the brick walkway, staring at the glossy black front door with its polished brass knocker, and reminded herself to breathe.

Slowly, she made her way up the steps. She'd never lived in this house. She'd spent a few weekends and holidays here, but it had never been home. Not like it had been to Grant and Erin. Not like the old ranch where she and her father had lived after the divorce—after the family home had been sold.

Deep down, she knew she had to take her share of the blame for broken relationships with her family. Grant was right. She'd been the one to take off for parts unknown. Initially, she'd been the one to sever ties. They'd had no idea what had happened. The loss. The heartbreak. That was on her.

She pushed aside the past and braced for emotional impact.

The second she pressed the doorbell, she heard voices hush inside.

Footsteps. A creak of wood.

Then the door swung open, revealing Erin—flawless in a beige wrap dress, blonde hair—obviously from a bottle since Erin was a natural brunette—swept into a loose twist. The transformation had begun when Chad entered the picture, and Erin gradually started lightening her hair until she looked nothing like the sister Riley remembered. Their father had confided once how hard it was to watch Chad reshape Erin into the woman he thought she should be, beginning with the demand that brunettes weren't sophisticated enough for his social circle.

"Wow, I can't believe you're here," she said, not moving to let Riley in.

Riley smiled without showing any teeth. "Hi, Erin. Good to see you, too."

Erin inched closer, her arms opening, and she pulled Riley in for a hug. The first one in God only knew how long. "It's so hard to believe he's gone."

"I know."

Riley leaned into the embrace, feeling every ounce of it. The moment wasn't full of love. But it was something real. Something she could hold on to and maybe build on.

"We're in the dining room." Erin stepped back, gesturing toward the hallway. "I should warn you... Mom's not handling your return well."

Riley recoiled, jerking her head back to study her sister. "What's that supposed to mean? I've tried calling. She hasn't answered or called me back."

"I don't want to fight." Erin raised her hands. "She's just being Mom. Acting as if it were her husband who died." Erin rolled her eyes. "But I suppose she's thinking about Parker's cancer. He's in remission, but it still weighs on her."

"I'm sure it does."

"Also, please don't start in on Chad." Erin swiped at her cheeks. "Not today of all days. We can talk about all that another time. I'm open to a conversation if you're going to be in town long enough to have it." She leaned closer. "Without Chad around," she whispered.

Riley's lips parted, and she let out an audible gasp. The memory of Chad's unwelcome hands when she'd been a teenager came flooding back, along with the pain of Erin not believing her when Riley had tried to warn her. Erin had called Riley a liar. Said she was just trying to sabotage her happiness. But now, hearing the desperation in her sister's voice, Riley wondered if Erin was finally ready to admit she'd been wrong about him.

"Okay," was all she could manage.

"Come on." Her sister looped her arm through Riley's and tugged her toward the dining room.

The air inside smelled like lemon polish and cinnamon potpourri. Her mother sat at the head of the table, a glass of white wine in hand despite the early hour. Parker, her second husband, stood behind her chair, a hand resting lightly on her shoulder like he was there for show, not support.

"Riley." Parker quickly made his way around the table and pulled her in for an awkward hug." It's good to see you again after all these years, although I do wish the circumstances were different. I'm so sorry about your father." He kissed her cheek.

"Thank you. How are you feeling?"

"Still tired but doing much better." Parker smiled weakly. "I enjoyed all the gift baskets and postcards. That was thoughtful." He turned and went back to his position where her mom still hadn't bothered to acknowledge her presence.

Grant and his wife, Kelly, sat on one side of the table, and Erin slipped into a chair on the other side. Chad, Erin's husband, offered a polite smile but looked away immediately. Riley's chest tightened. Seeing him again stirred old wounds she'd wished were healed.

"None of us were sure you'd make it," Elizabeth said, setting down her glass. She rose, smoothing down the front of her black dress. She blew out a strong breath through her nose and approached Riley. "I thought your calls and texts were telling me that you'd decided to stay in whatever country you've been living in these days." Her words were clipped, bitter, and they had a chilling bite to them. "But I'm glad you managed to find time in your busy schedule to come. Your father would be happy for that." She brushed her bright red lips against Riley's cheek before sitting back down.

Her mom could always hand out a good sideways compliment while scolding you in the same breath.

"I got in yesterday," Riley replied. "I wanted to settle in before seeing everyone, though I've been in constant contact with Grant and Erin."

Grant smiled at her. "You look good, little sis." He reached out, took her hand, and squeezed. "I told you that you could've stayed with us. If you change your mind, that offer still stands." After all the tension, all the stilled conversations and carefully worded texts, this simple gesture felt like a lifeline. Maybe her father's death had reminded them both of what really mattered—that broken as they might be, they were family.

"Thanks. But for now, I'm good at the inn."

"Is that where you're really staying?" Her mother asked. "Because I heard you were seen with Bryson Boone this morning." She waved a judgmental finger toward the window. "I saw the Stone Bridge Winery truck pull in the driveway. One can only assume you borrowed it from *them*, which means you're staying there."

"They loaned it to me," Riley said, her jaw clenched. "But I'm not staying there, not that it's any of your business."

"It is when you treat your bro—"

"Not the time for this." Kelly interrupted her mother-in-law. Turning back toward Riley, she added, "We've just been going over the final plans for Dad's celebration. We've postponed the ceremony to next week, but the date isn't confirmed, yet. However, the florist is taken care of, and the vineyard is letting us use the west lawn, free of charge. We're grateful for that."

Riley's gaze flicked to Grant. "Bryson's winery?" Of all the things that had been discussed this morning, she was a little surprised by this revelation. Maybe the Boones thought she knew.

Grant stiffened. "It's what Dad wanted. He specified it in his will. Though I'm not sure how I feel about that considering he died there."

"It's a beautiful location," Kelly offered. "We thought it would be nice to keep things simple and intimate. Just family and a few of your father's closest friends."

"I still think the country club would be better. I'm sure we can all agree that the outdoor gardens there are spectacular. The food is the best in town," her mother said. "Grant, that won't be a problem, financially, will it?"

Riley clenched her hands in her lap. Her father wasn't even buried yet, and her mother was trying to rewrite his final wishes to suit her own vision of what was appropriate. Her father had wanted to be remembered among the vines he'd cherished. He wanted simplicity, intimacy, and her mother was trying to turn his memorial into a social event.

"Not the point, mother." Grant's eyes narrowed to slits, his mouth pressing into a hard line. "Dad had some pretty specific wishes. I intend to honor them. Not to mention,

Walter and Dad have been close since grade school, and wasn't Walter in your wedding?"

"I just thought, with how you and Bryson are, that it would be better to have it somewhere else." Her mother lowered her chin and sniffled.

Always the actress.

"This isn't about me. Or Byson. It's about Dad and doing what he'd want."

Her mother swept one hand through the air while lifting the other to dab at her cheek.

"I'd like to help," Riley said. "He was my dad, too."

A heavy silence fell. Grant and Erin stole glances before shifting their gazes to their mother, who stared into her wine glass before taking a long, slow sip. Chad coughed. Or maybe it was a grunt.

"There's not much left to do," her mother said with a dismissive wave. "The details are in place. Decisions already made—even if I'm not on board with them."

"There are a few things that haven't been secured yet. And we needed to stay on top of the details. There are many ways you can help," Erin offered.

"I know the last two days were tough on you with travel and stuff, but I sent you a long email about the plans," Grant said. "The only things set in stone are the things Dad laid out in his will." He met her gaze. "If there's something you'd like to change, or want to add, let us know."

"Thanks." Riley felt a rush of unexpected gratitude toward her siblings. They were trying—really trying—to include her, to make up for years of distance. It was more consideration than she'd expected. But standing there in her mother's dining room, she still felt like an outsider looking in, unsure of her place in the family she'd walked away from so long ago. "Whatever needs doing, I can help."

"Right, because you've been around to help with anything for the last twelve years," her mother said flatly. "You don't get to just show up after over a decade and act like you know what your father would have wanted."

"Elizabeth, that's not fair. She's always—"

"Do *not* make excuses for my daughter." Her mother lifted her wine glass and took a long sip, glaring at her husband, before shifting it back to Riley. "You didn't even come home for his birthday last year. Or the year before that. Or ever. When was the last time you even saw him?"

"Less than a year ago." She stiffened her spine. "But I think you know that." God, she hated her mother's games. Everyone in this room knew about her trips with her father. But her mother preferred to perpetuate the concept that Riley had run off and never once looked back.

"Fighting isn't getting us anywhere," Grant said, running his fingers through his hair. "Riley's here, and we all know Dad would want her to be a part of this. Erin and I, despite our differences, want her to be involved. He was our father."

Wow. Grant had never stood up for her, except for maybe when a bully had picked on her at school. And that hadn't happened often.

"You don't know the first thing about him, or any of us. You disappeared because you thought we were beneath you. That this town was beneath you." Her mother's conviction was as sharp as her nails.

Riley clenched her fists. "You don't have the first clue as to why I left, and that has nothing to do with Dad's funeral plans. I'm here now. Dad would want all of us to get along. For him," Riley snapped, the heat rising fast.

"What do you know about getting along. Every time I call, you're usually too busy or start a fight." Her mother reached for the bottle and topped off her glass.

"That's not true," Riley said.

"Please, Mom," Erin whispered. "This isn't about you or the past. It's about Dad."

"Since when do you take… oh, never mind. Your little sister is always working on half-truths and even fewer facts," her mother said.

Riley took a breath. "Fine. But let's not rewrite history."

"We're not here to start a war," Parker said, trying to smooth things over. "We're here to honor Sean."

Chad cleared his throat. "Why don't we focus on what still needs to be done? We haven't finalized the music. Or the eulogy."

"I don't want to give the eulogy, but I'd like to say something at the service," Riley said quickly.

"No." Her mom's answer came without hesitation. "That won't be happening. You've been silent for twelve years, and that's the way it's going to stay."

"Mother." Grant leaned back and folded his arms across his chest and stared at her. "That's not true. Besides, Erin and I discussed this last night. We thought it would be nice if the three of us said something together. We're his children. That's how it should be. A formal eulogy can be given by…" he let out an exasperated sigh, "… Walter. They were very close, and while we all know I'm not a fan of the Boones, it's what Dad wanted."

Well, hell just froze over.

"So, no one has any consideration for my feelings in this." Her mother had the audacity to wipe her tearless cheeks. She'd mastered the art of the fake cry years ago. It had always grated on Riley's last nerve.

"We're trying to think about everyone," Grant said, softly.

"She has no idea what she's put this family through. I bet she doesn't even know your kids' names," her mother said.

Erin gasped, clutching her pendant. "Of course, she does. She speaks to them on Fa—"

"Grant's are Jessica and Randy, and Erin's are Nathan and Willa. I even know about when—"

"Just because you spent a few hours having the Boones fill you in on our lives doesn't mean you know us anymore. Do you know how heartbreaking that is for a mother?"

The words hit Riley like a knife. Each one designed to cut deep. She'd tried so hard to stay connected, to remember birthdays and milestones from thousands of miles away. But her mother was right—knowing facts wasn't the same as being present. All those FaceTime calls and carefully remembered details couldn't make up for missing first steps, school plays, scraped knees that needed bandaging. The guilt she'd been carrying for twelve years crashed over her with fresh intensity.

"That's enough, Mom," Grant said. "We're all upset, and this isn't helping."

"Let's all take a moment to settle down." Parker pulled out the chair next to his wife and took her hand. "We need to really consider what Sean would want here and set aside our personal feelings for the next few days. We can deal with those later."

Riley took in a shaky breath, grateful for Parker's intervention. "You're right. Dad wouldn't want us fighting." She looked around the table at her siblings, seeing exhaustion in their faces that probably matched her own. "We're all grieving. We're all hurting. Maybe we can just... try to get through this together?"

"Agreed." Grant held her gaze and smiled. It wasn't a big one, but it was enough. "For Dad."

"Well, you can agree to that all you want, but we're still in a holding pattern." Elizabeth set her wine glass down. "Has anyone heard if the ME has released your father's body yet? Kind of hard to have a funeral without one."

Riley bit down on the inside of her cheek. Sometimes her mother just didn't know when to zip it.

"No. Still waiting," Grant said.

"This is ridiculous. I don't understand." Her mother took a nice, long, sip of her wine... more like half the glass.

"Doctor Gavin is still deciding if he's going to do an autopsy or not," Grant said.

If there was ever a time to bring this up, it was now. If she didn't, she'd never forgive herself. "I want to ask Doctor Gavin to just do the autopsy."

Grant's expression hardened.

Elizabeth's wine glass hit the table with a sharp clink. "How dare you. I bet you're the reason they're holding your father's body."

"Mom, she's not the reason." Grant ran a shaky hand over his face. "We all heard what the emergency doctor said, and we all spoke our piece on the matter. It's the ME's decision, unless one of us changes our mind."

Her mother slammed her fist on the table, abruptly standing. "I will not let you do that to your father," her voice rose, vibrating and bouncing off the walls. "He avoided surgery on his knee because he didn't want doctors opening him up. You have some nerve coming in here after everything—after being gone all this time—you think you know what he would've wanted? I might not have been married to him when he died, but I do have enough respect for the father of *my* children not to desecrate his body."

"I think Dad would've wanted the truth. He was always telling us kids how important the truth was," Erin said quietly, with her head down, fiddling with her nails like a terrified toddler.

"You're going to take her side in this?" Her mother's voice cracked with fury.

"It's not about sides, Ma." Erin lifted her gaze. "It's about knowing what happened. About finding out why Daddy died before he even turned seventy. We all know heart disease runs in the family, but what if it's something else? Something that could affect *your* grandchildren?"

"I think Dad would understand if we requested one," Riley added.

Her mother pointed her polished finger in Riley's direction. "Maybe if you had been here—if you'd cared at all—you'd know more about your father. You would've also known he wasn't well. He'd been tired. Complaining of chest pains. Your brother had been bugging him to go to the doctor, but he wouldn't."

"That's not quite what—"

"Your father was a stubborn old man," her mom interrupted Grant.

"That doesn't mean we don't all deserve answers," Riley said. The tears came fast, hot, and silent.

"I've had enough. Get out," her mother said with more bite to her words than the day Riley left for Alaska. "This is my house, and I will not be disrespected. You've caused enough trouble, and you've only been back one day." She sat down and snagged her wine. "Grant, Erin, please talk some sense into your little sister before it's too late."

Riley couldn't form words. She couldn't argue, nor did she have the strength to do so. She turned and walked out, blinking back tears as she shut the front door behind her. The afternoon sun burned against her skin as she crossed the path to where she'd parked Bryson's truck.

"Riley, wait up," Grant called as he jogged in her direction. "I'm sorry about what Mom did back there."

"That wasn't about Dad. That was about her, and me, and the fact that I was so angry at her for betraying him all those years ago." Riley leaned against the side of the pickup. "She's never let it go that I chose to live with Dad."

"And you've never forgiven her." Grant eyes narrowed, slightly. "You've always come at the rest of us like we're the grudge-holders. But you took off and barely looked back. Mom's hurt, and it comes out sideways and all dramatic."

Riley glanced toward the sky as a few big white puffy clouds waltzed across the sun, sending its rays cascading down toward earth like long legs moving with the music. "I know the three of us don't have a great relationship, but at least we try. We always call on birthdays, holidays, and sometimes even send texts for no reason. Hell, you and I even saw each other a few times when you traveled over-seas. I get that we have more problems than most families, but I do try with her, Grant. I really do. And I kept her secret."

"You told the Boones."

"Jesus, they already knew."

"Not the point." Grant riffled his fingers through his thick, curly hair. "Mom has always been jealous of Brea. You spent more time in that house as a kid than at home with her. She felt like you didn't like her. I can't say I didn't have similar feelings. Always being pitted against a kid a couple of years younger."

"You still have issues with Bryson."

Grant lowered his chin. "He broke my sister's heart. He's the reason you took off to Alaska. He married someone who used to be your best friend. Why would I want to be kind to that man?"

When Grant put it in those terms, it was hard not to push past all the bullshit and accept his point of view on things. But he wasn't working with all the information, and she wasn't about to explain them. "I appreciate you having my back and sticking up for me with Mom."

"She can be a lot." He smiled. "However, I don't agree with you regarding pushing an autopsy."

"I don't need your permission to call Doctor Gavin and ask him to do it."

"No, I suppose you don't. But I'm asking you not to make that call."

"Can I ask you something?"

"Sure," he said.

"Outside of Dad's weirdness with doctors, why don't

you want it, because you all but accused Bryson of having something to do with Dad's death?"

Grant let out a long breath. "I had to put blame somewhere, and Bryson is an easy target for me."

"So, you don't hold him responsible?"

"Not like you're making it sound. I just don't like that Dad was out there doing hard labor sometimes."

Her brother was a lot of things, but he did have a heart. "How did he look that morning? Mom keeps saying he was sick. She said you and Erin saw it, knew it. But neither of you are really jumping on that bandwagon."

"Look, Dad appeared tired that morning. I've said that all along, and I've wanted him to go to a doctor for a checkup. He was getting up there in age. His hip bothered him sometimes. He didn't move quite as fast anymore. He wasn't a spring chicken." Grant rubbed his chest. "Kelly wants me to go see a heart specialist. She's been reading about this thing called a widow maker. Everyone thinks that's what killed Grandpa, and if it's what got Dad, she's all freaked out about me."

"Can't hurt to see one." It was impossible to miss the worry etched in the lines around her brother's eyes. "But all the more reason to call the ME. I just don't want this to be one more reason we don't speak to each other."

He reached out and placed a gentle hand on her shoulder. "I honestly want to put the past behind us. And it's not that I don't want to know, it's Mom. It's a delicate balance. We both know how she can get, and I'm the one who has to manage that."

"I know. And I'm sorry she does that to you, but I need to make that call."

"And I'll avoid telling her." He grinned.

"I'm looking forward to seeing my nieces and nephews. I haven't even met Erin's youngest, and that's one of my biggest regrets in life." She raised up on tiptoe and kissed her brother's cheek.

"I'd better get back in there. Erin isn't strong enough these days to handle Mom."

"Is something going on with Erin?"

"That's not my story to tell." Grant glanced over his shoulder.

"You two were always as thick as thieves. You never gave up each other's secrets."

"And I wouldn't break your confidence, either." He hugged her, though it was a bit awkward. Grant had never been the kind of man to show affection through physical contact. Turning, he jogged back toward the house.

She climbed inside the vehicle and stared at the steering wheel with her heart still thumping wildly out of control. Searching through her text string with Bryson, she found the doctor's number.

"Doctor Gavin's office, how may I direct your call?" a woman asked.

"This Riley Callahan. Is Doctor Gavin available?"

"You're in luck. He's standing right in front of me. Hang on."

A few seconds ticked by.

"Miss Callahan, this is Dr. Gavin. How can I help you?

"Um, yes. I wanted to speak with you about my father's death," she managed, fighting tears. "About Sean Callahan and formally requesting an autopsy."

"Is this Erin?"

"No, this is his youngest daughter, Riley."

"I see," he said. "I was just about to call your brother. Considering everything, I feel it's necessary to do an autopsy on your father."

Her heart thumped so loudly, it was a wonder she could hear any other sounds. "Is there something that swayed your decision?"

"Not any one thing, but without you filling out proper documentation, I can't discuss any of the details with you," the doctor said. "Would you like me to call the rest of the family and inform them of my decision?"

"I appreciate that. Thank you." No way was Riley going to inform anyone in her family about the autopsy. She'd already rocked the boat enough as it was regarding that topic. The doctor could deliver that news and while she was certain her mother would blame her, Riley at least felt like she stood a chance with her siblings.

"My pleasure. We'll be in touch." The line went dead.

Riley blew out a puff of air. She stared at her phone, shaking in her hand. All the emotions of the day hit her like a tornado. She didn't want to call *him*. Didn't want to need *him*.

But her fingers moved anyway.

He answered on the second ring. "Riley? Are you okay?"

"Oddly, I'm not horrible," she whispered. "But I could use a friend. Are you busy?"

"I'm at the tasting room in town," he said softly. "I can't leave right at the moment."

"Can I meet you there?"

"Of course."

"Thank you." She hung up before she cried again.

Then she shifted the truck into gear and headed into town. So many mistakes. Too many regrets blowing in the breeze. Her life had been good. She loved traveling and exploring. She'd been grateful for all the incredible opportunities she'd been given.

But they'd come at a cost. A big one. And now, it was time to pay up.

Six

The Stone Bridge Winery tasting room buzzed with the lazy hum of a mid-afternoon lull—soft conversation, the clink of glass against wood, and the faint echo of soft country music curling through the speakers. Sunlight poured through the tall front windows, warming the reclaimed redwood floors and casting tawny lines across the marble-topped bar.

Bryson moved easily behind the counter, pouring a 2020 estate Syrah into two wide-bowled glasses and sliding them across to a couple seated near the middle. They were in town from Sacramento—mid-forties, friendly, inquisitive, the kind who asked all the right questions and genuinely wanted to know more than what the tasting notes had to say.

"This one's a personal favorite," Bryson said, resting his palms on the bar. "Sean, one of the wine stewards, used to tell people it tasted like twilight on the back porch—blackberries, leather, and the smell of firewood."

The couple chuckled. The woman swirled the glass under her nose, impressed. "He sounds like a storyteller."

Bryson's smile tightened just a fraction. "He was." The past tense still caught him off guard. "Enjoy, and please, let me know if I can get you anything else."

He moved down the bar to check on another guest, but his mind wandered to Sean—how he used to hold court at the far end of the bar, spinning tales about the vineyard's earliest harvests, wild spring storms, the fire that nearly destroyed it all, and the love he had for the land. People came back just to hear him talk. That kind of charisma couldn't be faked, and Bryson had learned a lot about life and the art of storytelling from the old man.

Bryson looked toward the empty corner, where Sean should've been, and something hollow opened in his chest. He'd been like a second father. And in the end, a dear friend. Mornings would be very different without him.

The front door creaked.

He turned—and there she was.

Riley stood in the doorway wearing the same jeans she'd had on last night and a light green shirt with her dark hair pulled back. Her beautiful blue eyes were swollen but defiant. She paused just inside the threshold, scanning the room as if she wasn't sure if she belonged there.

He was around the bar in seconds.

"Hey." He didn't give her time to speak. Instead, he pulled her into his arms, wrapping her in a fierce embrace, trying to absorb whatever bad emotions had been created by her family.

For a brief moment, she rested against him, then

pushed back, just enough to break the contact. "Don't," she whispered. "If I cry again, I won't stop."

Bryson didn't press, just placed a steady hand on her lower back and guided her toward the far end of the bar, where it was quieter.

"I miss him so much." She climbed up onto the stool. "I see him everywhere. I can't escape the memories. They're flooding my brain, and while I want to remember, I don't want to feel because when I let the emotions in, they're all about the things I did wrong."

"Riley, don't do that yourself. Your dad spoke so fondly of you. He would lean across this bar with his cell in hand and show all our customers the pictures you sent him. He was so very proud of you. Regardless of the rest of your family, he understood your need to see the world. To experience different places. It's who you are, and he never wanted to stifle that in you."

"Says the man who begged me to stay."

He moved back to the other side of the bar, keeping his gaze anywhere but locked on hers. It wasn't that he was avoiding her. But her words stung in ways he hadn't been prepared for. He had begged—desperately, pathetically— asking her to choose him over her dreams. Back then, he hadn't a clue how small he'd made her world, but that's exactly what he'd done. It didn't matter that in the end, he'd done the right thing, because the reality was—she'd left him no choice. "I just wanted you to come back... back to me."

"Let's not get into that. It's like talking in circles about something we can't change anyway," she said softly. "And I just had the weirdest experience at my mom's house. I don't even know how to process it."

"What happened?"

"So many things. But the good news is the doctor decided to do the autopsy."

"Without you having to ask?"

She nodded. "He didn't say much as to why, and while Grant and Erin are against it, they support me, and that's... something."

"Then what has you so upset?"

"My mother," she said softly. "I knew she'd be cold toward me, but I was totally unprepared for her to go off on me like she did. I also didn't expect for Grant and Erin to defend me. That was even stranger."

"I'm sorry you had to deal with your mom's bullshit this morning, but I'm glad your siblings are surprising you and supporting you."

"I did have a nice chat with Grant before I left." She pointed to a bottle behind the bar. "Can I have a glass of that Pinot?"

"Of course you can." He turned, pouring her favorite wine into a glass and setting it in front of her. "Do you want to talk about it?"

"Not really. Not in this moment. Honestly, I just wanted to be here and see you." She briefly looked away before meeting his gaze and chuckled. "Don't let it go to your head."

He tapped his temple. "Too late." Having her here, in his space, felt like the most natural thing in the world. Like no time had passed at all. It scared him how easily they'd fallen back into this rhythm. And how much he wanted to believe this could be more than just grief bringing her to his door. He leaned forward, resting his elbows on the counter.

"I'm honestly glad you felt safe coming here, even if it's not to talk, but just be."

"I needed to be where I don't feel like everything I say or do is being judged." She lifted her wine to her rosy lips and took a tiny sip. "Despite our differences, at least you're not being a total asshole."

Bryson reached out and took her hand. "Not the best compliment anyone has ever handed out, but I'll take it." He watched her composure finally shatter. She stared into her wine glass, tears forming and spilling over before she could stop them. Her whole body seemed to deflate, like she'd been holding herself together through sheer will and had finally run out of strength. "Hey," he said softly. "It's okay. I know it doesn't feel that way right now, but you're going to get through this."

"I'm falling apart." She wiped away a tear. "I can't breathe. There are ghosts in this town everywhere I turn. I knew coming back would be hard. Death. Grief. I didn't expect it to be easy. But I didn't expect to feel... to feel... so much and be so empty at the same time."

He opened his mouth to respond as the door opened again.

And in walked trouble.

Freaking Monica. Her timing was always so perfectly fucking bad. He knew she'd be in today. He'd been mentally preparing for that. However, it still shocked his system, especially with Riley sitting in front of him, looking like someone had ripped her heart out.

Monica smiled and waved. She wore heels too high for wine country and sunglasses too big for anyone except maybe a movie star—and she certainly wasn't that. Her pale blue sundress clung in all the places she wanted it to, and her hair was styled in those waves he knew took hours to create because when they were married, that style always made them late. But Monica had insisted it gave her that *runway* look.

Talk about a woman who cared about optics—and knew how to create drama.

Bryson's jaw clenched. He'd asked himself a million times what he'd ever seen in her, and he'd never been able to answer the question. She was shallow, only caring about appearances and money. Their relationship had been born out of lies, manipulation, and loneliness. It had been difficult from the beginning.

The marriage barely lasted two years, but it was still about five years of his life that he couldn't get back.

"Fuck," he muttered.

"What?" Riley glanced over her shoulder. "Of course, she'd show up," Riley mumbled under her breath. "She always did have impeccable timing." She raised her glass and gulped down half her wine. "Except for when she was one of my best friends, then she was always too busy. Funny how that worked out."

"I'm sorry," Bryson mumbled. "I'll do my best to get rid of her as quickly as possible."

"Bryson." Monica cooed, making a beeline for the bar like she owned the place. "I'm here for my wine and tasting boards. I also wanted to ask you about the garden party tomorrow. I hope you're coming. You never did respond to the invitation or my personal note." She gave him a smile that had once made his knees weak because she was a knockout, which made him about as shallow as her.

"Sorry. I can't." He stepped away from Riley with reluctance and forced a half-smile because that was all Monica deserved.

He waved to Olivia, one of the waitstaff. "Can you go get the order for Ms. Gilford?" No way was he leaving these two women alone. Thank the good Lord Monica had changed her name when they divorced. She hadn't wanted to, but because she'd signed a prenup, if she wanted a dime of that settlement, she'd had to.

"On it, Boss." Olivia shuffled off to the backroom.

Monica's eyes flicked to Riley and narrowed. "Oh. I didn't realize you had... company."

"It's a tasting room, Monica. I always have company," he said, cocking his head. "And that's not how I would describe Riley."

"Right," Monica said with distain dripping off every letter of the word. "When did you get back into town? And are you staying long? Is there a reason for your visit, because it's been like forever, and didn't you say you'd never return to this devil of a town?"

Riley raised an eyebrow, glancing between Bryson and Monica.

"Jesus, Monica. How could you not know? Or is your heart really that black?"

Monica gasped, placing her hand over her cleavage. "No need to be so rude. I simply asked a question. A valid one, I might add."

Bryson threaded his fingers through his hair. "Her father just passed away the other day."

"Sean died?" Monica blinked, doing her best to look shocked—but she didn't pull it off. "I've been so busy with the party, I've hardly been out of the house or even looked at my phone much. I've barely had time to breathe."

Bryson believed that like he believed the sky was pink.

Monica turned to Riley and dared to inch closer. That wasn't good. "I'm so sorry for your loss. Please let me know when the service will be. I'll be sure to make a donation to whatever charity your family chooses and to send flowers to your mother."

"Thanks." Lifting her glass, Riley took a sip, silently dismissing Monica.

Monica shifted her weight and folded her arms, doing her best to draw more attention to her breasts.

Bryson didn't take the bait.

"I can't believe you're not coming to the party," Monica said. "It's going to be bigger than last year. Anyone who's anybody in this town is coming. And of course, I'm only serving wines from your vineyard. Your 2019 Pinot is still my favorite."

"You should try expanding your palate. We live in wine country. There are other good ones out there," Bryson said flatly just as Oliva returned with her order. "Here you go. Have a nice day."

Monica batted her fake eyelashes. "You know, we should really catch up. Maybe we could have dinner one night this week."

He cocked a brow. "What happened to what's his name?"

Monica tapped her long, polished nails on the counter. "Oh, that ended a while ago. Anyway, I was really hoping you could be my escort to my party—which I asked you about in my note." She leaned over the bar and curled her fingers around his biceps.

Her touch sent a wave of disgust through him. Monica had never understood boundaries, had never accepted that he wasn't interested. And having this happen in front of Riley—the woman he'd actually loved, the one he'd lost partly because of Monica's interference—made his stomach turn. He could only imagine what Riley was thinking. He pulled back from Monica's grip.

"You don't have to be so cold. I was just being friendly," Monica said in a sing-song voice, which she thought was seductive and inviting.

It was annoying.

"You always are when you're between boyfriends," he said. "But you're not getting another round with me. Not now. Not ever. I don't know how else to make that clear to you."

Monica laughed lightly, but the sound rang hollow. "You always say that, and yet, you always come back."

"That's not—"

"I'll see you soon," Monica said, cutting him off. She turned and headed toward the door, then hesitated, glancing back toward Riley. "Well. Best of luck." Her voice dripped with sugar-covered venom. "It can't be easy for you, being second choice, knowing he'll always come back to me."

Riley stiffened but said nothing.

Bryson closed his eyes for a long moment. Exhaling sharply, he dragged a hand through his hair as he lifted his gaze. "She's full of shit."

Riley was already gathering her bag. "You know, I

shouldn't be mad, and maybe I wouldn't be if it weren't for the day I've had. But really? Now, she's your go-to when you get bored and want a little action? You can do so much better."

"Oh, for fuck's sake. I haven't been with Monica since *before* our divorce."

"Yeah. Sure." Riley stood. "And you didn't kiss her before I lost… never mind. It doesn't matter."

"Riley—"

"You said she was in the past."

"She is."

"Then why does she still talk to you like you're hers? Why does she think she can come in here and throw jabs at me like I was just some passing fling?"

"Because she's insecure as hell, and you were a ghost in our marriage," Bryson snapped. "She's desperate. And jealous. And I only speak to her when I'm forced."

"But she still thinks she has a shot. That says more than you want to admit."

Bryson braced his hands against the bar. "You think I'd let you walk back into my life if I were still hung up on Monica? You think I'd—"

"A kiss to heal old wounds doesn't mean I'm in your life," Riley said, her voice cracking. "Everything about this town feels like it's closing in around me. And then she walks in like a shadow from the worst part of our past—"

"I'm not the same guy I was back then."

"And I'm not the same girl," she whispered. "But I don't make the same mistakes either."

The silence that followed was jagged.

"I need to go." Riley downed the last drop of wine.

"Ry—please don't walk away like this."

"I have to," she said. "I'm two seconds from saying things I can't unsay. And we both did that enough twelve years ago."

The door shut behind her with a soft creak.

Bryson stood in the tasting room, surrounded by half-finished wine flights and the hum of muted conversation, feeling more alone than he had in years.

But no way in hell was he going to let that feeling settle. Nope. He wasn't going to let her leave without saying a few things. Not this time.

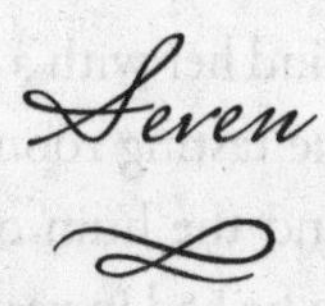

Seven

As soon as the door rattled shut behind her, Riley stopped on the sidewalk and pulled in a deep breath. The air was thick with the scent of sun-warmed grapes drifting in from the vineyard—a fragrance she'd once thought of as home. Growing up, that smell had been her calm in the middle of chaos.

She pulled out her phone and scrolled to Mateo's name.

"Oh, no you don't," Bryson's voice called from behind her.

She froze, her thumb hovering over the screen.

"I get that after you bury your father, you'll probably hop a plane and vanish into some exotic mountainside again," he went on, stepping closer. "Fine. But while you're here? You don't get to waltz into my tasting room, drop a grenade, and then disappear just because Monica decided to be—" he paused, his jaw tightening, "—herself."

"I'm not running," she said, exhaling hard, flexing her fingers. Half of her wanted to shove him aside and storm off. The other half wanted to collapse into him. "I just can't deal with her. Or you. Not after my mother made it sound like my existence was the reason we can't breathe the same air. And then Monica..." Riley's voice cracked, tears stinging her eyes before they spilled over. "She turned my dad's death into some inconvenience for her damn garden party—and a reason to take a shot at—"

"Hey." Bryson stepped in, brushing the tears from her cheek with his thumb. "I'm sorry she rattled you. That was cruel—*she* was cruel. And, yes, it was intentional. She's... good at that now. Too good. She's not the same person you knew back then. She's shallow, selfish, and the only person she cares about is the one in the mirror."

"Sounds like my mother." The words tasted bitter in her mouth. Monica had become exactly what Riley had spent twelve years running from—someone who used cruelty as currency and saw other people as obstacles to whatever she wanted.

"Listen, I can see if one of my siblings can cover for me here. Or you can come back in and hang out. We've got some great flatbreads. I don't want you to be alone."

"No. I'll be fine. I just need space."

He hesitated, brow furrowing in that way she remembered from years ago.

"I hate that look," she said quietly. "It means you're about to dig up something heavy."

"Considering what just happened, I don't believe you and I have completely cleared the air. And since you've always mattered to me, I want us to be able to be friends. It's important to me. I think we need to have the Monica talk."

"Is that kinda like a TED Talk?"

"You've always been adorable when you're deflecting," he said, amusement glimmering in his eyes. "But I'm serious. I don't want us to be at odds every time we cross paths with her, and it will happen. I need you to hear my side, and I want to hear yours. In the past, I don't think either one of us stopped to listen to what the other was saying. Instead, we flung hurtful words at each other. I'd like to move beyond that."

"I honestly don't know if I have the bandwidth for it. I'm running on fumes, and there's no gas station in sight for what I need." Only, she wasn't exactly sure what she needed. She swallowed. Hard. If her father were around, this would be exactly the kind of thing she'd talk to him about. A blanket woven of clarity and determination settled around her shoulders. The gaping hole left by her father's loss made some things clearer than they'd ever been before, and one of those things was that life was too short to walk around with open wounds. She and Bryson both deserved to heal

"But..." She took a breath then lifted her gaze to his. "Okay. Just not today. I'm gonna head back to the inn, take a nice, long, hot bath, read a book, drink some wine that your mom brought over, order room service, and crash."

"Sounds like a perfect night." He lifted her chin with his thumb. "Call me if you need anything. I don't care what time it is. I'm here for you." He leaned in and brushed his warm lips against hers.

Her heart stuttered in her chest. The kiss was so achingly familiar, like coming home and saying goodbye all at once. It stirred feelings she'd spent years burying, and for one dangerous moment, she wanted to pull him closer instead of letting him go.

"I'll talk to you later," he said. He stepped back inside, leaving her alone on the sidewalk.

The last time her emotions had swung this wildly, she'd been eighteen and boarding a plane for Alaska. But she wasn't that reckless girl anymore. She was thirty-five, a woman who'd seen the world, who should know how to steady herself. Bryson was right—if she didn't face her past, it would eat away at her until there was nothing left.

She looked down at her phone. "Shit." She pressed it to her ear. "Mateo?"

"Well, hello there," his voice boomed, dripping with amusement.

Her eyes narrowed. "You didn't just listen to that whole conversation."

"I plead the fifth," he said, laughing. "Isn't that what you Americans say?"

"You get some weird pleasure out of other people's drama."

"Reality TV is my cardio. And that Bryson guy? Hot voice, solid man vibes. But this Monica chick—spill the tea."

"How's everything there?" She'd been accused of being the queen of redirection. She might as well wear the crown for a little while longer.

"You didn't call to talk about me. What's going on?"

"Fine. Trying to navigate all this... is harder than I thought. Throw in an ex–best friend who married and divorced my ex-boyfriend, and it's more drama than your Real Housewives marathon."

"Ouch."

She glanced up the street and froze. "And speaking of Stone Bridge's latest real housewife drama—Monica. She's standing in front of a shop with someone I don't recognize. God, why am I still letting her get to me?"

"Because you've never dealt with it," Mateo said. "And you're still in love with the man she married."

"I liked it better when all we talked about was my lack of a smile."

"I'm just saying... be careful with yourself."

"Crap. She's headed this way. I'm hanging up."

"You'd better call me later."

She ended the call and rounded the corner—straight into someone.

"Whoa—sorry," she said, looking up. "Sandy?"

"Holy shit," Sandy said, stepping back to take her in. She was in a crisp Stone Bridge PD uniform, her blonde hair pulled into a sleek ponytail. "I'd heard you were back in town."

"Just got back the other day," Riley said.

"I'm so sorry about your father. He was such a great man. My oldest loves him."

"You have kids?"

"Two." Sandy's smile was about as wide as a human could possibly make it. "A boy and a girl. One's three and the other four months."

"Crazy personal question, but are you and—?"

"Are you asking if I stayed with Pauly? God, no. That romance died out faster than the ink dried on our diplomas." Sandy smiled. "I met my husband, Mason, about eight years ago. He was here on a golf trip with friends. It was a crazy romance. We married just a year after we got together."

"What does he do that he could just pack up from wherever he lived and join you here?"

"He's in sales. A manufacturer's rep. He works from home but has to travel a lot. Now that I'm the Police Chief, with better hours, our life is a little easier with the kids. But it's still hard, because Mason's gone a few days almost every week." Sandy had been a ball of energy in high school, always wearing a huge grin on her face. Not much had changed.

"Sounds like a wonderful life."

The sound of Monica's voice filled the air. Riley cringed, forcing herself not to glance over her shoulder. The rhythm of high heels clicking on the pavement got closer and closer, grating on her last nerve.

"I'm sorry. I need to—"

"Hi Sandy," Monica's high-pitched voice hit Riley's ears like a cannonball. "And Riley. Hmmm, did something happen?"

Sandy's face lit up like a damn Christmas Tree. "Oh, we're just catching up. But I was heading toward that fancy SUV of yours to give you a ticket. You've got about three minutes before I refuse to turn my back." She pointed a finger. "You're parked in a no-parking zone."

"So sorry. There were no spots left." Monica held up the platter she'd picked up from Bryson. "I just had to pop in real quick and get this. I've been so busy with the Garden Party planning that I didn't have any time to prepare for a little gathering I'm having this evening."

"Right." Sandy cocked her head. "Better scoot. I'm not

in a good mood today, and don't like being taken advantage of by people I used to be friends with a long time ago." She waved her hand as if she were asking a toddler to run along.

"I'm going." Monica leisurely strolled down the street with her hips swaying like she was trying to get someone's attention.

"How do you do that with a smile on your face?" Riley asked.

"There are moments I don't smile, but you should have seen the one I sported the day I arrested Robert Wilkerson." Sandy chuckled.

"Wait. What? He was arrested?"

"Oh, boy. Your mother didn't tell you?"

Riley shook her head.

"Ponzi scheme. Sadly, your mom invested and he's now in federal prison."

"Jesus. I had no idea." While she and her family weren't close, that was something she figured her brother and sister would've mentioned. Unless her mom had begged them not to—though, the only way she'd do that was to protect her reputation. Knowing those two, they would've kept their promise to her while she constantly bothered them, worrying they'd spill her dirty little secret.

"It rocked the entire town," Sandy said. "Do you have time for a cup of coffee?"

"I'd love that."

They fell into step, walking toward the local diner. Once inside, cups in hand, they slid into a corner booth.

"Can I ask you a question?" Riley asked.

"Of course."

"I was told that you viewed the security cameras at the Stone Bridge Winery the day my father died."

Sandy's smile disappeared, and she cleared her throat. "I looked at the footage. We couldn't see the area where your father collapsed." Sandy reached across the table and took Riley's hand.

"Why did you do that? The Boones keep saying stuff about standard procedure, but a cop asking questions and viewing security footage...Well, it feels like an investigation."

"When someone dies alone, we ask questions," Sandy said. "When your family mentioned that Sean wouldn't want an autopsy, the ME asked me to check things out." Her expression grew more serious. "His job is to help the family have peace. Knowing how a loved one passed often fills that space."

"I know," Riley said.

"If there is anything I can do—not just as the police chief, but as a friend—please don't hesitate to reach out."

"Thanks. I'll do that."

A few beats of silence settled between them. It wasn't uncomfortable. It was just... nice.

"So," Sandy said, wrapping both hands around her mug, "Monica."

Riley groaned. "Can we not?"

"Oh, but we really should. A lot has changed when it comes to her," Sandy said with a smirk. "When you left, she was still mostly kind and hanging out with the same crowd. But getting her claws into Bryson changed her. I'm not sure if it was because of his last name and what she thought that meant. Or the money. She acted like she was better than everyone else and burned plenty of bridges in the process."

Riley palmed her mug, staring into the dark liquid. "I don't mean to sound like a gossip, but I'm surprised by the idea that people like Kim, Stephanie, and Mae aren't her besties anymore—or at least that's what Bryson hinted at. The five of us were all so tight until... well, you know."

"Nobody here really likes Monica anymore. It's more like they tolerate her. Kim will still have lunch with her on occasion, but that's only because Kim doesn't know how to say no. Mae avoids her like the plague. And Stephanie? She's polite but distant."

Riley raised a brow. "And Bryson?"

Sandy sighed. "I don't think Bryson was ever happy when he was with her. I know he was absolutely miserable when they were married. We all saw it. He wouldn't admit it, but I think he married her to punish himself for... well, for everything that happened with you."

The words landed like pebbles in Riley's stomach—small but rippling out in every direction. "Punish himself? That sounds dramatic."

Sandy lifted one shoulder. "Maybe. But it's like he wanted to feel pain, and she was one way to do it. At least, at first. When the dust settled, I think he thought it was... safe. Predictable."

"Monica?" Riley scoffed. "Safe?"

Sandy's lips curved in a humorless smile. "Safe in the sense that she didn't matter to him the way you did. He could keep her at arm's length. Give her a few charities to work. Let her have the spotlight there, and he could live his days in the vines. Trouble was, Monica's not the type to be tossed aside. She wanted her man to dress her up and show her off."

"That sounds horrible... for Bryson," Riley said, picturing Monica's sharp-edged smile.

"When she realized Bryson wasn't going to worship her the way she wanted, she started playing the crowd—charming the people she could use, icing out the ones she couldn't. That's why most of us don't bother with her anymore. It's exhausting." Sandy laughed.

"I can't believe Kim still puts up with her. She always called us out on our shit. Besides, she never liked overly pretentious people."

Sandy snorted. "Kim's a good egg, and she'll often tell Monica she's being an ass. She's the kind of person who'll hold the door open for someone who just shoved her all while giving a lecture on being a butthead. But even Kim's patience has limits. I think she's getting close to them."

"What about Mae?" Riley asked.

"She's in full avoidance mode. If she sees Monica in the grocery store, she'll leave a full cart in the aisle and come back later. I've seen her do it."

Riley laughed. "Some things never change. Mae and I were shopping in one of the boutiques once and ran into her ex with his latest conquest, and she ran out with her shirt half done up because we'd been trying on clothes."

"That's Mae." Sandy leaned in, lowering her voice even though the diner was only half full. "You should know, though, Monica still talks about you."

Riley's stomach tightened. "Oh, I can imagine."

"It's not even original anymore. Same tired digs—how you left, how you couldn't hack it here, how you ran away when things got hard. She spins it like she's the authority on your life."

Riley rolled her eyes. "Classic Monica. Rewrite the story until she's the hero, but I don't like being at the center of it and certainly can't deal with it this week."

"Let her talk," Sandy said, sitting back. "Most people don't buy her version anymore. They've seen too much. And besides—" she gave Riley a knowing look "—you're back now. That alone changes the narrative."

Riley tapped her nails against her cup, thinking about that. She hadn't come back to change anyone's mind. She wasn't here to win a popularity contest. But the idea that her presence could shift the balance in any narrative— maybe that wasn't the worst thing. It was already moving in the right direction with her siblings. Things weren't half as tense with Bryson as she'd envisioned.

And this chance meeting with Sandy? Well, it was damn refreshing.

"Tell me about Stephanie," Riley said. "I haven't spoken to anyone since I left."

Sandy hesitated. "Steph's fine. Married, two kids, runs the gift shop on Main. She's... careful. Doesn't get involved in much anymore. I think she's still figuring out where she fits, you know? For a while, she trash-talked you with Monica, but she was in the wedding, and I think she got caught up in it all. When shit hit the fan, and Bryson literally threw Monica out of the family mansion, Steph felt like she'd betrayed you. But I'll admit, everyone was hurt that you didn't reach out, Steph maybe a little more than most. But that might have been because you two were pretty close."

"I was close with all of them, but yeah, I can understand that."

They fell into an easy silence for a moment, sipping coffee, watching a couple of teenagers outside loiter by the bike rack.

Finally, Sandy said, "Look, Riley. People have long memories here, but they're not unshakable. You left on weird terms. But you didn't burn the place down when you did. You might be surprised at how many folks are glad to see you back—me included."

Riley smiled faintly. "Thanks."

Sandy's grin widened. "Just... be ready. Stone Bridge loves its drama and secrets. This town was built on them. And with you and Bryson in the same zip code, Monica's going to make sure you're the headliner. And not in a good way."

Riley shook her head, but she couldn't quite suppress her own smile. "Let her try."

The Rusted Rail was half-lit and half-empty, the way Bryson liked it. But that would change in less than an hour, considering it was Friday night. The low hum of conversation blended with the crackle of an old jukebox in the corner, warbling out a country ballad that had probably been stuck on repeat since before he was born. The air smelled of hoops, fried food, and that faint metallic tang of spilled beer soaked into the floorboards over decades.

He sat at the far end of the bar, a bottle of lager sweating in front of him, watching the condensation pool into a ring on the wood. Most people eyed him suspiciously when he ordered a cold brew. As if a man who owned a winery couldn't enjoy anything other than vino. Truth be told, Bryson sometimes got sick of wine and needed a change of pace, if only to cleanse his palate.

Tonight, however, he wished he'd ordered that nice Pinot they had staring him down from behind the counter like they were in a showdown at high noon.

He glanced at his watch. Mason was late. No surprise there—between the kids, the job, and Sandy's knack for finding "one last errand," Mason almost always ran behind on the rare occasion he found a free night for some much-needed male bonding.

The door creaked open behind him, letting in a draft of cooler night air. Bryson turned slightly—and stilled.

Grant Callahan. Wonderful. Bryson wasn't in the mood for angry banter that teetered on the edge of angsty adolescent behavior. He was still reeling over his encounter with Monica, which included the three texts she'd sent shortly after. One had been begging him to reconsider his attendance at the garden party as her date. She made some ploy about how the optics would be good for both of them. A united front would bring in more money for the charity. Utter bullshit.

The other two texts were regarding Riley, and those had totally churned his stomach. Monica—and her insecurities —was fishing for information, and he wasn't about to feed her and her self-doubt.

Grant glanced around the bar, and the moment he spotted Bryson, Grant moved through the crowd like a ripple disturbing still water. Broad shoulders, crisp shirt, a face that carried the Boone-Callahan small-town legacy in the hard set of his jaw, as if they were the Hatfields and McCoys. For a heartbeat, they just looked at each other like they used on the football field during practice. Tight, angry, and ready to tackle. Which was funny, since they'd both been quarterbacks.

"Bryson," Grant said, striding over. His voice was controlled, but tight, like a rope stretched to its limit.

"Grant." Bryson kept his tone neutral. No point giving him more to work with.

Grant stopped just short of crowding his space. "Have you seen or spoken to Riley?"

"You're looking for her *here*?"

"No, but since I saw you, I'd thought I'd ask. You two seem to be spending a lot of time together. Which shouldn't surprise me but somehow does."

"I'm not sure if that's a compliment or a dig." Bryson took a slow pull from his beer. "Last I saw, she was leaving the tasting room. Said she was headed back to the Stone Bridge Inn to relax."

Grant's gaze didn't move, but something behind it flickered—restlessness, maybe. Unease. It was the same look Grant used to get when he was stuck sitting the bench during games. What transpired after those games was never good. Arguments. Fights, usually involving fists. Followed up by a good lecture from both their parents. "She didn't stop anywhere on the way?"

"Not that I know of." Bryson studied Grant. He had dark circles under his eyes, which wasn't surprising, all things considered. "Something wrong? Did something happen?"

"I just wanted to check in with her." Grant's gaze continued to dart around the bar. The man was on edge, only Bryson had no idea about what, and that was never a good sign. "When our mom found out about the autopsy, she went into one of her rants. I'm worried she might have called Riley and said a few things she shouldn't have."

"I assume you've tried calling," Bryson said.

"Of course. I've been trying to reach her for hours. I figured she was with you." Grant let out a long breath, looking Bryson up and down. "Did you two get into a fight, because if she took off again because of you, we're gonna have a problem."

Of course, everything was Bryson's fault. Grant had a knack for making Bryson his fall guy. Whether it was on the field or in life, Bryson was the reason something didn't work out for Grant.

However, Bryson wasn't going to be the one to tell Grant about the run-in with Monica. That would cause fists to fly, and Bryson hadn't thrown a punch since he'd been in his early twenties. He'd like to believe he'd... matured.

"When she left, she said she wanted to relax in a nice, long, hot bath. That's all I know." He raised his hands like he was waving a white flag. "Swear."

The door to the bar swung open again, letting in Mason, a gust of cooler air, and the smell of woodsmoke from outside. Mason's ball cap was turned backward, his cheeks flushed from the night air.

Bryson smiled. He had backup, and Mason was a nice stabilizer. He hadn't lived in Stone Bridge long. Only since he'd married Sandy, but he'd become a staple in the community. He fit in—better than some people born and raised.

"Sorry I'm late," Mason said, clapping Bryson on the shoulder. "Had to drop the kids at my mother-in-law's—Sandy's heading over to the winery to take another look at the security footage. She said she spoke to you, your father, and Devon about it."

"She did. My dad's waiting for her." Bryson grimaced.

Grant's head turned sharply. "Wait. Why? Did something else happen at the winery?"

Mason blinked, shifting his gaze between Bryson and Grant. "Not sure. She didn't say. My wife tries not to bring her job home. While it's a small town and not much happens—we have a rule—home is family."

"That's a good rule to have," Bryson said. "Impossible for my family. Though, we try not to talk business at the dinner table."

"I'd like to know if this has anything to do with my dad," Grant said. "I think I have that right."

Bryson met Grant's stare. This was not going to end well. "All I know is that Sandy called asking if she could take another look at our camera footage from that day."

Grant's jaw clenched. "Or maybe you're stirring up trouble where it's not needed. Putting ideas in someone's head. You've always been good at that."

Bryson's fingers tightened around the bottle. "Why would I want the cops poking around my business? That's not a good look for me."

"Maybe not. But me and Riley?" Grant tapped his finger against his chest. "We've been getting along lately. And you've always had a way of coming between us. I'm not going to let that happen again. You broke her heart once, Boone—you've got no right to meddle, now. You lost that chance when you didn't fight for her and married someone else. Married Monica of all people."

The words cut deep because they carried the weight of truth. Bryson had lost the right to protect her when he'd let her walk away. When he'd married Monica instead of waiting. Instead of hoping. Instead of fighting. Grant was throwing his biggest failure back in his face, and Bryson couldn't argue with any of it.

Bryson set his beer down hard enough to rattle it on the bar. "I'm not meddling. I'm just being a friend. I'm glad you've set your differences aside. I certainly don't want to derail that. I want to champion it. But she's really struggling. And this town, we both know how unforgiving it can be."

Grant stepped in, just enough for the air between them to thicken. "She doesn't need you playing hero. You're not very good at it. You failed her twelve years ago, and I don't want to lose my sister again because you're not man enough to do the right thing."

Before Bryson could even form a coherent thought, Mason's voice cut through, firm and even. "All right, enough chest pounding. I don't want to have to call my wife. She breaks up enough fights between grown-ass men. I don't need her to do it between you two."

Grant gave Bryson one last look—cold, flat—and stepped back. "If you see Riley before I do, please tell her to call me back. I just need to know she's okay."

"I will." Bryson watched Grant leave, the door swinging shut in his wake.

Mason waved to the bartender and pointed to Bryson's beer, holding up two fingers. "The two of you are idiots. He's holding onto a grudge that's not his burden to carry, and he's pissed over the fact he actually likes you and can't admit it." Mason slid onto the stool beside Bryson. "And you. Jesus. You're behaving like my toddler in pre-meltdown mode, waffling between knowing how to do the right thing, and all the brain cells misfiring right before the explosion of tears and there's no going back."

Bryson shook his head, though his pulse was still running hot. "Grant's always been territorial. With Riley, with everything. And yeah... maybe I don't always handle things with him well. But I'm not letting him decide what she needs. Not when he gets in my face like that."

"You don't get to decide, either." Mason arched a brow. "You're just as territorial as he is. It's like watching two gorillas get ready to rip the other's head off."

"I wouldn't go that far."

"I would," Mason said. "I wasn't here twelve years ago. I didn't see what went down. But I felt all those years slam into your backside during that conversation. And you tossed all that angst right back in Grant's face." Mason drummed his fingers on the counter. "It was like a damn tennis match, and now I have whiplash."

"I don't even know what that means," Bryson said before tipping his beer and finishing it. He shoved the bottle aside and snagged the fresh beer.

Mason studied him for a moment. "You still care about her."

Bryson didn't deny it. Couldn't. "Of course I care. I've always cared. That's never been the problem." He rubbed his jaw. "Right now, I kind of wish I didn't still care so damn much," he admitted.

"Do you still love her?" Mason asked.

Bryson let out a dry, sarcastic chuckle. "I don't know. She was my first. Don't we always love our first?"

"God, no," Mason said. "My first love turned out to be a crazed psychopath. And I'm not exaggerating. She's actually in prison for stalking me."

Bryson nearly choked on his beer. The confession hit him like a curveball. "How did I not know this?"

Mason shrugged. "I don't talk about it. I used to be embarrassed by it. Like I'd done something wrong. I was nineteen when Ellie and I started dating." He shook his head. "I was such a late bloomer, and she was so fucking gorgeous. I couldn't believe she wanted me. All the attention she showered me with? I thought I was the luckiest man in the world. A year into the relationship, I was terrified. She was so jealous. So controlling. I couldn't even go fishing with my buddies without her freaking out. We broke up, and it got worse. She would do the craziest shit. It took four years of hell before she was arrested. I worry about when she gets out—about what she might do. Especially now that I've got kids."

"You're married to a cop. Who, by the way, once stopped two grown men from raping a teenager—when she was only a teenager herself. Sandy's badass," Bryson said.

Mason smiled wide. "You don't have to tell me how great my wife is. But Ellie's nuts. And that does scare me. But my point is, I don't have any feelings for that woman. Not even empathy." He lifted a finger. "Actually, I do have one emotion for her. I loathe her. And I don't dislike people. Not even Grant."

"You've always liked Grant, and don't tell me otherwise." Bryson laughed. "Even I can admit he's not that bad. The problem with Grant is that he was raised by a mother who doesn't believe he could do anything wrong. She put him on this weird pedestal, constantly kicked him off it in private, but led him to believe he was better than the rest of us. He's not really like that, but he's always been a mama's boy, and he'll do anything for that woman."

"Look at you—half defending him." Mason tipped his beer. "Your dad really wanted me on that revitalization committee. There were a few people who didn't. Thought that because I wasn't born and raised here, I didn't belong. Grant's only concern was how much I traveled. He voted yes." Mason leaned closer. "And now your father has roped me into looking at the books with him and Mayor Jessip, and I feel like I'm betraying Grant. We're not close, but we've played golf. We have drinks." Mason raised his index finger to his lips. "Walter said you knew, but don't say anything. He called me earlier. Sunday, I'll be at his home office staring at ledgers. For some reason, your old man thinks I'm great with numbers because I can sell someone a free bottle of water for forty bucks."

Bryson tossed his head back and laughed. Finding a friend like Mason was like finding a perfectly balanced wine after too many bitter tastings. A good man. A great father. A kind soul. And a really kick ass salesman. No one knew how much money he made, because he lived modestly. They had to because of his wife's job. But everyone knew Mason was loaded.

Bryson cleared his throat. "Do you think someone stole money from the town?" he asked.

"I really don't know yet. Haven't had the opportunity to dig. However, this joint isn't the place to discuss this, and we've gotten sidetracked," Mason said. "Seeing Riley again has affected you deeply."

"I won't deny that." Bryson fiddled with the label on his beer. "She was my best friend all through grade school. My girlfriend for five years. Then everything went to shit, and she took off." The truth of it sat like a stone in his chest—he'd always known this was temporary, that she'd disappear again as soon as her father was buried. She was a bird that couldn't be caged, and he was a man whose roots ran too deep to follow. "Doesn't matter how much I care. She's just gonna leave again." He lifted his beer. "And I'm going to stay right here."

"Do you want her to stay? Would you want to rekindle that romance if she did?"

"Now that's a loaded question." Memories flooded Bryson's brain. "But yeah, if she stayed, I'd want to see if there was a spark left to ignite."

"Then you'd better make her want to stay," Mason said. "Because from where I'm sitting, that's the only move you've got."

Bryson stared at the bottle in front of him, the glass cold against his palm. He wanted to believe Mason was wrong. But deep down, he knew the man was right.

Eight

The chair was deep enough to swallow her, the kind of comfort she could lose hours in if she let herself. Riley sat sideways in it, knees hugged to her chest, a half-empty wine glass on the windowsill. Her favorite Pinot. The very first wine she'd ever tasted at seventeen. Outside, the half-moon draped the vineyard in an eerie white glow, and every vine danced in the breeze.

She remembered sitting in a very different chair—harder, splintered from years of use—on the porch of her childhood home. She'd been maybe ten, swinging her legs, waiting for her father to come home from his shift. The smell of crushed grapes had been thick in the air that evening, drifting in from the winery, a comfort she hadn't understood then but had carried with her everywhere since.

Now, that same scent crept through the partially-opened window, and instead of comfort, it carried an ache. She reached for her wine and took a slow sip, staring past the rows of vines, wondering if it would ever feel like home again.

Her phone buzzed against her thigh. Grant. She'd been avoiding him. Avoiding everyone.

She hesitated, thumb hovering over the screen. Their last conversation had ended well enough, but one never knew. However, this was all about new beginnings. Fresh starts. Mending fences. She owed it to her family to try more than she ever had before. She swiped to answer. "Hey, big brother."

"You busy?" His voice was tight.

"No. What's going on?"

His sigh was heavy, like a dense fog, thick and difficult to see through.

She sat up taller.

"This autopsy... Sandy poking around the vineyard... now Mom's dragged Erin and me into the middle of everything."

Riley felt like she was drowning in regret. She'd come home to bury her father and somehow managed to turn his death into a battleground. Her mother's histrionics, the family taking sides, Grant looking like he was ready to crack —all because she'd needed answers that maybe weren't hers to seek.

"I'm getting it from all sides. I can't take the pressure anymore. I feel like I'm going to explode. I just know that it will be at the wrong person," Grant said.

She set her glass on the coaster. "What can I do to help?"

"It's not that. Mom's gone off the rails." He didn't even try to soften it. "Erin and I knew she wouldn't welcome you with open arms. The longer you stayed away, the more bitter she's become."

The words confirmed what Riley had always known but never wanted to face—that her mother's love came with terms and conditions. Stay close, follow the rules, be the daughter her mother wanted, or forfeit your place in the family. Riley had chosen freedom over approval, and now she was paying the price her mother had always promised she would.

"Erin and I, we never wanted you to stay away. For our relationship with you to suffer. We're tired. We want to make things right with you. To see you. To have you in our lives. Our kids' lives."

All this time, she'd been the one keeping the distance, thinking she was protecting everyone from more disappointment. But her siblings had wanted her. They'd been waiting for her to come home.

"But then mom gets involved, and she clings to her pain like she won it in a war. She can't let it go. One wrong move and you're out. She even said she'd stop seeing my children if I didn't either get you to start making the right decisions or stop talking to you. Can you imagine? My kids are old enough to have some understanding of emotional blackmail, but not so old that this wouldn't mess with how they process love, like it did with us."

The words hit Riley like ice water. Her mother was holding Grant's children hostage to force him to choose sides. Those kids would grow up thinking love was conditional, that family came with threats and ultimatums— exactly the toxic legacy Elizabeth had passed down to her own children. "Grant—"

"I'm tired," he cut her off. "Tired of being the one holding it all together while you blow back into town after years away and start stirring things up. And I'm pissed, because it feels like you're still choosing the Boones over your own family. Just like before."

"That's not fair," she said, heat rising in her chest. "I'm choosing us. How can you not see that? And dad. All I want to know is how he died."

"You think I don't want that too?" His voice cracked, low and raw. "You think I'm not hurting? You think I didn't love him?"

She closed her eyes. Grant had always been the kind of person to lash out at others when he hurt and right now, he was carrying a heavy burden. "I never said you didn't."

"Jesus, Ry. I know. I'm sorry. I was so angry. You left. You didn't call. You didn't write. It took us a couple of years for us to manage a single call without one of us hanging up. And now you're back, and it's done something to Mom. I can't explain, but that's what Erin and I have to deal with." He sighed. "There's a part of me that wishes I could just walk away from that, like you can. But I can't."

"I get I have some big boundaries and higher walls," she said quietly. "It's the only way I can survive Mom without feeling like I'm not a worthy human."

"I know that feeling, but I guess I handled it differently. I'm sorry I came into this conversation so hot," he said. "To be fully transparent, I just ran into Bryson, and we had... words."

"What does that mean?"

" Same thing it always does. I say something stupid that I'll regret later... this is later. I'm just trying to deal with my grief... and mom... and that's—"

"A lot. I get it. I do. She threw me out of her house."

Grant chuckled. "I was there, remember?"

For a long beat, neither of them spoke, and all she could do was remember her mother's cruel words on that fateful day. Her calling Riley ungrateful. The accusatory tone. The shrill of her voice had haunted her dreams for years.

The sound of a TV droned in the background and the muffled thud of something—maybe a cupboard door—closing. She and Grant had made so much progress since she'd been home, and she wasn't ready to lose that connection while it was still so fragile and new.

In an effort to keep him talking, and because she genuinely wanted to know, she asked, "Care to tell me about Robert Wilkerson and how Mom got involved with that?"

He exhaled loudly. "The Ponzi scheme... I warned her. Robert was bad news even in college. I cut ties with him for a reason. But she didn't listen, and when it blew up, she was humiliated. Still is. Now she just blames everyone else—like she always has."

A wry smile tugged at Riley's mouth. "Sounds familiar."

"What the hell is that supposed to mean?" he muttered, but there wasn't much bite behind it.

"I'm just saying, maybe the two of you are more alike than you realize. We all have a little piece of her in us. Look at me. I push people away and slam the doors behind them."

"I suppose that's true." He sighed again, softer this time. "We've got to stop making this harder on each other than it already is."

"That would be Mom, and there's nothing we can do

about her," she said. "But... we can call a truce and find better ways to communicate.

Another pause. "I can do that."

After they'd said goodnight and ended the call, she sat there for a long moment, phone resting on her knee. It wasn't forgiveness, but it was something.

She texted Erin: *Coffee tomorrow? My treat. Stone Bridge Café?*

A reply came almost instantly: *9 a.m.*

Setting the phone aside, she leaned back into the chair, gaze drifting toward the vineyard. The light was starting to soften, the sky turning that rich, burnished color that always made her think of endings.

A knock startled her.

Standing, she smoothed her sweater out of habit. She checked the peep hole before opening the door. Bryson stood there—hands in his pockets, eyes warm and safe in a way that made her breath catch.

"Hey," he said, voice low.

Her hand tightened on the doorframe, something unsteady sparking in her chest. "Hey." She leaned against the frame for a heartbeat longer than necessary, taking him in—the way the fading light caught in his hair, the faint crease between his brows like he'd been debating something the whole way over. "What are you doing here?" she asked, softer than she'd meant to.

His mouth tipped into that slow, crooked smile that used to undo her. "Thought you might need some company."

A dozen responses crowded her throat, but instead, she stepped back, opening the door wider. "Come in."

As he crossed the threshold, the air shifted, warmer somehow, threaded with the familiar scent of his cologne. She closed the door behind him, allowing her fingers to brush the wood just long enough to ground herself before she turned to face him.

"Bryson..." she started, but the words tangled. There were too many things she wanted to say and not nearly enough courage to say them all.

Unreadable, he held her gaze. "We need to talk. But first, maybe we just... sit."

Something in her shifted. Stilled. All the anger from earlier, when Monica had glided into the tasting room like a whispered threat, vanished. It didn't matter anymore. Monica had never actually been the problem, and that was a cold, hard truth that Riley had to come to terms with.

Bryson leaned back in the chair, letting the silence sit between them. The lamplight spilled gold over the table, catching in Riley's hair and painting the strands a gleaming amber. Outside, a light drizzle tapped a steady rhythm on the partially open window, the scent of damp earth sneaking in.

She sat curled into her chair, one leg tucked under her, a half-full wineglass cradled loosely in her fingers. Her eyes were far away—not cold, but shuttered, the same glint he remembered seeing when she was trying to hold her ground.

"Monica wasn't the real problem," she said finally, her voice so soft he almost had to lean in to catch it. "I mean that kiss, it hurt, but I knew you would never cheat on me. Never initiate anything with someone else. Not even when we were broken up, because we were never really broken up for long."

He tilted his head and cracked a smile. "No, not really, and I know she was just a symptom of bigger issues."

She fixed her gaze somewhere over his shoulder. "It was everything. My family. This town. It felt like the walls were closing in. I needed to breathe. To see something beyond the same roads, the same people who all thought they knew everything about me. I couldn't do that here. I know I've said that a thousand times, but it's true."

His mind flickered to summer nights, years ago, the two of them stretched out on the hood of his truck, watching the sky turn to velvet while she talked about the places she wanted to go. Paris. Patagonia. Anywhere. Back then, he thought love would be enough to keep her here.

"And I never made that decision easy for you, did I?" he asked.

Her eyes met his, then — steady, unflinching. "You were here. Rooted. It's not a bad thing. It's who you are. But I think... even if nothing else had happened, we were always headed in different directions, no matter how much we loved each other."

He let out a breath, slow and deliberate. "Deep down, I always knew that. I'd try to tell myself that if I traveled with you for a year, you'd be able to get it out of your system, and we'd come back. But then, I'd see how utterly selfish and arrogant that was of me. Letting you go was the only option. It was the right thing for both of us, even if it hurt like hell."

She hesitated, her fingers twisting together. "I cried for months. I loved you so much, but I couldn't come back. Not then."

He studied her for a moment, seeing both the woman in front of him and the girl who used to run barefoot through the vineyard, her laughter carrying over the rows like music. "So, where are you headed next?"

Her mouth curved, but it wasn't a smile. "I don't know. I've been chasing so many different places, I'm not sure I even know what I want anymore. Maybe it's not about the next adventure. Maybe it's about... finding a place that feels like mine."

A small, dangerous flicker of hope caught in his chest. "And maybe that place is here," he said before he could stop himself.

Her gaze softened, but she didn't commit. "I'm actually not totally terrified of that idea. So, maybe."

The word "maybe" hit him harder than any definitive no could have. It meant she was considering it—actually considering staying. The possibility bloomed in his chest like warmth after being cold for too long. He smiled faintly. "I'll take 'maybe.'"

Something shifted in the air—the kind of shift he felt in his bones. The tension wasn't sharp anymore. It was warm, magnetic, drawing him toward her like gravity.

He rose slowly, crossing the space between them. He pressed his hand against her cheek, her skin was warm beneath his palm. She leaned into him without hesitation, and for a second, she was eighteen again, tasting summer on her lips in the back of his truck, thinking he could keep her forever.

The first kiss was tentative, meant to test the ground—but the moment her lips moved against his, the years between them vanished. She breathed in sharply, curling her hand into the front of his shirt like she used to when she wanted him closer but wouldn't say it.

The second kiss was deeper, slower—his thumb stroking the curve of her jaw as his other hand slid around her waist. She rose from the chair, and he pulled her in, her body fitting against his, the way it always had—perfectly, like no time had passed at all.

They broke apart just long enough to breathe, foreheads touching, both of them smiling in that quiet, intoxicating way that said they knew exactly where this was going.

"You're dangerous," she whispered, almost laughing.

"Only for you," he murmured, brushing his lips over hers again.

It was hungry, insistent, the kind of need that made thought scatter.

She gasped when he angled his head, his mouth tracing the corner of her lips before returning to fully claim them.

His heart thrummed in his chest, reverberating through his very core as she kissed him back, her teeth nipping gently at his lower lip. A wild gust of wind swept the rain against the window, the scent of the storm mingling with the taste of her on his lips. He craved her like a man who'd been denied wine for centuries, yearning for the lush oasis only she could provide.

Her hair was soft and warm in his fingers, the strands sliding silkily across his skin. A vague hint of Pinot wafted from her glass, mellowing into the comfortable mustiness of the inn around them. They were alone, enveloped by the thrum of the rain and their shared past, their shared dreams.

He slid his palms over the curve of her waist, pressing gently into the softness of her. Slipping his hand beneath her shirt, he searched for bare skin.

His breath hitched as his fingers met the silk edge of her bra, the thin barrier between him and the intimacy he yearned for. It was too much and not nearly enough. Her heartbeat thrummed under his palm, mirroring his own rhythm, frantic and wild. He pulled back slightly, watching her, drinking in her flushed cheeks, her parted lips whispering his name like a prayer.

With a newfound urgency, he drew her close, pulling her shirt over her head, the lamplight casting a gentle glow on her skin. His gaze lingered on her, taking in every curve and line he'd memorized so long ago. Her chest rose and fell with rapid breaths, her stomach bare and smooth beneath his hands. He traced the line of her collarbone, his fingertips barely grazing her skin, and she shivered, her eyes fluttering shut.

He leaned closer, his lips seeking the tender hollow of her throat, relishing the way she gasped. The sweet scent of her skin mingled with the distant musk of the wooden rafters and the heavy smell of rain-soaked earth from outside. As his mouth worked lower, he delighted in the way she clung to him, her fingers digging into his shoulders. Trailing kisses across her chest, he slipped a hand around her back, unclasping her bra. She sighed, her breath hitching as the cool inn air touched her skin, bare and vulnerable.

"I think we should move to the bed," he whispered.

For a moment, he held her gaze, drinking in the shared desire that shimmered in the depths of her eyes.

"Sounds like a solid plan." A slight blush crept to her cheeks, painting them an enchanting shade of rose. Gathering her into his arms, he carried her towards the bed, her body warm and pliant against his. The mattress creaked in protest as he gently set her down, his eyes raking over her once more. The sight of her laid out before him coaxed a low growl from his throat.

He pulled his wallet from his pocket and opened the billfold, tossing a condom on the nightstand.

"Good call," she whispered as he eased in next to her.

Her chest rose and fell in rapid succession, the steady rhythm fascinating, hypnotizing. He marveled, not for the first time, at how perfectly she fit with him, into him, around him. The scent of her mingling with the earthiness of the vineyard easing in through the window was heady, intoxicating. It filled his senses, leaving no space for anything but her. She was his sun, his moon, his stars, his sky. For a moment, he paused, his gaze feasting on every inch. If she decided to leave again, and this moment was all he ever had with her again, would it be enough?

His fingers traced a slow, torturous path down her chest, skimming over the swell of her breasts. She gasped, a soft, pleasured sound that echoed in the silence, bouncing off the old inn's walls. The sound teetered on the precipice of a moan, sending an answering ripple of desire through his veins.

He trailed his mouth lazily over the sensitive skin of her collarbone, savoring the salty-sweet taste of her. Her breath hitched, a soft whimper escaping from between her lips as he descended lower, the valley between her breasts, the altar he worshiped at. He could feel her pulse race beneath his fingers, a silent testament to her arousal. A moan escaped his lips, the sound primal, filled with raw desire, reverberating around the small room.

Taking her nipple into his mouth, he gently swirled his tongue, until he couldn't stand it a second longer. He sucked, hard, needing more.

She arched into him, gripping his shoulders, her breath gusted past his ear like a breeze rustling through the vines.

Her hands, fingers splayed wide, threaded through his hair as she made a soft, pleading sound, urging him on. His hand moved down her stomach, tracing the buttons of her jeans. Her hips lifted off the bed slightly, seeking the pressure, wanting more.

Taking the unspoken invitation, he moved his hand lower, dipping into the waistband of her jeans. He could almost taste the anticipation in the air, the seconds ticking by like hours as he slowly unbuttoned her pants, sliding them off her hips, tossing them aside.

"God, you're so beautiful," he murmured.

A soft sigh escaped her as he moved in closer, his hands exploring the familiar yet exciting realms of her body. His fingers brushed along the edge of her panties, his own breath hitching at the contact. The sight of her beneath him was turning him inside out. She was a vision and she left him feeling vulnerable in ways he hadn't thought possible.

"Bryson," she whispered, her voice a soft melody that fluttered over the drumming rain outside. "Don't make me beg."

He licked his lips. "I always liked it when you did that."

"Just remember what they say about payback."

He groaned as he gently removed her lacy thong.

The tips of his fingers traced over the soft skin of her thighs, eliciting a shiver from her, her muscles tensing under his touch. His fingers flirted dangerously close to her core, her soft gasps and whimpers only stoking his desire.

He dared to glance at her face, her cheeks flushed and her eyes half-lidded. Her lips parted, and she breathed out his name, like a plea, like a command, all at once.

"Bryson."

With that, he moved closer, his fingers exploring her, her hips lifting to meet his hand. Her body was a furnace, and he was being sucked into the flame. He reveled in it, the intensity of her desire burning his fingers as he delved deeper. Her whimpers turned into soft cries, her back arching off the bed like a bowstring pulled taut.

The primal need was potent, blurring his rational thoughts. All he could focus on was her—the taste of her under his tongue, the softness of her body against his, the intoxicating scent of her arousal. The world outside ceased to exist.

He didn't rush, not with this. Every caress was purposeful, every stroke aimed to elicit a response. Her hips rose off the bed, chasing the pleasure he bestowed. His name ripped from her throat as he pushed a finger inside and brushed his tongue over her swollen clit, an echoing plea for more. He obliged, adding another, the squelching sound of her arousal filling the room.

When he added a third finger, her legs trembled around

him, and her nails dug into his scalp. Her body was coiling, wound tight like a spring.

He could feel her pulse around his fingers, her body convulsing with a pleasure so intense it was almost debilitating. Her release took her, consumed her entirely, and he rode it with her, his own body responding to the pleasure coursing through hers.

He took a moment to just watch her. Splayed out beneath him, her body glowed under the dim light of the lamp. He leaned down to kiss her. It was a heady mix, the tang of their arousal, the dull hint of Pinot, and her own sweet taste. He could get drunk on her alone.

"Your turn," she said, her eyes glinting with a promise of a night well spent.

"If you insist." He tore off his shirt and tossed it to the floor.

She made a grab for the buckle of his jeans, her fingers trembling slightly. He bit back a groan as her hands moved over him, anticipation tightening the coil in his gut.

With a determined tug, his jeans and boxers were discarded on the floor, his arousal freed from its confinement. Her fingers circled his length, her eyes never leaving his. The sight was intoxicating.

She leaned forward, her tongue darting out, licking his tip before taking him into her mouth.

Holding his breath, he did his best to maintain control. It wasn't easy. She glanced up at him, and he all but came undone.

"I need you to stop," he managed.

"If I must." She kissed her way up his chest.

He reveled in the momentary respite, his heart pounding, his breath coming in short gasps. He wanted this. Needed this. But it wasn't just about the physical pleasure. It was about the connection, their shared past, their love.

He pressed her onto her back, fumbled with the necessary protection, then he pushed inside. It felt like he'd come home.

She gripped his shoulders, her nails digging into his flesh, marking him as hers. He moved faster, harder, his body seeking the release that he craved. Raw pleasure spiked through him with every thrust, overwhelming him almost as much as the profound connection that drew them together. This was more than just a physical act—it was about reclaiming their love, rekindling the flame that had never truly gone out.

He could see his own pleasure mirrored in her eyes, the clenching of her body beneath him a clear indication that she was as lost in this moment as he was. Greedily, eagerly, she met every thrust, her hips grinding up to meet his with an intensity that spurred him on. He kissed her then, claiming her mouth in a heated dance of tongues, consumed by her taste, by her feel... by her.

Her climax hit, a violent shudder wracking her body taking him over the edge with her. Their bodies fused together, lost in a kaleidoscope of pleasure, as they rode out the aftermath together.

The silence that followed was only interrupted by the sound of their ragged breaths as they held each other, their bodies still entwined, the scent of their lovemaking hanging heavy in the air. Her fingers traced lazy patterns over his chest, her head nestled comfortably in the crook of his arm. He pressed a soft kiss to the top of her head, his heart filling with an emotion so profound it was almost over-whelming.

He wasn't sure what the future held for them. Later, they'd have to face reality, face the world with all its challenges. But for now, for this moment, it was just them, here in this room, tangled between the sheets, basking in the afterglow of their shared passion, their shared history.

"Not to scare you or anything, but you should know that I still love you," he murmured, his lips brushing against her hair. She smiled against his chest, her hand squeezing his in response.

His heart swelled with a certain peace, something he hadn't felt in a long time. The storm outside echoed his thundering heartbeat, a rhythm that pulsed with love and longing. There was a world outside the inn, one filled with complications and hardships, but it didn't matter. Right now, all that mattered was Riley. Her warmth. Her love. Her understanding.

"I never stopped loving you," she whispered back.

He held her close, cherishing the feel of her in his arms, the taste of her still on his lips. Whatever happened next—whether she stayed or left—whether they reunited or fell apart— didn't matter. All he knew was that he loved her, and she loved him. And in that moment, it was enough.

"Hey, Ry?"

"What?"

"Can I stay here tonight? I really don't want to get out of this bed."

She laughed, but before she could answer, her phone buzzed. "Ugh." She sat up. "I think I left my cell on the table by the window."

"I'll get it." Bryson slipped from the bed, hiked up his boxers, and padded across the room. "Um, who is Mateo, and should I be jealous?"

Riley burst out laughing. "God, no. Feel free to answer it. He's got a bit of a man crush on you."

"Not fair. I don't even know who this dude is." He tapped the green button as he made his way back to bed, but not before snagging the bottle of wine and the glass. They could share. "Hey, Mateo," Bryson said.

"Who is this?"

"Bryson and you're on speaker with Riley."

"Good to know. I was beginning to think my girl had been kidnapped," Mateo said.

"Let's get one thing straight. She's my girl," Bryson said as he topped off the glass, took a sip, and then handed it to Riley, who had turned about five shades of red. "Now, what can we do for you?"

"Riley?"

"Mateo?"

"Permission to speak freely?" Mateo asked.

Bryson liked this guy already.

"Of course. But now you're freaking me out. Is everything okay?" She handed the glass back to Bryson and sat up, clutching the sheets to her chest.

"Yeah. But you got a letter today, and I don't know how to tell you this," Mateo said in a much softer voice.

Bryson held her gaze.

"It's from your dad," Mateo murmured.

Riley covered her mouth and gasped. A tear slipped free and landed on the sheet. And then another one. Followed by a trail of many more.

Bryson twisted his body, setting the wine on the night-stand. He wrapped his arm around Riley, tugging her close to his chest, kissing her temple. "Mateo, we're gonna have to call you—"

"No. I want you to open the letter and read it." She wiped her face, but she didn't leave Bryson's embrace.

"Are you sure?" Mateo asked. "I feel like I'd be invading your privacy."

"No. It's okay. I need to know. It's probably just my dad being my dad. But it will help." She sighed, resting her head on Bryson's shoulder. "Rip it open."

"Okay," Mateo said.

"Hey, kiddo,

I've been meaning to write you anyway, but something's been on my mind, and I just don't know where to turn or who to talk to.

You know me—I've never been one to stir the pot unless there's a good reason. Back when I was still on the revitaliza-tion committee, I noticed a few things in the books that didn't quite add up. At the time, I chalked it up to slow paperwork or human error. But I've learned some things since I left, and I can't believe it.

I don't want to drag you into this, but what I can tell you is that a lot more money has gone missing from that fund, and it's got Grant's name all over it. I don't understand it. Your brother's done well for himself. He's smart. He's not someone who needs to cut corners. He's opening a second spa since he's making money hand over fist. It just doesn't make sense. I didn't want to take it to anyone on the revitalization committee. Not until I've had a chance to speak with Grant. I don't want to believe he had anything to do with this. It's not like him. I know he can be a little entitled sometimes, but he's a good man.

I asked Grant for a meeting. I want to hear what he has to say. For all I know, everyone's already looking into it, and I'm just being paranoid—and I have to consider where I got this information from. Although they wouldn't point the finger at Grant unless they thought something was up. I'm so distraught.

I hate dropping this on you, especially from so far away, but I've always wanted you to know the truth when it comes to family matters. No matter what happens, you should be proud of the life you've built and the person you are. I sure am.

Love you always,
Dad"

"When was that letter dated?" Bryson asked.

"Two days before he died."

Riley sucked in a deep breath. "There is no way Grant stole that money. Or that he...I can't even say it out loud."

"Mateo, can you scan that letter in and send it to Riley's phone? I'll also forward my contact information so you can drop it in the mail. Send it the fastest way you can. I'll pay for it."

"Sure, no problem," Mateo said. "Riley, are you gonna be okay?"

Riley plopped back onto the pillow, covering her eyes. "I have no idea. This doesn't make any sense."

"You take good care of that girl of ours," Mateo said.

"I will. Don't you worry." Bryson ended the call, setting the phone on the nightstand. He pulled Riley into his arms. "Once I get that letter, we're gonna need to give it to Sandy, and I don't want you staying in this inn all alone. Tomorrow morning, you're moving into the main house with me."

She groaned. "Do you really believe my brother is capable of embezzlement?"

"Capable? Yeah. He's smarter than most. But would he? That's the problem. I don't see the motivation. But my dad? He's looking at the books. There's a problem there, and people on that committee know it. Sean knew it, and now he's dead."

Bryson couldn't believe the words that slipped between his lips. But what was worse were the thoughts tumbling through his brain.

Nine

The steam from her coffee curled up in delicate ribbons, dissolving into the cool morning air. Riley sat on the Boone's wide front porch, the fancy modern chair creaking under her as she leaned forward, elbows resting on her knees.

Next door, though more like a half city block away, her childhood home stood in soft shadow, the early light just starting to spill over the roofline. From this distance, it looked the same—the faded clapboard siding, the slanted porch roof, the way the maple in the front yard arched over the driveway like a guardian. But up close, she knew every paint chip and warped board told a different story.

Before her parents' divorce, that house had been everything—birthday parties in the backyard, her dad grilling while her mom sipped Chardonnay and complained about the mosquitoes. Sleepovers with friends in the living room. The clatter of dishes during dinner, her dad making corny jokes until Grant rolled his eyes.

She took a sip of coffee, trying to ground herself in the

bitter warmth, but the memories pressed harder. Her gaze drifted to the narrow strip of grass that marked the property line. On impulse, she rose from the chair, bare feet brushing over the weathered porch boards. She stepped off onto the cool dew-covered lawn and walked toward it, heart tugging in a hundred directions.

She had no idea who lived there now, but it looked as though it needed some tender loving care. Grant had told her it had changed owners twice. Bryson had mentioned that if it went on the market again, his family would buy it, fix it up, and make another guest house out of it.

"Thinking about jumping the fence?"

She turned toward the deep voice, finding Walter stepping out onto the porch, coffee mug in hand, his frame filling the doorway. He wore faded jeans and a colorful flannel, no different from how she remembered him from high school—steady, grounded, with eyes that saw too much and judged too little.

He'd always been like a second father, and she'd loved sitting in the back, out near the vineyard, in front of a bonfire, listening to her dad and Walter tell stories from when they were little. How there hadn't been as many rows, how they'd both loved the crush pad, and when they got older, tasting the wine with their fathers. It was a great tradition.

"I was just... looking," Riley said, brushing a strand of hair behind her ear as she made her way back toward the porch. "I heard if that place goes up for sale, you'd snatch it up. But I can't imagine why you'd need another guest house."

Walter gave her a small smile, the kind that didn't ask

for more than she wanted to give. "I honestly have no idea what I'd do with it." He laughed. "But I'm more determined now than ever. To me, that was Sean's place. And I wouldn't mind honoring him... somehow."

"My dad loved that house. It was hard for him to sell it, but my mom didn't want it, and he couldn't ... I'm sorry. I shouldn't be going on about this."

"No need to apologize."

Riley settled back into her chair. "I don't want to be alone. Not yet. But staying here... I feel like I'm intruding."

"You're always welcome." With a quiet grunt, Walter lowered himself into the chair beside her. "From the moment Bryson dragged you across the yard as fast as those little legs of yours would take you when you were all of maybe two, you've been family to us."

She let his words sit for a moment before the weight of the other thing she'd been holding pressed forward. "Walter... about that letter my dad sent."

"No point in worrying too much about that right now."

"But the implications of it all. What it could mean about my father's death."

Walter glanced up. "The police are looking into the embezzlement. The autopsy report will tell us what caused your father's death, and honestly, there's no reason to believe it was anything other than a heart attack."

"Do you believe that? Can you say, with certainty, that someone stealing money—potentially my brother—the letter, and my dad dropping dead doesn't feel like a scene from a true crime novel or something?"

Walter shifted. "I've been staring at those books for a

few weeks. Something isn't right. But I don't have the full picture. We're gonna get that today. Do I believe your brother would steal from the town?" He rubbed his jaw. "That's a tough one. Grant did some stupid things when he was a boy. But all teenagers do that." He lowered his gaze. "Like when I caught you and Bryson taking my sports car out for a joy ride."

She laughed, waving her hand. "In my defense, Bryson told me he had your permission."

"I don't doubt that. He was trying to impress his girl-friend...among other things."

Heat rose from Riley's toes to her cheeks.

"But there's motivation behind all our actions. I don't see what Grant has to gain from stealing from our community. It makes no sense. Not even to fund his second spa. He had more than enough money to do that. It's why I'd like to have a conversation with him... after I've had a chance to make some more notes. Perhaps on Monday, after all the drama from the garden party has died down."

Riley groaned. "I'm so glad I'm not attending that."

"I wish I wasn't." Walter sighed. "Monica has taken all the joy out of it for Brea and me." He winced and leaned forward. "I'm sorry. I shouldn't have mentioned her name."

"It's fine. I'm sure Bryson told you about my run-in with her."

"He mentioned it," Walter admitted. "She's a sore subject for everyone in this family, but I can't imagine that was easy for you. She tends to believe she still has some rights to our name, this family... and Bryson."

"Yeah, she made that perfectly clear."

"You're the better woman." Walter patted her hand. "If

it makes you feel any better, my son nearly jilted her. But his sense of honor got in the way."

The screen door banged lightly, and Bryson stepped out. His hair was damp, his jaw tight, and he moved like someone already carrying too much on his shoulders. "Seriously?" he said, looking at Walter. "You encouraged Devon to have the conversation?"

Walter frowned. "I'm not sure I know what you're talking about."

"Emery Tate," Bryson said, planting a hand on the porch rail. "That isn't okay, Dad. I don't care if she grew up in Stone Bridge. The scandal that blew up her career in wine auctions and fine vintages should be enough reason to shut the door before she even steps through it."

Walter's expression didn't shift much. "It's an interview. People make mistakes. You know I believe in second chances. And there's no reason you can't be at the interview, asking questions."

Bryson shook his head, clearly not convinced, but Walter stood, clapped his son on the shoulder, and said to Riley, "We'll talk later."

Then he disappeared inside, leaving her with the distinct impression there was more to that conversation than she understood.

Bryson dropped into the chair Walter had vacated, muttering something under his breath before glancing at her. "I can't believe the nerve of my brother. And my father is too kind."

"I'm clueless," she said, curiosity flickering to life. "Who's Emery Tate?"

"You don't remember her?"

"Name's familiar... wait. Did she graduate with Devon and Grant?"

"She did, and she was nice enough back then. Built a brilliant career," Bryson said. "I'll admit, she's smart. Damn smart. But she blew it all up. No one will even look at her resume. And the last few weeks, Devon's been slipping out of meetings, taking private calls when he should be dealing with winery business. I thought it was some girl he's been secretly dating because he's always been weird about that. I wouldn't be surprised if he's slept with Emery. She's so his type."

"Wow. This really has your panties in a twist."

"Yeah. It does. My brother sometimes lets his love life interfere with business." Bryson sighed. "Devon's my best friend. Always has been, despite being three years older. But sometimes, he thinks with the wrong head."

She burst out laughing. "That's really mature."

"More mature than my brother, right now." He sighed. "Sorry. I just don't believe that hiring someone with that kind of baggage is a good look for us. We've had some issues with Winston Callaway lately."

"As in Callaway wines?"

Bryson leaned back and folded his arms. "Our biggest competitor in the space we're in. Just little things, but it's enough to get my hackles up."

"I'm sorry you're having to deal with that. But like your dad said, it's all just a conversation right now."

Bryson shot her a weary look.

She shrugged.

"So, what were you and my dad discussing?" he asked.

"The embezzlement. What it means and what it doesn't, and where my mind keeps going."

Bryson nodded slowly. "I spoke to Sandy a bit ago. They're gonna take another look at everything."

She let out a breath. "I feel like I'm keeping secrets from Grant and Erin, and considering we're all sort of getting along for the first time in years, keeping secrets sucks."

"Sometimes, it's not keeping something from someone," Bryson said. "It's holding it long enough to make sure you're telling the right truth."

"You sound like your father."

Bryson chuckled. "He's not the worst person to emulate."

The morning light spilling over the vines and the distant hum of the town waking up in the background.

"Speaking of the truth," Bryson said, setting his mug down, "Monica's been texting me. Like nonstop."

Riley groaned. "Of course she has. What does she want now?"

"In one text, she actually asked what time she could expect to be picked up and told me the color of her dress so we could match." He closed his eyes for a moment. "I damn near told her to fuck off but thought better of it."

"You don't swear all that often."

Opening his eyes, he met Riley's. "Oh, you should have heard us fight." He laughed. "At first, my mom would remind me that no lady deserved to be spoken to like that. Then, my darling mother said, '*That* woman is no lady.'

"Sounds like Brea."

"Anyway, I'm not answering Monica. She's not worth

my time. It's a non-issue, despite being annoying. But, given everything else. I just wanted you to know."

"Annoying's putting it mildly," she said. "And thank you for telling me."

"The only thing that bothers me right now is seeing you hurting," he said, his gaze holding hers.

Her chest tightened. She sipped her coffee to keep from saying something she wasn't ready to voice. "You always were good at knowing when to say the right thing."

"And you always hated admitting it." He grinned, and for a heartbeat, the heaviness surrounding them eased.

She turned her head toward her old house again, knowing breakfast with Erin was going to be its own battle. But for now, on the Boone porch, she let herself breathe.

The smell of fresh ground coffee beans and warm cinnamon wrapped around Riley the moment she stepped inside Stone Bridge Café. The place hadn't changed much —the same mismatched wooden tables, the same chalk-board menu with flourishes that leaned more artistic than legible, the same hum of locals greeting each other like family.

She ordered a latte and found a small corner table by the window. From here, she could see the ebb and flow of Main Street—shopkeepers sweeping their stoops, a couple of early tourists lingering outside the bakery to take pictures of the hand-painted sign. Her gaze caught on the gift shop two doors down, its front windows filled with postcards, pottery, and handmade soaps.

Stephanie's shop.

As if summoned by thought, the door chimed, and there she was—Stephanie Wilcox, hair a little shorter now, swept back in a loose braid, wearing jeans and a floral blouse. She spotted Riley instantly, hesitated for half a breath, then made her way over.

"Well, if it isn't Stone Bridge's most elusive wanderer," Stephanie said with a smile that didn't quite hide her nerves.

Riley rose enough to give her a quick hug. "Steph. You look... good."

"You're kind to say so, but most days I look in the mirror and all I see is tired. I'm fueled by caffeine and two hours of sleep thanks to my youngest deciding 3 a.m. is a great time to redecorate her room with finger paint."

Riley covered her mouth and let out a snort. "I'm sorry. I shouldn't laugh, but all I can think about is the time we thought it would be fun to paint your mother's garage. Like a mural was all the rage, and we did so with her permanent spray paint."

"Good Lord. We were maybe eight, and my mom didn't know whether to skin us alive or burst out laughing because our masterpiece looked more like a penis than a rocket." Steph shook her head. "Mind if I sit for a minute?"

"No. Please, join me. That is, until my sister arrives. Erin still believes that being a half hour late is in the window of being on time."

"Sounds like your sister." Steph slid into the chair across from her. Her hair color was the same, but styled shorter, more sophisticated. And she carried herself with a sense of maturity that came with age and living. "I'm so sorry about your dad. It's been such a shock to the community. He was such a sweet man. He'd wander into the gift shop, smile, and tell me a story about my past. He was so kind. I really loved that man."

"Thank you. He always said you were unicorns and rainbows... until someone fed you sugar."

They both laughed.

"How long are you in town?" Steph asked.

Riley hesitated. "Not sure yet."

Stephanie glanced at her mug before looking back up. "Have you seen any of the old gang?"

"I had coffee with Sandy the other day." Riley traced a finger along the rim of her cup. "Can't believe she's the Police Chief. And of course, I've seen Bryson. He's the one who first got hold of me when my dad died."

"I've been meaning to say this for a long time," Stephanie said, leaning forward. "I felt like I betrayed you. Standing up for Monica at her wedding to Bryson... it wasn't because I picked her over you. At the time, it felt like the whole town had, and I just... got swept along. But I regret it. Every damn day."

Riley studied her, the sincerity in her voice cutting through years of distance. "Monica's good at making people think they don't have a choice."

Stephanie's mouth twisted. "I had a choice. I just made the wrong one. I don't really talk to her anymore. Had enough of her crap a few years back. We run into each other at parties sometimes, but since I had kids, I've got little built-in bundles of excuses."

That made Riley huff a short laugh. "I ran into Monica, and it wasn't pretty. Bryson was there. We had words. She treated me like sloppy seconds. Shoved her big ass boobs practically in the man's face. Bryson looked like he wanted to die, but it was at the tasting room, so he had to be polite."

"He's usually kind." Steph leaned forward. "Except, once, he got really drunk and told her off... in front of the whole town... including her mom. Everyone clapped. It was awesome."

"We're like teenagers all over again. This is so petty."

"I know, right?" Steph leaned back. "I do my best to avoid that drama." She pulled out her cell. "These two take up all my time, and I love them so much I could cry."

"Wow. They're so cute."

They talked for a few more minutes about Stephanie's kids, the shop, and small-town life before Stephanie checked the time and sighed. "I should get back before my part-time help burns the place down. But I'm glad I saw you." She reached across the table, squeezing Riley's hand. "Really glad."

"Me too, and I'd like to do it again before I leave."

"I'd love that."

When Stephanie left, Riley sat back, letting the moment settle. The past here wasn't all bad. But it was tangled, and she wasn't sure how many knots she had the patience to untie.

The door opened again. This time it was Erin. Her blonde hair was pulled back in a low ponytail, her face bare of makeup, the shadows under her eyes more pronounced than Riley remembered. Erin spotted her and made her way over, her smile small but genuine.

"I'm so glad you reached out," Erin said as she slid into

the seat Stephanie had just vacated. "I'm sorry I'm late. I had dropped the kids off at Mom's, and that was a whole thing. Next time we get together, we'll do it with my babies. They're so excited to see you."

"I can't wait."

They ordered breakfast, the clink of silverware and hiss of the espresso machine filling the gaps between pleasantries. But it didn't take long for Erin to lean forward, her voice low. "I'm having a hard time. With all of it. Dad's gone, Mom's acting... well, like Mom. And Grant's... I don't know. He's taking it from all sides, and he's more than twitchy. He's downright moody."

Riley kept her face neutral, though her mind flicked immediately to her father's note, and the missing money. "I'm sure it's a lot for him, too," she said carefully.

Erin sighed, rubbing her forehead. "I know Grant has made his share of mistakes, but he's under so much pressure from Mom about you." She glanced up, meeting Riley's gaze. "It's so tough to balance. Grant and I both regret so many things about your departure. We were hurt, and we listened to Mom, who cares more about appearances than she does her own children." Erin lifted her napkin and dabbed her eyes.

"Wow. That's a big statement coming from you."

"Mom's so good at manipulating," Erin added quickly. "It's just... now, it feels gross. This pressure to 'choose' and I hate it. She's furious you're staying at the Boones'."

"Wait. What? I've been staying at Stone Bridge Inn."

"She drove by this morning. Saw you and Bryson carrying your bag up the front porch." Erin shook her head.

"She thinks it's disloyal. Me, I'm glad. I'm not like her, or even Grant in that way. I've always liked Bryson."

Riley's stomach twisted. "I'm not choosing sides. I just... didn't want to be alone, and Grant really needs to get over this thing with Bryson. There's no reason for it. They're grown men."

"Oh, he knows that. He tries. But it's not easy when Mom's telling him Bryson pushed you out of town. That Bryson broke your heart when he cheated on you."

"That's not what happened."

"We all know that now, including Grant. But Mom sometimes whispers half-truths about Bryson. Things that happened, and then she gets all quiet and tells us she can't dare say anything else. That it would be gossip, but that there's so much more, and she knows things, but then doesn't say anything." Erin hesitated, her fingers tightening around her coffee cup. "I haven't exactly been a great sister to you over the years."

Riley blinked, surprised. "Where's this coming from?"

"From the fact that I finally see our mother for who she is. That my marriage is in shambles," Erin said, her voice cracking. "Chad's cheating on me. And the worst part? I believe it now—what you said when you were sixteen. Maybe I even believed it then. That he was the one who made the pass at you. Not the other way around."

Riley swallowed hard, the old hurt pressing at the edges of her chest. "Erin..."

"I defended him because I didn't want to admit the boy I loved would do such a thing to my little sister. And now..." She let out a bitter laugh. "Now, I'm living with the consequences. Mom thinks I'm overreacting, says Chad provides a good life, and I'm just being dramatic."

"That sounds like Mom," Riley murmured.

"She doesn't see how miserable I am. And Dad's not here for me to talk to anymore. He always made me feel like I could figure things out. Now I just feel... lost."

Riley reached across the table, covering her sister's hand with her own. "You're not alone. You've got me. Always."

Erin's eyes filled, but she didn't look away. "I don't deserve it, but... thank you."

They sat there for a moment, holding onto each other across the table, two women who'd spent too long on opposite sides of old wounds finding some common ground at last.

But under the warmth of it, Riley felt the secret in her chest like a stone — heavy, unmoving, impossible to set down. Because Erin trusted her now. And when the truth about the money came out, that trust might be the first casualty.

Erin swiped at her eyes, managing a shaky smile. "At least now we can all just... focus on grieving Dad. No more drama. No more fights."

Riley forced a nod, her throat tightening.

While Erin was clinging to the hope for peace, Riley knew the undercurrent running beneath their family was anything but calm. Secrets didn't stay buried in Stone Bridge—they had a way of surfacing when you least wanted them to. And when this one came up for air, she wasn't sure who would still be standing beside her.

Bryson's father's home office smelled faintly of tobacco and old books, even though his dad hadn't smoked in decades. The big oak desk occupied half the room, its surface a mess of neatly stacked ledgers, printouts, and an open laptop Mason had brought from home. Sunlight slanted in through the tall window, catching in the dust motes that swirled lazily in the air.

Bryson leaned against the doorframe, mug of coffee in hand. "You planning on building a fortress with all that paper, Dad?"

Walter glanced up from his reading glasses. "If it keeps you out of my office, maybe." He smiled, but it didn't quite reach his eyes.

From where he sat at the desk, Mason smirked. "I think Bryson's just trying to keep you too busy to notice that Riley's moved into his wing of the house."

Bryson narrowed his eyes. "She's not—"

"Oh, she's taken up residence," Walter cut in, clearly enjoying himself now. "And I gotta say, it's been a long time since I've seen you looking this happy over a house-guest." His father smiled a little too widely. "Can't imagine why."

Bryson ignored them both and crossed the room, setting his coffee down next to the laptop. "What have you found?"

The teasing faded quickly, replaced by a thick, tense quiet. Mason tapped the ledger in front of him. "Here's the problem. We have checks from the revitalization fund ledger, signed by Grant. Not a big deal. Only, some aren't logged in the right place. Or the amounts don't match. Or some are cashed or deposited into an account with a routing number that traces back to a small credit union in Modesto."

Bryson frowned. "Modesto? That's a hell of a drive for someone who lives here."

Walter shifted through another stack. "It's the same routing number on every suspicious transaction. And whoever did it, covered their tracks well enough that it looks like the money was moved into a legitimate vendor account before being transferred again, only the money is still missing."

"And it's damning news for Grant," Mason said flatly. "From where I'm sitting, if I took this to my wife right now, Grant's gonna have to answer for every cent."

Bryson rubbed the back of his neck, trying to push away the instinct to defend Riley's brother. "It doesn't make sense. Grant's not broke— far from it. He's got the business, the house, the image. What the hell would be the motive?"

"I borrowed money to start this winery when I was twenty-two because my father wanted to teach me the value of a dollar. And we don't know all there is to know about Grant and his finances. Just because his business appears to be solvent doesn't mean it is. He's expanding, but we don't know what that looks like on the inside." Walter rubbed his temples. "And there's greed. That doesn't always make sense."

"Okay, all of that is logical, except Grant's never been greedy, except maybe on the football field," Bryson said. "I can't even say the man's thirsty for attention. He's a little arrogant. Kind of a dick, but that's pretty much reserved for me. He's got a great wife, who loves him and is amazing.

Two beautiful kids. And no one to tell him he needs to borrow money to expand a business, like Grandpa did to you."

"Maybe he started gambling, because we're all missing something, and, you know, we're not the ones wearing the badge." Mason leaned back, arms crossed. "Sandy's going to want to see this, herself. But I can tell you right now, she's gonna push to bring Grant in for questioning, and we can't stand in her way."

Bryson's head came up. "Questioning? Already?"

"I know my wife," Mason said. "The amount taken isn't pocket change. We're talking felony-level theft from a community fund. If it wasn't him, someone went out of their way to make it look like him. Not to mention, he's got to know these numbers don't add up." Mason waved a hand. "Too many questions with too many dollars missing. We've got to call my wife, now."

Walter took off his glasses, rubbing at the bridge of his nose. "Let me talk to him first. I've known Grant his whole life—"

"No." Mason's tone was firm. "Not only will that give him, or someone else, time to come up with a story, or to cover their tracks, this is a police matter now. If we start tipping people off before we've got them in the room, we risk losing any chance of getting the truth. You know that."

Bryson glanced between them, the knot in his gut tightening. He didn't want to imagine the look on Riley's face when she found out her brother was being questioned for stealing from the town fund. And he sure as hell didn't want to picture what it would do to her to know the evidence was this strong.

Walter exhaled heavily and pushed back from the desk. "All right. Call the chief."

Mason picked up his phone, his expression grim as he dialed. "This isn't gonna be pretty," he said, stepping onto the patio.

Bryson moved to the window, staring out at the vineyards rolling away in orderly rows. Nothing about this felt right—not the numbers, not the lack of motive, not the way Grant fit into it. But the evidence was staring them in the face, and now there was no turning back. He shifted toward the desk, jaw set. "This just sucks. Riley doesn't need to deal with this on top of her father's death."

"Hopefully it's something that can be cleared up easily," his dad said.

Hope was an endangered commodity these days.

Ten

R iley's fingers curled around the edges of a book, the spine warm from the afternoon sun filtering through the screened porch. Beyond it, the Boone vineyard stretched toward the tree line, rows of vines dense and proud, as if nothing in the world could unearth their roots.

But Riley couldn't shake the sensation that doom lurked in the shadows. That her family hung in the delicate balance between grief and mending the traumas of the past. She slipped the letter from her father, which Bryson had printed, from the pages of her book, and unfolded it, staring at the words on the pages. Her dad's neat hand-writing stared back, haunting, tormenting her as if he'd reached out from the grave.

Her dad, even though he hadn't wanted her to leave at the tender age of eighteen, had driven her to the airport. He'd handed her a card, stuffed with a lovely note, filled with encouragement and love, along with a check for a thousand dollars. He'd told her that there was more if she ever needed it. To never hesitate to call if she got into financial trouble or just needed an ear. He'd always be there.

And his parting words had been that he loved her, and she'd always have a safe place to return when she was ready.

There was a huge part of her that regretted she'd never taken the risk to come home, if even for a visit. What had she been so afraid of? Her family? Bryson? Could they really hurt her anymore?

The truth was she'd been a coward in so many ways.

She could jump from a perfectly good airplane without a second thought. She had no problem flinging herself across time and space on a zipline. Or dangling upside down from a tree without worrying if the rope would hold. She enjoyed teetering between having one foot on a clearly-marked path to a death wish and the other one planted firmly in the dirt of real life. It was a weird way to live, and she knew it. But it had been her life for twelve years. And she'd truly loved every second of it. It filled her heart in ways Stone Bridge hadn't.

She'd done and seen so much of the world. She'd experienced more than most.

A concept her father seemed to have understood and accepted.

Sean Callahan had been bound to Stone Bridge out of love and obligation to his family. But also because of a connection to something bigger. He loved this winery— this land—and taking what he'd called his dream job ten years ago had made him come alive in ways that she hadn't expected. She loved that for him because for years, she'd watched him be everything to everyone else, and yet, never quite be good enough.

Except when it came to her. He'd always been the best in her eyes.

But unlike her father, she couldn't stay in a town that had betrayed her.

However, being at the Boone residence gave her a sense of belonging again. A thought that both brought her comfort and a tinge of resentment.

Relying on Bryson again stirred things deep in her core she hadn't wanted to face. Things that she'd known had always been there—buried so deep she could pretend they held no power over her anymore.

But they did.

Stone Bridge was still her home. She'd left a tiny piece of herself behind, and it was as if by being here again, she'd collected it, making herself whole.

Laughter broke the stillness, drawing her gaze to the far edge of the back lawn. Bryson and Deven raced each other down a dirt path between the last row of vines and the edge of the grass. Deven surged ahead, but Bryson lunged at him with a sideways tackle, sending both men tumbling into the grass in a flurry of flailing limbs and breathless laughter.

For a moment, it was just like high school. Summer heat. Bare arms. Boys chasing each other like dogs off-leash. She felt the ache of it in her chest. A tickle of a giggle stirred in her throat as Bryson pressed on his brother's back, before jumping to his feet and taking off again—Devon calling Bryson a few choice words in his wake.

It amazed her how easily they went from being in an argument over something like hiring Emery Tate to acting like best friends.

"Ah, my boys are still idiots," came a voice from behind her.

Riley turned just as Brea stepped through the sliding glass door, all elegance in a pale green sundress and strappy wedges that didn't belong anywhere near a vineyard. Her hair was swept up into some kind of soft knot that probably took twenty minutes and six pins to pull off he casual style. Riley smiled despite herself. "You look amazing."

Brea gave a theatrical sigh and collapsed into the chair beside her. "Technically, I'm underdressed, under perfumed, carrying way too few dollar signs dangling from my ears, neck, and wrists, and over this entire ordeal. But thank you because that was exactly the look I was going for."

"And where are we headed this evening?"

Brea cocked a brow. "Monica's party." She groaned. "If I hear the words 'artisan' or 'bespoke' one more time, I'm going to throw myself into the fountain. Yes, the one she had craned in from Tuscany because the decor at the country club wasn't... quite right. That woman is ridiculous."

Riley laughed. "That can't be real."

"Oh, it is. There's a plaque. With a quote. In Latin." Brea waved her hand. "Pardon my French, dear. But that girl is a fucking disaster wrapped in a spray tan and a fake personality. I'm not sure she's ever going to understand that it doesn't matter how many designer labels she drapes herself in or how many high-end bags she owns. At the end of the day, dog shit is still gonna smell like dog shit no matter how much expensive perfume she sprays on it."

Brea leaned forward. "I can't stand that little bitch, but

I smile, I pretend, and I try not to toss sand." She gestured loosely at her outfit. "Again, it's why I'm dressed in clothing barely worth noting. It'll make Monica clench in all places she doesn't want to. She'll believe I'm poking fun at her party because I didn't break out the crown jewels and let her borrow them."

"Sounds like a little mockery is going on."

"I know. I shouldn't. But I can't help myself these days." Brea stretched her legs out, examining her painted toenails with a little frown. "I should've gone with coral. Monica hates that color. Says it's not bold enough. I'll give her bold. But too late now, and no, I'm not bitter. Not one bit. But since both of us can agree we don't like her, I can be honest about it."

Riley absently turned the book over. "You don't have to go."

"I do." Brea's voice softened. "It's for the youth arts fund. Bryson's grandmother helped start that charity. And if I don't go, Monica wins. It's childish, I know. But for a few long years, I put up with her trying to be a Boone. Our family name comes with responsibility. Our ancestry goes back to the beginning of this town. I get it sounds as pretentious as she is. However, we take pride in our community. In giving back. In being real, decent, honest people. She does not. I can't let her win."

"And here, I was told we don't keep score."

Brea gave her a sharp, sideways glance. "Oh, honey. We're always keeping score."

Riley snorted. "Well, then maybe I should go."

Brea's eyes widened like someone had lit a fuse, and

immediately Riley regretted her quick retort. "Now we're talking."

"I was joking." Riley pursed her lips.

"But you're thinking about it." Brea leaned in conspiratorially. "Because I know exactly what would happen if you walked into that party on Bryson's arm." She winked. "Especially since you've put a smile on my son's face as big as the sky since you waltzed in here today with him carrying your luggage right up into his bedroom." She leaned in closer. "And don't try to tell me you're staying in one of the other rooms. I wasn't born yesterday, and I'd be insulted if you tried to tell me otherwise."

Riley's cheeks flushed.

"Now, what do you say about coming to that party? I could use someone to commiserate with."

"I'm not trying to start a war."

"You wouldn't be starting it. You'd just be reminding everyone Monica didn't win the last one." Brea nodded toward Bryson and Devon. "Look at them. You're telling me you don't want to walk into that overpriced garden party and watch Monica's lips curl like she's just bitten into a lemon wedge, all while desperately trying to save face?" She sighed. "I'm not normally a mean girl, and I don't hold grudges. But I haven't been able to let go of this one. Walter believes it's because Monica enjoyed undermining me publicly when she was married to Bryson, and I had no choice half the time but to bite my tongue."

"I've never known you to keep your thoughts to yourself."

"It was a difficult time for Bryson, and I didn't want to make it worse."

Riley glanced to the field where Bryson and Deven were still roughhousing like they were sixteen again. Bryson's head was tipped back in laughter, his T-shirt clinging to his back, sun catching in his hair.

"What do you say? It's for a good cause, and considering all you've been through, it would be good for you to get out and do something fun," Brea said. "If, once you get there and you're not feeling it, Bryson will take you home."

Riley's lips curled. "I don't have anything to wear."

"I've got the perfect dress for you."

Skeptical, Riley turned to face her. "Please tell me it doesn't have sequins."

Brea smirked. "It's vintage. Deep plum. Wrap-style. Subtle slit. Monica will think it's new off the Paris runway and spend all night trying to figure out if it's Dior or Valentino while steaming because I never once let her borrow from my collection."

Riley raised a brow. "And it's just... in your closet?"

"It's from my 'just in case I have to destroy someone' section," Brea said matter-of-factly. "Every woman should have one."

Riley laughed, harder this time. "You're terrifying."

"I'm a Boone," Brea replied, brushing imaginary lint from her lap. "Being terrifying is practically a family motto." She batted her eyelashes. "Monica's mother once compared me to Morticia from the Addams Family. She meant it as an insult. I took it as a compliment. The highest kind."

"You've always known how to make me smile."

They sat in companionable silence for a beat, watching the brothers disappear down a row of vines again. The breeze carried the scent of ripening grapes and summer dust, mixing with the lightest hint of Brea's perfume.

Riley rested a hand on the book. Everything with her dad and the funeral was on pause since the body had yet to be released. She might as well try to have a nice evening. If she sat around here all night, she'd only drive herself crazy with questions she couldn't answer. "Bryson's never liked putting on a suit."

Brea's head whipped toward her so fast Riley thought she might pull something. "If you go, wearing that dress I just told you about, he'll go. Trust me on that." She pointed to her son. "Because the only thing he'll be thinking about all night is how to get it off you."

Riley tried to hide her smile. "Won't we be late?"

"I don't mind. Besides, I enjoy making an entrance." Brea patted her knee. "But we'd better hurry. Can't be too late."

Just then, Riley's phone buzzed beside her. She glanced down at the screen.

Bryson: *Be right there. Just after one last race.*

Riley smiled and typed a quick reply.

Riley: *Better hurry. You need a shower, a shave, and a decent suit. We're going to Monica's party.*

"Oh my." Brea pointed. "Bryson's about to..." Brea turned her head.

Riley grimaced as Bryson stood in the yard, staring at his phone, as Devon tackled him. "Hopefully, that didn't leave a mark."

"Let's get you all dolled up," Brea said, taking Riley's hand. "We've got a party to go to."

Riley swallowed, wondering if she'd ever be able to

backpedal her way out of this one. But maybe this was exactly what she needed to get her mind off Grant and everything else surrounding her family.

Bryson had faced barrel-aged tempers, harvests from hell, and the heartbreak of watching the love of his life walk away. However, none of it had prepared him for the sight of Riley standing in the foyer, wearing a purple dress that looked like it had been designed with only her in mind.

His breath caught in his throat as his heart dropped to his toes. The room spun and faded in the background.

His mother leaned closer, squeezing his shoulder. "What do you think?"

He opened his mouth, but nothing came out.

"This party's going to be bloody hellish," Devon said as he passed him on the staircase, babbling something about Monica's poor taste in menus and artisanal cheese displays.

His mother chuckled as she strolled down the steps, toward Riley, leaving him standing there like an idiot.

Bryson's mouth dried out. The air thinned. And for a second, all the years between him and Riley disappeared in a swirl of purple fabric.

He gripped the banister, taking the steps slowly, praying he didn't face-plant on the marble floor.

The dress clung to her curves in ways that made his brain go sideways. Her hair was down, loose and soft around her shoulders, and her makeup was just enough to highlight her eyes. She was poised, calm—and utterly devastating.

Only, now, he really didn't want to go to the party. He wanted to rip that dress off her and ravish her in unspeakable ways.

Riley looked up and smiled. "Hey, you."

He forced his feet to keep moving. "You look..." He trailed off, because 'like every mistake I made twelve years ago' didn't sound like a compliment. "Incredible. Beautiful. Amazing..."

A little smile touched her lips. "You clean up pretty well yourself." She winked.

"Ready for this?" Bryson asked.

"No," Riley said, taking his hand and pressing it against her cheek. "But I'm not wasting this dress, so let's go before I change my mind."

Taking her by the hand, he led her outside and opened the passenger door to his truck.

"We're not going with your parents?"

"My mom insisted we drive separately." He chuckled. "She thought we might want to slip out early and have some alone time."

"I've blushed more times today than I did during the entirety of high school, when your parents kept catching us with your hand up my shirt."

"I was obsessed with your breasts." He leaned closer, taking her chin with his thumb and forefinger. He brushed his mouth over her lips in a gentle kiss. Every nerve ending in his body ignited. She was the kindling to his fire. He pulled away before things got out of control. "I still am." Gently, he closed the door and jogged around the hood.

Slipping behind the steering wheel, he sucked in a few deep breaths and eased out behind his parents' big, dark

SUV. "Not to sour the mood, but I can't believe we're all going to this. Since the divorce, it's usually just my parents who go. If one of my sisters, or Devon, is dating someone who has to be there, then they'll make an appearance, but we haven't all attended since I was married to Monica." He shook his head. "And the last time I was at the event, it didn't go well."

"Really?" She turned her head and twirled a few stray strands of hair between her fingers. "Do tell."

"Not much to tell other than Monica was mad over... something. I was drinking. A lot. And she took my wine glass from my hand and tossed it in my face. I laughed. She yelled. I kicked her out that weekend and filed for divorce the following Monday. She spent the next year begging me to take her back."

"Come on." Riley lowered her chin. "I'm sure if you dig deep enough, you can remember whatever it was you were fighting about."

"Sure. It was always the same fight. Or a variation of the same thing. She wanted me to spend less time in the vineyard. She wanted me to spend more time taking her to fancy parties. To the country club. She wanted to be on display, and I thought that was gross. But the biggest thing we fought about was *you* and the fact that I was still pining for you."

Bryson stole a quick glance at Riley, who'd folded her arms and squinted. "And she wasn't wrong. At first, I did my best to forget about you. But in the back of my mind, I thought you'd get the travel bug out of your system and come back. When I realized that wasn't happening, I let

Monica talk me into a proposal I didn't want to make. It went downhill from there."

"That's no reason to get married. Now, I'm questioning my decision to go to this damn thing—not to mention yours. It's like we're only going to toss something in her face."

"I'm sorry. That's not why I agreed to go." He reached across the cab and took her hand.

"Maybe not, but it's kind of why I did." She squeezed his hand, feeling the weight of her own pettiness. "And I'm better than that."

He kissed the center of her palm. "She has the ability to bring out the worst in everyone. This was a charity started by my family, and somehow, hers has taken it over. It's been a bone of contention for my mom. Not that she wants to plan and run the event. But it's the fact that Monica, of all people, is butchering it." Bryson let out a long breath. "It used to be held at the winery. It wasn't this excessive black-tie event."

"I remember." Riley smiled at the memory. "There'd be food trucks, and a band, and even a non-scary clown that did those balloon animals for us kids. When did it change?"

"It was the year my mom's father died, and things were just too much for my parents. Monica and I were engaged, so it seemed like the right thing to do. The following year, my mom had to have surgery, and things just got out of hand from there."

"Your family should take it back," Riley huffed.

"That would mean fighting Monica and her mother, and no one has it in them to do that. They're exhausting.

Not to mention all my mother cares about is that the people of Stone Bridge open their wallets."

They rolled to a stop in front of the country club. A big white tent stretched across the side yard with twinkle lights and an actual arch of imported roses. Music wafted from somewhere behind the hedges, and servers glided around like they were auditioning for a period drama.

"I've always hated coming to the club." Riley hesitated, her fingers tightening slightly against his arm. "I feel out of place."

He leaned closer. "We can leave," he whispered. "It's not my cup of tea, either."

"Nope." She gave a breathy laugh. "I'm not backing out."

As soon as they stepped past the arch and under the massive tent that overlooked the eighteenth green, the world seemed to slow. Heads turned. Whispers rippled. Monica's curated crowd took notice.

"Riley." Erin scurried across the room, leaving her husband to deal with a couple Riley didn't recognize. "I didn't think you were coming." She kissed Riley's cheek."

"Bryson's mom talked me into it."

"She has the wickedest sense of humor." Erin smiled. "Hello, Bryson."

Inwardly, Bryson groaned as Grant and his wife, Kelly, strode across the room. Grant was an impressive man, no doubt. His wife was stunningly beautiful in a red strapless dress with her dark hair pulled back in a tight ponytail at the nape of her neck and a single strand of pearls around her neck. They looked like a power couple, and in many ways, they were.

Kelly didn't come from money. Her family lived on the outskirts of town in a modest home. Her dad had worked with Sean at the power company—blue collar. They lived a quiet and comfortable life. Bryson remembered when Grant got married. His mother hadn't been happy. Kelly wasn't the pedigree that Elizabeth had wanted for her son.

Not like Chad, who came from a long line of high-priced lawyers.

But eventually, Elizabeth had seemed to accept Grant's choice in life partner.

Bryson quickly put a protective arm around Riley's waist.

"Hey, little sis," Grant said, leaning in to kiss Riley's cheek. "You look fantastic."

"Thanks." Riley smiled, though Bryson could tell it was forced.

So was Grant's. Of course, Bryson was on edge.

"Boone." Grant nodded. "Surprised to see you here tonight."

Bryson shrugged. "Your sister twisted my arm."

"Crap," Riley whispered. "Here comes Mother."

"Don't let her get to you." Grant's tone carried both affection and brotherly concern.

Elizabeth approached with her usual regal disdain, Parker one step behind her, sporting a half smile, which made Bryson feel bad for the man. Not just because of the cancer, but because he always seemed to do whatever Elizabeth wanted. As if "yes, dear" was the only response he was allowed to give.

Something Bryson never quite understood.

"Well, this is certainly unexpected," Elizabeth said, her

gaze traveling from Riley's dress to Bryson's arm. "I'm shocked to see you here. And with him." She gave Bryson the once over, her gaze filled with disgust. "Your father died while working—"

"Hello, Mother," Riley said, her voice even, but she wasn't sure her tone could be considered polite. "I'd appreciate it if you didn't go slinging accusations like they're appetizers. No one in Bryson's family did anything wrong."

"Guess we'll find out for sure since you pushed the autopsy, which is probably a good thing. I'm sure Bryson worked your dad to the bone." Elizabeth's gaze slithered up and down Riley. "You look... like someone else's idea of appropriate." Elizabeth stuck her nose in the air. "That dress doesn't quite hang on you properly. A little tight in the waist. A little too big in the bust. You always did have an odd-shaped body."

Fury surged through Bryson as he watched Elizabeth systematically tear Riley apart. This was psychological warfare, designed to make Riley feel small and unwelcome. He'd forgotten that Elizabeth could wield cruelty like a scalpel, cutting with surgical precision. "She looks perfect. Beautiful."

Elizabeth's mouth thinned. "So, we're visiting old ghosts, Bryson? Because that's all she is. She'll vanish in the light of day. She always does. And like usual, she'll take something that doesn't belong to her." Elizabeth lowered her chin. "You're lucky Parker talked me out of calling the police. I wonder what the statute of limitations is for theft."

"What's that supposed to mean?" Riley asked through her clenched jaw.

"Why, my favorite diamond earrings, child. They went missing the day you left all those years ago."

Parker cleared his throat. "I think it's best if we take a walk around the room, dear."

Elizabeth turned on her heel, retreating toward the champagne like a queen returning to her throne.

"What on earth is she talking about?" Riley asked, staring at Grant.

"I honestly don't know." Grant glanced over his shoulder. "That's the first time I'm hearing this."

"She mentioned it to me," Erin said. "Also told me that her favorite crystal figure went missing the day Riley came over for funeral planning."

"Excuse me?" Riley blinked. "Why didn't you tell me that the other day?"

"I'm sorry," Erin murmured. "I don't believe her," she rushed to say. "I'm sure she either misplaced them, or she's lying about it. She has a bizarre relationship with the truth and likes to attack when she's hurt."

"That's a cruel thing to do," Bryson said

Grant glanced toward his wife. "Not the first time Mom's accused Riley of something like that."

The old familiar anger rose from Riley's toes and snaked a path through her system. "I never stole money from—"

"Relax, Riley." Grant waved his hand. "I believe you."

"Seriously?" Riley's voice rose in obvious frustration. "Because you've always taken her side when it comes to that summer fundraiser."

"I was a kid. I didn't want to believe what you were saying about Mom and Parker." Grant rubbed the back of his neck with a shaky hand. "Don't take this the wrong way, but I also weirdly understood Mom. While she always acted like she was better than, she never felt good enough—not for this town. But I can't begin to fathom her behavior toward you since you've come home. But she's being more repugnant than usual."

Bryson wanted to add how Grant wasn't behaving completely like himself but decided to keep his mouth closed. Sandy was still reviewing those documents and speaking with some of the committee members. Bryson was walking a fine line and didn't want to trip up.

"We'd better go mingle, sweetheart." Grant took Kelly's hand. "I'll see you later." He turned and headed toward a group of people from his business.

"I better get back to my husband before he gets upset." Erin smiled weakly.

Riley took her hand and squeezed. "Let's talk tomorrow."

Bryson sighed. Every family had its drama, but this one had way too much, and he was pretty sure there was about to be a whole lot more. "Still time to turn around and leave," he offered. He honestly didn't want to be at this damn party. While he was friendly with many townspeople, being around Monica and her family wouldn't be a cake walk. If he managed not to stick his foot in his mouth, it would be a fucking miracle.

"No way." Her gaze shifted toward Monica. "I know that makes me look like a catty person, but she started it the other day at the tasting room."

"You're not catty. You're simply letting her know that she can't rattle you, and I'm all for that." He pressed his hand against the small of her back and guided her through the crowd. They settled near the silent auction table. One of the waitstaff strolled by with a tray of red and white wines. He lifted two glasses of red and handed one to Riley. "Here she comes. Kick me if I start saying something too rude."

"I will not," she said with a laugh.

"Wonderful." Bryson lifted the glass, swirled, sniffed, and took a sip. "Jesus. It's warm. I've told her a million times to chill it slightly before letting it breathe. She's the only person I know who manages to ruin my wine."

"Don't let that destroy your night. The wine still tastes delicious."

"Sorry. I'll work on adjusting my attitude."

Monica floated up to them, looking like a perfume ad, glass of white in one hand—with a fucking ice cube in it— her smile tight as piano wire. "Well," she said. "This is bold, brazen, and brave."

"Not sure what you mean by that." Riley said, cool and composed. Out of the corner of her eye, she saw Brea leaning against the bar. She raised her glass and winked.

God, Brea was such an amazing woman. Strong, confident, and even though she sometimes permitted others to get under her skin, she never allowed it to show.

"I wasn't expecting you—with him, since he was supposed to be my date." Monica's eyes dragged over her like a scanner.

Bryson shifted, but Riley gave him a small squeeze—as if to say, "Don't engage."

"Not sure what gave you the idea that Bryson would be your date, because he asked me before I came back to town." Riley smiled sweetly at Monica, and it was clear

Monica wanted to claw out her eyes. But Riley kept smiling that fake-ass, sugary smile. "He called me while I was in Patagonia to catch up, and when I told him I was coming home, he insisted I attend with him. Isn't that just the sweetest?"

Holy crap. Riley had never been one to lie. She'd also never been very good at it, but right now, she sounded a bit like his mother when she wanted to get under someone's skin.

Monica's lips parted in what looked like shock. Sadly, it only lasted a split second. "Wherever did you find that dress? Or did Brea donate it to the cause? She's got a closet full of things she doesn't wear because they're either not designer, or so last season. They hang on her rack until she decides where she's going to donate it."

"Oh, this one was meant just for me," Riley replied. "Something about it being from her special collection."

Oh boy, did that dig land exactly where it was intended. Bryson bit the inside of his cheek to hide his grin.

Clearly stunned, Monica blinked, tilted her head, her smile weak. "Well, I hope you enjoy the party. There's an auction starting. Try not to accidentally outbid anyone." She showed her teeth in what might have been a smile—or maybe it was meant to be a threat. "Wouldn't want Bryson here to have to play hero since you don't have the money."

"At least the money I have wasn't from a divorce settlement," Riley said smoothly. "And I will enjoy the wine. It's from Stone Bridge Winery, after all."

Monica's lips parted. She blinked. Once. Then twice. Then it was like rapid-fire blinking for a good half a minute before she cleared her throat and closed her mouth. "Enjoy your evening." Monica spun on her heel and disappeared into the crowd.

Riley exhaled, laughing a little. "I can't believe I just did that."

"I can't believe I kept my mouth shut through that entire exchange."

"I'm just glad she didn't pour wine on your mother's dress. This thing must be worth a fortune." Riley leaned into Bryson.

"My mother never lent anything to Monica. No dresses. No jewelry. Not even a sweatshirt when we were sitting around the fire pit at night."

"Brea did mention something about that when she offered to let me borrow this one."

The band began to play a slow, familiar melody—something from their high school years. He remembered how he'd stepped on Riley's feet when they'd danced and how she'd laughed and tried to teach him to follow the rhythm.

"Dance with me?" he asked, extending his hand.

She laughed. "Do you remember prom? How you kept apologizing every time you stepped on my dress?"

"It's not the memory that I enjoy thinking about the most." He winked, taking her hand."

She smiled and let him lead her to the dance floor. This time was different—he spun her around smoothly, dipped her once, and twirled her back into his arms with practiced confidence.

Having her this close again felt like coming home and losing his mind all at once. The familiar scent of her hair, the way she fit perfectly against him—it was dangerous territory, but he couldn't bring himself to care.

"Oh my. Where'd you learn to do that?" she asked, gripping his shoulders and looking up at him with surprise.

He grimaced, embarrassed by the admission he knew was coming. "You don't want to know."

"Oh, my god. You took dancing lessons for your wedding, didn't you?"

"Guilty as—" he stopped moving as he noticed Sandy, in full uniform, speaking with Grant. "Shit."

Riley spun. "No!" She took two steps. But Bryson pulled her tight to his chest. "She's here to arrest him."

"I doubt that. But I have to admit, hauling him down for questioning during a charity fundraiser definitely makes quite a statement."

"I need to go speak—"

"Now is not the right time," Bryson said. "It looks like a conversation. And they're taking it outside."

"Well, then I'm going outside."

"I don't think that's a good—"

"That's my brother. It's not up for discussion."

Bryson scanned the room for his father. Once he found him, he pointed toward the main entrance as he chased after Riley. Whatever this was, and regardless of Grant's guilt or innocence, Bryson was going to make sure Riley wasn't collateral damage.

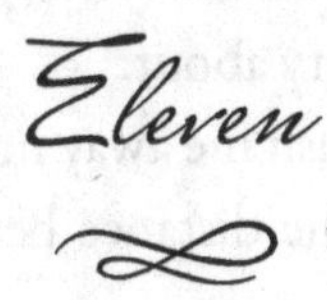

Eleven

Riley's heels struck the tile in a rapid staccato as she raced through the country club's main entrance, the cool night air hitting her face like a slap. She paused just as Grant's black SUV pulled into the circular drive, its headlights cutting through the amber glow of the security lights. Sandy's patrol car sat behind it like a predator waiting to pounce.

Grant stood off to the side, his bow tie hanging loose around his neck, one hand clasped firmly around Kelly's. Even from a distance, Riley could see the tension radiating from his shoulders.

A valet hopped out and handed Grant his keys.

"Grant," she called, breathless, as she approached, her voice carrying across the nearly empty drive.

He turned and attempted a smile, but it was all wrong —too tight, too forced, and the way his brow furrowed told Riley everything she needed to know. Her brother wasn't just worried.

He was terrified.

"What's going on?"

"Go back inside." His voice carried that big-brother authority she remembered from childhood, but underneath it was something she'd never heard before—defeat. "It's nothing for you to worry about."

"Don't you dare push me away now. We've come too far for that." She closed the distance between them, her dress rustling against her legs.

Grant glanced at Sandy, who stood beside her patrol car with the practiced patience of someone who'd done this dance before. "Can I have a moment with my family?"

Sandy checked her watch. "A few minutes. But remember what I told you about—"

"I got it." Grant sucked in a breath that seemed to rattle in his chest. He lifted his gaze over Riley's head toward the country club, where warm light spilled from the windows and the faint sound of conversation drifted on the night air.

"Talk to me," Riley demanded, crossing her arms.

Warm fabric settled around her shoulders, and she jerked back, startled. She touched the cloth—Bryson's jacket, carrying the familiar scent of cedar and something distinctly him. His fingers found hers, lacing their hands together with the easy familiarity of muscle memory. The simple contact sent a surge of strength shooting through her veins.

Walter appeared beside Bryson, looking every inch the distinguished vintner in his perfectly tailored tuxedo. He said nothing, but his mere presence spoke volumes—the Boones standing with the Callahans, just like the distant times of their ancestors.

The sound of heels clicking on concrete echoed from

the direction of the club, accompanied by the low hum of voices that made Riley's skin crawl. Half the town was probably pressed against the windows by now.

"Sandy just needs to have a chat with me about some committee business," Grant said, his tone carefully neutral.

"That committee business wouldn't happen to involve what Mason and my dad have been digging into, would it?" Bryson's voice carried an edge that made Riley glance at him sharply.

Grant's jaw worked for a moment. "This isn't the time or place to get into it. We can talk after I get back."

"This is harassment!" Elizabeth's voice rang across the parking lot like a dinner bell, and Riley's stomach dropped. Her mother swept into view as if she were making a grand entrance at the Met Gala, her midnight blue evening gown billowing dramatically in the night breeze. She positioned herself near the valet stand like she was claiming territory. "Sandy, you have no right to storm into a charity event and drag an innocent man away like some common criminal."

"Ma'am, Mr. Callahan isn't under arrest," Sandy replied, her voice carrying a maddeningly professional calm Riley hadn't remembered from high school. "We're just going to have a conversation."

"A conversation that can't wait until Monday morning?" Elizabeth's voice rose another octave. "At the police station, no less?"

Chad emerged from the crowd, his tuxedo jacket draped over one arm, sweat beading along his hairline despite the cool evening air, like a shark scenting blood. "Grant, you shouldn't say another word without legal representation. Let me handle this."

Kelly's laugh was sharp enough to cut glass. "If we needed a lawyer, it wouldn't be you." She turned to face Chad directly, and Riley was surprised by the steel in her sister-in-law's usually gentle voice. "Grant made it very clear he doesn't want you anywhere near this situation."

Chad pushed closer, ignoring Kelly entirely. "Sandy, what exactly are the charges here? Are you planning on booking my client?"

"Your client?" Grant's voice dropped to the dangerous quiet tone Riley remembered from their childhood fights. "Did you miss the part where my wife just told you that you're not my attorney?" He moved to the passenger side of his SUV and helped Kelly inside with exaggerated courtesy. "Besides, you've got bigger problems to worry about than my legal representation."

"What's that supposed to mean?" Chad's face flushed red in the security lighting.

Grant straightened slowly, and Riley caught a glimpse of the man who'd once been quarterback of the football team—confident, ruthless when cornered. "It means maybe you should spend less time chasing after other people's legal problems and more time explaining to your wife why that blonde in the red dress was practically sitting in your lap during the silent auction."

The parking lot went dead silent. Riley watched the color drain from Chad's face as every eye in the vicinity turned to him like spotlights.

"Time to go," Sandy announced, sliding behind the wheel of her patrol car.

Grant walked over to Riley and took both her hands in

his—a gesture so tender and protective it made her throat tight. "I'll call you in the morning, little sis."

He turned to Bryson, and for a moment, the years fell away. They weren't two men with a complicated history—they were just her brother and... well Bryson. "Take care of her."

"You know I will."

Walter stepped forward, pressing a small piece of paper into Grant's palm. "Harlan Maddox. He's my attorney and a good friend. Call him—it can't hurt to have someone in your corner."

"I appreciate it." Grant pocketed the paper, climbed into his SUV, and followed Sandy's patrol car into the night, leaving behind the acrid smell of exhaust and the weight of unfinished conversations.

Riley sagged against Bryson, feeling like all her bones had turned to water. The country club parking lot, which moments before had seemed with the elegant aftermath of a successful charity event, now felt like a crime scene. Groups of well-dressed guests huddled together in the fluorescent light, their voices carrying snippets of speculation and barely concealed excitement.

"Riley," Erin's voice cut through the chaos. She stumbled toward them in her emerald gown, holding up her hem with one hand, clutching a small, beaded purse in the other. "Did Sandy really arrest Grant?"

"No," Bryson said, his arm tightening around Riley's waist. "But honestly, we're not sure what's happening."

"This is absolutely ridiculous," Elizabeth announced to anyone within earshot, her voice carrying across the parking lot like a town crier. "Grant Callahan is one of the most respected men in this community." She fumbled in her purse, producing a delicate lace handkerchief that she pressed to her eyes with theatrical precision. "Chad, what are you still doing here? Get down to that police station, and make sure Sandy doesn't try to railroad him."

The parking lot had filled with curious onlookers—apparently half of Stone Bridge's social elite had abandoned the charity event to witness the drama firsthand. They clustered in small groups, pointing and whispering with the shameless hunger of people who'd just discovered the juiciest gossip of the year.

Erin found Riley's hand, gripping tight. Her sister's palm was ice-cold and trembling.

Chad dug into his pocket and pulled out a valet ticket, scanning the crowd with the desperate look of a man searching for an escape route. His eyes locked onto someone in the distance, and he raised his hand in a subtle signal.

Riley followed his gaze and felt Erin's grip tighten to the point of pain.

"Don't wait up," Chad said, his voice flat as he stared directly at Erin. "I have no idea how long this is going to take."

"It won't take any time at all," Bryson said, his voice carrying that deceptively casual tone that meant he was furious. "Since it was made abundantly clear that Grant doesn't want you there."

Chad's face twisted with something ugly. "Mind your own damn business, Boone."

He snatched his keys from the valet without offering a

tip, slid into his silver Porsche, and peeled out with enough force to leave rubber on the asphalt.

"Come on, Erin." Elizabeth reached for her younger daughter with jewelry-laden fingers. "Let's go get the children. You can all stay with me tonight."

"No." Erin's voice was barely above a whisper, but it carried absolute finality.

Elizabeth's mouth fell open in a perfect O of surprise, her hand fluttering to the strand of pearls at her throat. "Sweetheart, you shouldn't be alone after hearing... well, whatever that was about."

"We both know exactly where he's spending the night," Erin said, her voice gaining strength. "And if I need company, I'll call Riley."

Elizabeth's face shuttled through several expressions before settling into cold fury. "Not even home a week, and you're already tearing this family apart." She turned, lifting her chin like a queen dismissing her court and swept back toward the country club's entrance.

"There's plenty of room at our place," Walter offered. "Brea and I would be more than happy to have you and the children stay."

Erin smoothed down the front of her dress with shaking hands. "Thank you, but I'll be fine. The kids are already asleep and there are... things I need to deal with." She kissed Riley's cheek, her lips cold against Riley's skin. "Let's talk tomorrow?"

"Call me if you need anything," Riley said. "Anything at all."

"Same goes for us," Bryson added, his voice gentle.

Riley wrapped her arm around Bryson's waist and let

her head fall against his shoulder, breathing in his familiar scent. "This whole thing is insane. I don't know what to think or feel about any of it."

He pressed his lips to her temple, the gesture so natural it made her chest ache with longing. "Unfortunately, there's nothing we can do until Grant tells us what happened."

As guests began to trickle back into the country club, their voices buzzing with excitement over the evening's unexpected entertainment, Riley stared at the spot where Grant's taillights had disappeared into the darkness.

Whatever was happening at the police station right now, she knew one thing with absolute certainty—when her brother walked out of there, the fault lines running through her family would be deeper and more treacherous than ever.

The house was quiet—the kind of heavy, middle-of-the-night—early morning silence where the air felt still enough to hold secrets. Bryson had finally gotten Riley to drift off upstairs, curled into the right side of his bed, hair spilling across the pillow like a ribbon of ink. He'd stayed with her until her breathing slowed, until her restless shifting stopped, until her tears dried. Only then, had he slipped out.

Now, he sat at the kitchen table, nursing a cooling mug of coffee, the darkness outside fading into the muted gray of early morning. Across from him, Walter sipped from his own cup, reading glasses low on his nose, the half-folded newspaper spread across the counter.

The Boone homestead had been updated into a family estate when Bryson had been a baby. Still, in the early hours, he could feel the bones of what it used to be like—wood beams overhead, faint scents of yeast and oak from the cellar, the clock ticking on the wall in slow, deliberate beats.

Walter set down his cup and studied him. "You look like hell."

Bryson smiled humorlessly. "Thanks. I'll have that stitched on a pillow."

"How's Riley?" Walter asked, folding the paper and setting it aside.

"She cried herself to sleep," Bryson admitted. "For her dad. For Grant. For... all of it. I stayed until she let go, but I don't think I even dozed."

Walter's gaze softened. "You're a good man."

He looked away, toward the back door, where the porch light painted a dull square on the floorboards. "Some days, I wonder."

"You wonder too much," Walter said, leaning back in his chair. "You've always been harder on yourself than anyone else could be. I think Riley sees that. Always has."

Bryson huffed out a breath. "Yeah, and look where that got us."

"Where it got you," Walter said, "was older. Smarter. Maybe ready to do it differently."

Bryson didn't answer, but his father's words lodged in his chest. "I do still love her."

"Tell me something I don't know."

"She still loves me."

His father chuckled, shaking his head. "That's obvious."

"She's not sure what she wants." Bryson palmed his mug, staring into the liquid. "She's had an amazing life, and I'm grateful for that. I'd hate it if she were miserable. Outside of my marriage to Monica, my life hasn't been horrible."

"No." His father leaned back, resting one arm on the counter. "But you've had a big hole in your chest."

"She has too, but maybe less because of me, and more because of her family."

"Don't sell yourself short."

"I'm not." He reached across the counter, snagging one of the muffins his father had pulled from the cupboard earlier. "We've come to terms with our past. We put it all out there. Worked through it. In the end, her chasing her dreams was the right thing, and we both know it."

"I feel a but coming."

"It's not that. It's just that since she's been back, she's feeling a little more grounded here. She'd made some good headway with Grant and Erin. She wants her family back in her life. She didn't come out and say she planned on staying. However, she did make it sound like it was an... option."

"And you're afraid this thing with Grant will make her run again."

Bryson shook his head. "She wants to find where she fits. To put roots in the ground." He lifted his gaze. "I'm worried that love isn't enough."

"Ah. I see." His father leaned forward, resting both

hands on the island. "Love is always *enough*." His dad tapped his temple. "It's our brain that meddles with our heart." His voice softened with the weight of experience. "When your mother and I first got together, she used to believe she wasn't good enough because she didn't come from money. That her family came from the wrong side of town. She used to constantly worry that people wouldn't accept her."

"But Grandma and Pops were so well-respected. They did so much for Stone Bridge. And they started that damn garden party."

His father chuckled. "They did. But it was a success in part because they weren't rich people putting on a show. They were regular folk raising money for people who had even less than they did."

"Most people—rich or poor—will open their wallets for a good cause."

"Most good people," his father said. "But rich folk often make it about themselves. When your mom and I took over, we kept up with the tradition of it being fun and for everyone. There wasn't a silent auction. There were no two-hundred-thousand-dollar prizes to bid on that only a handful of people could afford. And frankly, we raised just as much, if not more. It's why your mother's so bitter about it all."

"But anyone can donate."

"That's true, but half this town felt left out once Monica took over. They felt their three-hundred-dollar donation wasn't enough. Or that they'd be laughed at because they couldn't bid on the Porsche that the dealership donated. So, that's when your mom decided to start taking up a collection, matching whatever she manages to raise."

"That's usually one of the biggest donations, and it burns Monica's ass, because she thinks it takes away from others participating in her precious auction. Everyone wants to see how much Mom's going to raise."

"It gives your mother great satisfaction. And then she sends thank-you cards to each and every person. It's a win-win in her book," his father said. "But we've derailed a little."

His father rose and went to the small bookshelf in the corner. He lifted the latest family portrait. "Love isn't always easy." His dad set the picture in front of Bryson, tapping his finger on the image of him, and then his brother and his two sisters. "I fell in love with your mother, in part, because she took my breath away. She was not only the most beautiful woman I'd ever met, but more importantly, she's also the kindest, sweetest, most genuine person who won't ever let me get away with my own bullshit. Having a family with her has been the best thing I've ever done."

Jerking a thumb over his shoulder, he added, "I'm prouder of that than I am of what I did out there in the vines. I love this legacy. I'm grateful I can pass it down to my children. But none of it really matters without this." He traced his finger over the frame. "Love has to be enough."

"Can I ask you something?"

"Sure."

"What would you and Mom have done if one of us ever moved away?"

His father smiled. "We would've helped you pack your bags and then cried our eyes out in private." He sipped his coffee. "Where's this coming from? Are you considering leaving if Riley wants to?"

"I don't want to lose her again." Bryson sighed. "But I don't know if she's even mine to lose, and this winery is my life. I can't imagine being anywhere else. But I was curious, more than anything. I've never felt like I was obligated to be part of the family business. Or that you'd be disappointed if I hadn't."

"I love working side by side with my children," his father said. "But I'm amazed and in awe of the people you've become. That's more important. And if opportunity... or love..." he smiled. "Took you somewhere else, well, your mother and I would support you."

"One more question," Bryson said. "Why haven't you pressured any of us to get married or have children?"

His dad lowered his chin and lifted his mug. "You're joking, right? Your mother drops hints all the time."

"About finding partners to share our lives with, but not about kids."

"Because your life is not ours to live."

Bryson took a small bite of his muffin, chewing more on the love and respect he had for his parents than the food that went into his mouth. Growing up, there'd been expectations. Things like getting good grades, being a decent human, and following the rules were important, but his parents had given their children a lot of room to make mistakes.

And every single one of them had made plenty.

Bryson more than the rest.

The sound of knuckles on wood cut through the quiet —three sharp raps at the back door.

They exchanged a look.

"That's Grant. What's he doing here at this hour?" Walter rose, sliding the deadbolt back. The cold crept in as Grant stood on the back stoop, shoulders rounded, shirt wrinkled, and hair mussed like he'd run both hands through it a hundred times. His eyes were red-rimmed, shadows etched deep beneath them.

"Jesus," Walter murmured. "You look like death ran you over. Get in here."

Grant crossed the threshold, and the faint scent of earth and humid air clung to him.

"Coffee?" Walter offered.

"Black. Thanks," Grant said.

Bryson hooked his boot around the chair beside him and dragged it out. "Have a seat." Normally, one of them would start in on the sparing, but there was no point in beating a man when he was down. "Did you come here straight from the station?"

Grant lowered himself into it like his bones might shatter under his own weight. "No. I took my wife home, kissed my kids, then drove here."

Walter poured coffee into a thick ceramic mug and slid it over. "Would you like a muffin? Or I can whip up some eggs and sausage?"

Grant shook his head. "No thank you. Just the caffeine." He wrapped his hands around the mug, staring into it. "What a night."

Bryson leaned in, elbows braced on the table. "You doing okay?"

Grant snorted, his eyes stayed fixed on the coffee. "That's a relative term." A few moments of silence filled the kitchen before Grant said, "I knew about the missing money."

Bryson's jaw tightened. "Really? How long?"

"Few months. At first, I thought it was just a dumb mistake on my part. But I generally don't make those. So, ran all the numbers again. They didn't add up. It drove me crazy. I couldn't figure it out, and while I know you think I'm an arrogant ass, I'm really good at my job."

"I've never said you weren't," Bryson said.

"I was honestly shocked when I went through the books," his dad offered. "Mistakes I can understand, but the money trail makes some interesting loops, and you know what it looks like," Bryson's dad said.

"I've been digging for the last couple of months. Didn't want to say anything until I had proof. My name's on vendor approvals that don't exist. Transfers of funds. The checks..." Grant shook his head. "It looked bad. I wanted to find the problem before it went public. Before I went to anyone."

Walter's tone sharpened. "Why didn't you come to me?"

"Because you're on the committee," Grant shot back, frustration flaring before he caught himself. "You'd have to take it straight to a meeting. If it was just a screw-up, I'd take the heat. But deep down I knew it wasn't that, and I needed time to uncover... hell if I know."

Walter's gaze was steady. "Unfortunately, not coming forward didn't do you any favors."

Grant's grip tightened on the mug. "It's so much worse than I thought. The morning Dad died... we had a conversation about it." His voice cracked. "He'd already figured it out. Looked at some records, and it all pointed to me."

"How did he know?" Bryson asked.

"He didn't say, but it didn't matter. He might not be on the advisory board, but he still volunteered on the tourism and wine committee," Grant said. "We argued for a bit. I swore to him I didn't take it. I think he believed me. Or, at least, he wanted to."

Bryson watched Grant's shoulders sag, as if admitting that even Sean had doubts was the final straw.

"When I left, he was standing at the end of your driveway, coffee cup in hand, reminding me that I needed to tell someone. To work with someone to figure it out. That if I didn't do it, continuing to remain quiet would only make me look guilty."

"You told Sandy that?" Bryson asked.

"Yeah. But now, I can't tell if they think I'm lying. That they're wondering if maybe we argued and I..." Grant's words trailed off, swallowing hard. "I don't know what they think."

"What time did you leave your dad that morning?" his father asked.

"Around seven," Grant said.

"I found him a little after eight. That's a full hour, and we do have Sean walking up the field at seven ten," Bryson added.

Walter's jaw flexed. "The autopsy's Monday. We'll know more then."

"So, now you think I, or someone else, killed my father," Grant said, slamming his fist on the counter."

"That's not what I'm saying," Bryson's father said. "But

something doesn't add up, and until we know more, it's a waiting game."

"With my life teetering in the balance," Grant whispered. "The timing of my father's death has had me on edge."

"I don't mean to be accusatory, but asking the ME not to do an autopsy doesn't bode well for you." Bryson's father stood and leaned against the sink. He'd always been the kind of man who thought better on his feet.

"Jesus. I only did that because my dad really thinks cutting into the human body is a little psycho, and my mom's right there with him." Grant leaned back, rubbing his neck. "Should have seen her during Parker's cancer treatments. Either she was in everyone's face, telling them what to do, or more like what not to do, or she was nowhere to be found, only to come in later like a wrecking ball because she didn't like his treatment. Talk about crazy."

Bryson wasn't used to Grant discussing his mother in this fashion, so he let it slide right on by.

"I'm curious," Bryson's father started, "did Kelly know all this? Or did she find out when Sandy brought you in last night?"

"She's known everything from day one. I've never kept it from her."

"Did you call my attorney, Harlan?" Bryson's father asked. "Or did Chad show up and demand to represent you?"

"I didn't do anything wrong, except maybe not tell anyone about the missing money, but yeah, I know how it looks." Grant raked a hand down his face. "I won't use Chad—he's a crap lawyer and an even worse husband to

Erin. Been cheating on her for years. She doesn't need this. None of us do." He looked up at Bryson, voice rough. "I want Riley out of it. Keep her safe from this mess."

"I'm not lying to her," Bryson said flatly. "I tried hiding the truth once—that picture of me and Monica—and it blew up in my face. I'm not repeating history."

"You want to hear something funny about that one?" Grant asked.

"There's nothing amusing about what happened back then." Bryson glared, doing his best to keep his emotions in check. This was not the time to get into a brawl with Grant.

"I told Riley that either that picture was a fake or that Monica planted her lips on your mouth knowing someone was going to take that picture." He shrugged. "There's no way you'd ever do that. Not with anyone." Grant sighed. "But Riley and I were always fighting back then, and something else was going on with her. Nothing Erin and I said could console her."

Heart suddenly pounding, Bryson froze for a moment. His mind raced back to that phone call. *Bryson, I... I... lost the baby.* Riley's words tore through his system. He swallowed. Hard.

Grant snorted. "I never hated you, you know. Not completely. I just never thought you fought for her. And to me? That's not love. When my mom thought my wife was beneath me, I fought like hell. I might blame you for some things, but I'll tell you this—you're a hell of a lot better than Chad." He tapped his knuckles on the counter. "And I believe you loved her. Hell, I know you still do."

"I fought for her in my own way. Staying when she wanted the world wasn't easy. But back then? We were never going to meet in the middle. It's hard to love someone so much and know the best thing for them is to let them go. It was the right thing for Riley. I just behaved like an ass." Bryson's voice was quiet but firm.

Grant's gaze dropped. "I won't argue that point. But you've got another shot now. Don't screw it up."

"Never thought I'd see the day when you two agreed on anything," Bryson's father said. "Now, how about we discuss you and your attorney needs because you absolutely should have representation."

Grant groaned. "My mother has texted me five times. Chad, even more. As if that man could help me. I did leave a message with the guy you mentioned, but I haven't heard back yet."

"Harlan Maddox," Bryson's father said. "His firm can handle anything. He started out in the DA's office and moved over to private practice a few years ago. I use someone in his office for all my accounting needs, but he does handle criminal cases."

"I really don't like the way you put that," Grant said.

"Just being proactive." Walter leaned forward.

"You think he'd take me on?"

"If I ask him to," Bryson's dad said.

"So, you believe me?" Grant shifted his gaze between Bryson and his father.

"I do," Bryson spoke first. "You and I might have never gotten along, but I've never known you to lie. Not about important things. It makes no sense that you'd do this."

"That's just it, I wouldn't. I begged people not to invest in Robert Wilkerson's business. I knew it was a scheme. I distanced myself from him during college. He was always running a racket." He sighed. "I make good money. I've got no reason to steal from this community." Grant slumped in his seat. "I don't get it."

"What about enemies?" Bryson asked.

"Outside of you and your brother, not many," Grant said. "A few people in business, but that's less like enemies and more like we just don't see eye to eye."

"What about people who didn't take your advice about Robert?" Bryson's father asked.

Grant shrugged. "I don't think anyone blamed me for that, not even my mother, and she's the queen of blame."

Silence filled the kitchen—just the clock ticking and the hum of the fridge.

Walter finally spoke. "You need some rest. So, you're going to march yourself up to one of our guest rooms, climb into a bed, and sleep for a few hours. I'll call Harlan. See if he can make a Sunday house call."

Grant hesitated. "I'm too tired to argue. Thanks."

Bryson caught his father's eyes over Grant's bowed head. Walter's look said, "Help him."

But Bryson's gut whispered something different—that Grant's hadn't given them the whole story. That pieces were missing, things they didn't know. And until Monday's autopsy, those shadows were going to linger, no matter how much coffee they poured or how many reassurances they gave.

Twelve

Late afternoon sunlight spilled across the Boone backyard, bathing it in a honeyed glow, warm enough to coax the last lazy bees toward the flowering vines that climbed the surrounding fences. The air was rich with the scent of grass and the dusty, herbal aroma of the olive trees from the grove beyond. This had always been one of Riley's favorite times of the year. But today, everything just felt... wrong.

She sat at the long teak patio table with Erin, Kelly, and Brea, each of them cradling a glass of wine. Erin's kids, Nathan and Willa, were darting across the lawn, shrieking with laughter as Bryson and Devon chased them like the overgrown kids they were. Kelly's two, Jessica and Randy, joined in, weaving between lawn chairs and past the garden beds in a chaotic blur of limbs and giggles as if their world wasn't in turmoil. As if their father wasn't facing the biggest hurdle of his life.

On the far side of the house, behind the glass doors of the home office, Riley could just make out the shapes of

Grant, Harlan—the lawyer Bryson's dad had recommended —and Walter. Heads bent together, their silhouettes moved slowly, deliberation written in every gesture.

On the patio, the ladies tried to make the conversation lighter, but it proved impossible. Erin sighed as she leaned back in her chair, pulling her legs up under her. "Brea, thank you so much for letting us spend the day here. I can't remember the last time I walked the vines or just relaxed in the fresh air. I'd forgotten how beautiful it is."

"You're welcome anytime." Brea smiled. "I'm sorry your husband couldn't come."

"No, you're not, and neither am I." Erin huffed, looking down at her lap, hands crossed. "I'm sorry. That was rude."

"It's honest." Riley reached out and took her sister's hand. "No more pretending, right?"

"Maybe not with you. With Kelly. Or even the Boones." Erin stared out at the vineyard, her gaze following her young children, ten and eight. So young. So innocent. "But with them?" Erin shook her head, wiping a finger across her cheek as a single tear rolled down her cheek. "I don't know how I'm going to tell them I'm leaving their father. It's not like they don't know. Willa cries sometimes at night, asking why daddy leaves after dinner. Nathan acts out. But his aggression is pointed at me. He blames me for his father's physical and emotional absence."

"It's not your fault, sweetheart," Brea added softly. "And, I'm sorry to say, but it might get worse before it gets better. But as long as you don't make adult problems theirs, they'll adjust. Kids are resilient. What they need is love.

Understanding. And the truth, in an age-appropriate format."

"That's not going to be easy." Erin took a tiny sip of her wine. "And once my mother gets wind of my plans… God, that's going to be a mess. I know how she'll be, and because she likes to think I'm the one with the problems and constantly takes my husband's side, she'll put that on my children."

"You've got to create boundaries with her," Kelly said. "It's about the only thing Grant and I ever really fight hard about. He loves his mother, and she's been pulling at his strings for as long as I can remember. Standing up to her isn't easy. He did it for me, and he continues to do so for our children." She ran her hands up and down her thighs. "It's a delicate dance to keep her in our lives sometimes."

"I had no idea it was that bad." Riley shifted, staring at her sister-in-law. "No one ever mentioned this before—not Grant…or Dad…"

Kelly shrugged. "Grant and I kept our issues private. We didn't want it touching our kids. It started back in college when we started dating, and Elizabeth had a freaking meltdown over me. Grant told her that either she accepted he was going to marry me, or he would walk out of her life." Kelly waved a finger like it was a laser pointer and she was giving a keynote speech. "Just like you did. That really got to her, but she's been mostly okay. It's Grant who struggles with it. He's always missed you and hates the family dynamic but doesn't know how to change it. Years of hurt. Years of blaming people. Years of staring at Bryson, feeling as if things had been different there, you'd still be here."

"Jesus, that's a lot to take in." Riley swallowed hard. It

was a bitter pill, but she couldn't deny that this had been her brother's reality. "However, Grant has said some pretty crappy things to me when we've chatted on the phone."

"That's because his mother still knows how to get to him when it comes to you," Kelly said. "This isn't meant to hurt you, but it's hard when he's only seen you a few times in the last decade."

That stung. However, it was also the truth.

"Do you feel that way, Erin?" Riley asked.

"Sometimes, but I've been on this rollercoaster ride with Chad. It's all-consuming." Erin sighed. "But, I can't even think about that right now. Grant needs to be the focus. I don't believe for one second he did what he's being accused of."

"These aren't easy times for any of you," Brea said. "Just breathe. Tackle one thing at a time."

"My parents' divorce screwed all of us so much," Erin whispered. "We all handled it differently, but none of us well."

"But you're not them," Kelly said. "And you have support. Don't forget that."

"I can't believe I brought any of this up. I'm so sorry, Kel. You've got so much to worry about, right now." Erin sucked in a deep breath and let it out slowly.

This entire thing was messed up, but in a very real way, it was also what family was all about. Being there no matter what, and Riley wouldn't turn her back on her siblings now.

Her mother was an entirely different matter. Though currently, her mom wouldn't even respond to her texts or take her calls. She'd told Erin that she was too disappointed in her youngest child. If she only knew the entire clan had just enjoyed a barbecue at the Boones. Now that would really ignite a bomb.

"Mommy! Mommy!" Willa jumped and waved. "Watch this."

Erin sat up and covered her eyes, shading them from the afternoon sun. "I'm watching, baby."

Bryson snagged the football, pointed toward the far corner of the yard, and Willa took off running, glancing over her shoulder, and stretching out her arms. Bryson sent the ball sailing through the air, and Willa caught it.

"Did you see that, Mommy?" Willa yelled as she jumped up and down and pranced in a circle.

"Bravo!" Erin clapped.

"My turn!" Randy snatched the ball and tossed it to Devon.

"I swear, I have no idea how they have that much energy." Erin slumped back into the chair. "I'm exhausted just watching them."

"That's because you're old," Kelly teased, tucking a strand of hair behind her ear.

"Look who's talking." Erin rolled her eyes. "Thirty-three is not old. Two kids who think sleep is a government conspiracy... that's what's old."

Riley smiled faintly, letting the much-needed switch to easy banter warm her. She'd missed so much with her sister and Kelly. She wasn't jealous of their relationship. Not at all. She relished it. However, a sadness settled in her heart. She'd missed so many years, all because she'd been too hung up on past pains that could've been cleared up if she'd had the maturity and the courage to come home sooner.

That was on her. Not them.

She reached out and grabbed Erin's hand. "You're an amazing mother. I've always enjoyed the pictures and the stories, but meeting them? Spending time with them is like seeing the best parts of you," Riley said, meaning it.

Erin's dark circles and messy bun told a story of a woman barely able to keep it together, but there was love in every line of her sister's face when she looked toward the yard.

Bryson caught Riley's gaze across the lawn, grinned, then took off at a sprint, letting Willa tackle him around the knees. He fell into the grass with exaggerated defeat, Devon cheering the victory like a sideline coach.

Erin sipped her wine, watching them. "You know, for all their gruffness, those Boone boys are really just big kids."

Kelly laughed. "Makes them perfect uncles, though."

"One of my children would have to get married, have kids, blah, blah, blah, for that to happen." Brea waved a finger. "While their lives are not mine, and my purpose in life was as a mother, not necessarily a grandma, I'm always hopeful." She leaned over and winked at Riley.

"I'll drink to that." Kelly raised her glass.

"Me too." Erin clanked her glass against Kelly's, then Brea's.

"You people are crazy." Riley rolled her eyes. A few days ago, she would've boarded a plane so fast it made everyone's head spin. The mere thought of being with Bryson again seemed like a pipe dream. Absurd at best.

Now? Being in his arms again felt natural. Real. Waking up next to him was like coming back to the place she'd always belonged even though she'd gotten lost along the way. As if being home allowed her to rediscover all the possibilities she'd thought she'd left behind.

A lull settled between them, the hum of conversation drifting from the yard, the sound of kids' laughter floating up again.

Erin's cell vibrated on the coffee table. She lifted it and glanced at the screen. "Ugh."

"Who is it? Riley asked. "Chad?"

"No. But just as bad... It's Mom." Erin set the cell back on the table, face down. "She's been acting so strange lately." Her tone was careful, neutral in the way someone speaks when they're afraid of what's behind the question. "More short-tempered than usual. Distracted. And the way she accused you of stealing was disturbing. And not true. I found that crystal figure and waved it under her nose. She blew it off like I was the one lying. I'm getting tired of defending her to people."

Kelly let out a dry laugh. "And yet, she'll be the first to remind you she's never wrong—even when she is."

The truth of that statement hung in the air like smoke.

"I do remember happy times as a kid," Erin said. "But there was always this undercurrent of things not being good enough. Of mom wanting things to be different. I didn't understand back then. I remember Dad wanting to change careers. Wanting to work here. But mom didn't like the prospect. Not unless it was in sales. Something that would bring in money *and* respect.

Then, Dad was gone. She always said he was the one who left, but we all knew why he did. Mom and Parker..." Erin trailed off, then shook her head. "I like Parker. He's a good man. But doesn't have much of a backbone. Does whatever Mom tells him to. Anyway, I just hope she's not making all this worse. We all know how she can get. Mom spinning her weird version of the truth is the last thing Grant needs."

Riley swirled the wine in her glass. She'd never heard Erin speak this truthfully about her mother. It was refreshing, yet, at the same time, it was depressing as hell. "The problem is, there is so much stacked against Grant. I don't believe the evidence, but the optics aren't good."

Kelly's shoulders slumped with exhaustion. "He's been battling this alone for so long. It's been a living hell for him. He's wanted to talk to someone but was frightened that the second he spoke up, this would be exactly what happened. The letter Sean sent Riley made everything even worse."

"I wish I hadn't had Mateo open it," Riley managed.

"It would've made its way here, eventually," Brea said. "Best Grant be open and honest about everything now, then have something come crawling out of the woodwork later."

They all went quiet for a moment. The truth was, no one wanted to dwell on any of it—not on the fact that the medical examiner had come in on a Sunday to perform the autopsy, or that Grant's name hung in the air like smoke no one could quite see but everyone could smell.

Erin leaned forward, as if she could will them back to safer topics. "You know, Nathan's been begging to play football this fall. His dad's been practicing with him. We think he's got potential, but we don't want to build him up too much. That was so painful for Grant. He thought he was so good."

Kelly laughed. "Then Bryson waltzed out on that field

and took *all* the wind out of Grant's sails. He realizes now that his mother had given him a false sense of importance."

"Bryson went to the coach his freshman year and asked if he could sit the bench, giving up the starting position," Brea said. "He didn't want to take that from Grant because he was older. And Bryson knew he'd get his time eventually. To him, it was just a game."

Riley's chest tightened at the revelation. Bryson had been willing to sacrifice his own achievements for Grant—the guy who'd spent years resenting him, who'd made Bryson's life miserable whenever he got the chance. The selfishness of her mother's actions was staggering, and it made her think of all the times her mother had pitted the young boys against each other, had used competition and comparison as tools to control.

Brea shook her head. "While I thought that was kind of him, he earned that spot, and I told him so. Perhaps, I shouldn't have done that. We all make mistakes as parents. But most of us are doing the best we can."

The simple honesty in Brea's admission hit Riley hard. Here was a mother admitting uncertainty, acknowledging that maybe she'd made the wrong call. Riley couldn't remember her own mother ever expressing doubt about a parenting decision—Elizabeth's way was always the right way, the only way, and anyone who disagreed was simply wrong. Her father, though... he'd been different. He'd listened, had admitted when he didn't know something, had apologized when he made mistakes. He'd parented with humility and love, while her mother had wielded motherhood like a weapon, using guilt and manipulation to keep her children in line. The contrast had never felt starker.

The sun's light deepened, long shadows spilling across the grass. Bryson scooped up Willa and spun her until she shrieked. Devon and Randy tried to dogpile on him, only for him to spin away, laughing.

For all the heart-pounding adventures Riley had experienced, there was nothing in the world like this.

The sound of footsteps on gravel drew her attention toward the side gate. Sandy stepped into view wearing her uniform with her hair pulled into a low ponytail, expression unreadable.

Not even a hint of a smile. That couldn't be good.

Conversations stilled.

Sandy's gaze swept the yard and locked onto the glass doors of the office. "I need to speak to Grant," she said, her voice carrying softly across the patio.

The home office door opened, and Grant stepped out. His brows pulled together at the sight of Sandy. "Hey, Sandy. You've got news?"

Sandy's eyes flicked toward the kids playing in the grass. "Can we speak privately?"

Bryson caught the hint at once and strode across the yard, clapping his hands. "Alright, team—water break inside. And I have it on good authority that there are cookies and ice cream in the kitchen. Let's go."

The kids barreled past in a blur, Willa giving Riley a fist bump on her way inside.

When they were gone, Sandy turned back to Grant. "I have some bad news. The medical examiner finished the preliminary autopsy." She paused, as the weight of that settled. "There's more to be done. The labs and tox screens will take a week, maybe longer. However, because your father's death has been ruled suspicious, I need you to come back down to the station."

Kelly's hand shot to her mouth. "Suspicious? What does that mean?"

"It means I have more questions for your husband," Sandy said evenly.

"No," Riley whispered, grabbing Kelly's hand.

Erin inched closer, wrapping her arm around Kelly's waist.

Grant's expression shuttered, but a flicker of something —fear, disbelief—passed over his face. He looked at Kelly, then back to Sandy. "Am I under arrest?"

"No," Sandy said. "But you are a person of interest. I'd recommend bringing a lawyer with you."

Grant glanced over his shoulder.

Harlan slipped out the door, tucking a stack of papers under his arm. "Good evening, Chief." He motioned to the driveway. "I'll drive my client to the station."

"Alright," Sandy said. "I'll wait in my car and follow you."

"Can I have a moment with my wife?" Grant asked.

"Of course." Sandy looped her fingers into her belt and strolled back through the side gate.

Kelly raced toward Grant, throwing herself into his arms, sobbing.

"Hey. It's going to be okay." He cupped her face.

"It doesn't feel okay," Kelly whispered.

"Grant?" Walter called. He leaned against the side of the office door. "It's getting late, and we don't know how long this is going to take. Why don't Kelly and the kids stay here tonight? We've got plenty of room. It might make them feel a little safer, less alone... a little more removed from what's going on."

"I don't want to be a burden," Kelly said.

"It's no trouble." Walter jogged down the steps toward the couple. He rested a firm, fatherly hand on Grant's shoulder. "We'll take good care of your family."

Riley caught the subtext in Walter's careful words. What he wasn't saying—what none of them were saying—was that staying at the Boone house would keep Kelly and the kids safe from her mother's inevitable dramatics. Her mom would descend on Grant's house like a hurricane, wringing her hands and demanding answers no one could give, turning an already impossible situation into a three-ring circus. At least here, Kelly could process what was happening without having to manage Elizabeth's theatrics on top of everything else.

"Thanks." Grant waved.

Riley's heart ached. None of this made any sense.

"Grant..." Kelly's voice trembled.

"I'll be fine." Grant kissed his wife. "I'll be back as soon as I can." He took a step back, gave a quick wave to everyone else, and followed the same path Sandy had taken.

"That was the most horrible thing I've ever had to watch," Erin whispered. "Why do they think he had anything to do with Dad's death?"

"Grant might have been the last one to see him alive," Riley whispered.

Just then, Bryson stepped from the back of the house. He took Riley's hand and kissed it. "I'm going to the station. Grant's got a lot of friends in this town. But he chose us to be the ones to help him navigate this, and I'm not going to let him walk into that interview with just his lawyer."

Riley's heart thumped in her chest. She glanced up at Bryson. "Then I'm coming with you. I'm not sitting around here doing nothing."

"Neither one of you are going anywhere," Walter said with a firm tone. "Sandy will kick you out of that station faster than you walked into it."

"Grant didn't do anything, and he needs support." Riley blinked back tears.

Kelly closed the gap, taking her hand. "He knows we're all here for him."

"What you don't know is that Sandy called Harlan and gave him a heads-up," Walter said. "The ME classified the autopsy as suspicious. Toss in that damn letter Sean sent, and Grant is suspect number one. They've got nothing else and nowhere else to turn."

"You're not making this better," Kelly said softly.

Riley covered her face with her hands. "I refuse to listen to or believe a single word."

Bryson pulled her into his arms and held her close. "I love you," he whispered. I'm not going anywhere, and neither is anyone else in this family."

She heard the words but couldn't respond. All she could do was cry.

Thirteen

The Boone house had long since gone still, that late-night hush where every sound seemed to carry farther than it should. As a boy, Bryson loved the vastness of this place. He and his siblings used to pretend it was a hotel. They'd set up a check-in counter, and Devon was always the businessman, Hasley the princess, Ashley the famous actress. And Bryson was the owner of the world-famous hotel where everyone clamored for a room.

Those were the days.

Tonight, he found no comfort in the heart of his home.

Down the hall, Riley's soft, even breathing drifted to him from the guest wing. Bryson had walked her up earlier, lingering in the doorway until she was under the covers, the glassiness in her eyes dulled enough to let sleep take her. Now, hours later, he was in the study with a fire low in the grate, shadows haunting the corners like ghosts.

The Boone study had always been his father's domain —rich walnut shelves, deep leather chairs, and the scents of old paper and wood polish hanging in the air. Bryson sat behind the low table, working the cork from a bottle of their 2014 Pinot Noir Reserve, the pop loud in the silence. It was the kind of wine his father pulled from the shelf when days were long, and nights brought the kind of dense fog that couldn't be seen through. He poured the ruby liquid into two wide-bowled glasses, catching the firelight.

Across from him, Grant slouched into one of the big chairs, looking as though the weight of several weeks had been piled on top of him, brick by brick. His shirt was wrinkled and his hair pushed into uneven ridges.

Bryson handed him a glass. "Here. You look like you need it."

Grant took it, rolling the stem between his fingers before taking a sip. He closed his eyes briefly. "You know, I've always liked this stuff. Even back in high school. I used to pretend I hated it because... well, Mom."

Bryson leaned back into his chair. "Your mother enjoys decent wine, and she also seems to enjoy telling people our wine is swill and Winston Callaway's wine is the best wine in all of Napa Valley." Bryson lifted his glass, swirled it, watching the legs hold the side, pride swelling in his chest at his family's legacy. "Callaway Winery makes a decent blend. I won't deny that. However, I do believe ours is better."

Grant snorted.

"Of course, I'm biased."

"My mom taught us to hate anything with Boone on the label. But it was subtle at first. Underhanded digs. Sideways complements. It wasn't until you strolled onto that football field, that she insisted you stole my starting spot. Neither one of us was going to the NFL, but you were better. I knew that. However, I'd been built up just enough, and was too young, to know any better. I was also jealous." Grant gave a wry half-smile. "Mom, she developed this script for us, and I played my part perfectly. Riley refused. She and my mom were at odds over almost everything, but the tipping point had been our mother's affair with Parker." Grant lifted his glass and sipped. "Sometimes, Kelly and I drink this at home. If my mother knew, she'd probably disown me."

"Elizabeth won't even take Riley's calls right now."

"I don't understand that one." Grant leaned back. "But I suspect it has something to do with Ry staying here. My mother has always been so envious of Brea. They both grew up in the same part of town. Both had very little as children." Grant lifted his gaze and smiled. It was the first one he'd sported in days. "My mother-in-law, who was in the same grade as both Brea and my mom, once told me that my mom was all about your dad. Had a huge crush on him and did everything she could think of to get his attention. But nothing worked, so she started dating his best friend to get close. Thought that might work."

"What?" Bryson stared at Grant. He leaned forward. "My mom has always said that Elizabeth was interested in being *important,* but she never mentioned that she'd made advances toward my dad."

Grant shrugged. "It was a long time ago. But Victoria has no reason to lie. And my mom? Well, she doesn't like to lose. So, I bet if someone asked her, she'd say something to the tune of she'd never been interested in Walter. That he'd been after her."

Bryson chuckled. "I'm sorry, I shouldn't laugh."

"No need to apologize," Grant said. "It took me until I fell in love with the most wonderful human in the world to truly see my mom. But I do love her. For me, she wasn't the worst mother in the world. But it pains me how she put us in roles. I was the golden child—her favorite. Erin was the one she could mold into her little worker bee. The child who couldn't stand up to her."

"You couldn't either," Bryson said.

"Oh, I could. But I chose not to." He lifted a finger. "Once Riley was born, it was like the battlelines had been drawn. Me, Erin, and my mom, against Riley and my dad. It was the most fucked up family dynamic I've ever seen. But I was only four. I didn't know what it all meant. I just felt it. And when Riley left, I held onto that hurt like a badge of honor I wore with pride. I get that it's gross, and I'm working like hell to fix it. But it's hard with all this shit hanging over my head."

"Why didn't you talk to Riley when you got back from the station tonight?"

Grant's gaze stayed fixed on the wine in his glass. "Because I didn't have it in me to explain. She was already looking at me like she didn't know whether to hug me or slap me. Like she's stuck between this weird space where I'm innocent and guilty all at the same time. And I don't blame her for that. If you only look at the facts, I look guilty. I just didn't have it in me to go through it all with them."

Bryson set down his glass. "All she wants to do is support you. But she's scared. And confused. She doesn't understand why anyone would want to kill your father."

Grant's eyes flicked up to his, and something in them made Bryson's gut tighten.

"Here's what the outside world doesn't know. And I have no idea if Sandy will release this information or not. So, you shouldn't tell anyone." Grant's hand tightened around his wine glass, his gaze dropping. "They believe my father was poisoned. There were things both the ME and the doctor in the ER questioned, so it was only a matter of time before they went ahead and did the autopsy. The question is how someone could give my dad a substance that could kill him, and Sandy believes she knows that answer. She believes it was in his morning coffee." Grant sipped his wine, taking a moment to swallow, as if he were frightened of what was in the wine, the glass trembling faintly in his hand. "I'm the one who gave him the coffee."

Bryson went still. The fire popped softly. "What?"

"I handed him the very thing that killed him." Grant's voice was hoarse. "I might as well have poured it down his throat myself."

Bryson's fingers curled against the arm of his chair. "Where did you get the coffee?"

Grant lowered his head, tears dropping from his eyes like a leaky faucet. "From my mother." He set his glass on the coaster, rested his elbows on his knees, and cradled his cheeks.

The silence stretched. The fire's glow flickered against the gold in Bryson's glass, but his mind was already racing ahead—Elizabeth's name was a snake uncoiling in the middle of the room.

"My mother knew about the missing money." Grant leaned back and stared at the ceiling. "She called me that morning. Told me to pay it back. Said I had plenty of money to cover it. Which is true. It's not like I'm poor. But that's not the point. I didn't do it. And I told her that. Told her I was headed over to see Dad to have the same conversation."

Bryson held up his hand. "I'm sorry. I understand how your dad might have figured it out. He only left the board a short time ago and still volunteered on the Tourism and Wine committee. But your mom?"

"My father told her," Grant said. "Surprising but not totally shocking. Anyway, she asked if I would stop by to tighten a leaky faucet. Parker just doesn't have the strength to do anything around the house yet. It was on my way, so I did." Grant swiped at his face. "I didn't think anything of it when she shoved two mugs of coffee at me."

"You really think she put something in the coffee?" Bryson asked. "Jesus, what if you drank the wrong one?"

Grant snorted. "My dad drinks so much cream and sugar, it's gross. I like mine black, so she labeled them. My mom does stuff like that all the time."

"There was no coffee mug when I got there." Bryson leaned forward.

"Sandy didn't say anything about that." Grant sighed. "It's possible the police have it."

Bryson rubbed his temple. "Our security cameras don't overwrite for a full week. I'm sure Sandy will be requesting all of them now. But there are ways to skirt some of the cameras if someone knows where they are."

"You think someone came back on property and to get the mug?"

"It's possible someone picked it up and tossed it. But that mug had to go somewhere," Bryson said.

"It was one of those fancy paper ones my mother orders online. She gets them in bulk. That way, if someone wants a cup to go, she doesn't have to worry about her precious tumblers being taken."

"Sounds like Elizabeth." Bryson leaned against the desk. "Do you know if Sandy plans on bringing your mom in for questioning?"

Grant's jaw tightened. "Sandy said nothing makes sense about my mother killing my dad. No motive. But I still look guilty as hell for the embezzlement and murder. Checks with my name on them. Approvals I didn't sign. The letter my dad sent to Riley. And now? I'm the guy who handed him the poison." He rubbed both hands over his face, then let them fall into his lap, staring at the floor. "I keep replaying it. I should've poured it out. I should've made it myself. I should've done a hundred damn things differently. But I didn't. I just... trusted her." His voice cracked. "She's my mother."

Bryson stayed quiet for a beat, letting the weight of it hang between them. He understood the kind of loyalty that could blind a man, the way family could wrap a chain around his neck and still expect him to thank them for it. He'd been watching it unfold with Riley and her family for years, only he hadn't understood how deep the roots ran. Finally, he said, "We don't know anything for certain yet, except you didn't pour that poison. You didn't put it in his cup. You didn't kill your father."

Grant's laugh was brittle. "But in a way I did, because I handed it to him. How am I going to tell Erin? Her kids?

My kids? Riley? Deep down, I feel utterly responsible because it all started with me trying to handle this by myself."

Bryson leaned forward, elbows on his knees. "Then we find out the truth. About the money. About that coffee. We turn over every damn rock until we see what's underneath. And if your mom had a hand in either crime, you're not going down with her."

Grant's eyes went wide. "How could my mother have anything to do with money missing from the revitalization fund. She's not even on the board or a committee. And why would she?"

"This is going to sound crazy," Bryson said. "But cancer treatments aren't cheap, and your mom lost a good sum of money in Robert Wilkerson's Ponzi scheme. First, we hire someone to look into that." Bryson lowered his chin, hating himself by the minute. This was Grant's mother. But at the same time, it was also Grant's freedom. "And let's not forget, Monica is on the committee for the main street project."

"What does your ex-wife have to do with... oh, she had my mother's help on that project."

"Exactly," Bryson said. "Not to mention, Monica never liked your wife. She thought Kelly was an imposter. A poser."

"Kelly snubs Monica every chance she gets. Can't stand that woman," Grant said. "No one can. I'll never understand why you married her."

Bryson let out a long breath. "Trust me, man, it was the worst few years of my life, and I couldn't explain it if I tried."

"So, what are we doing?" Grant asked. "Hiring a PI to look into my mom?"

"I think that's the best course of action," Bryson said. "I'll talk to my dad in the morning."

The fire snapped softly in the grate. Grant leaned back, drained his glass in one swallow, and closed his eyes. For the first time, Bryson saw just how tired the man was—not just from the questioning, but from years of playing roles, keeping secrets, and living under the weight of someone else's expectations.

Grant peeked open one eye. "So, you and my sister, again, huh?"

Bryson smiled. It was hard not to. "I'm working on it."

"Don't fuck it up this time." Grant stood, slapping Bryson on the back. "And if you tell anyone that I wouldn't mind you as a brother-in-law, well, I won't deny it this time." Grant slipped out of the room and disappeared down the hallway.

Bryson corked the bottle, took the glasses, and headed toward the kitchen, where he found Riley sitting at the island with a bowl full of ice cream sprinkled with home-made cookies. "What are you doing out of bed?"

"I thought about eavesdropping on your and Grant's conversation and then decided that would be rude." She licked the spoon, scooped up some more, and offered him a bite. "Are you going to tell me about it?"

"I am," he said. Leaning forward, he ate the dessert she offered.

"All of it. Every detail. Nothing left out."

He nodded.

She stood, holding the bowl of ice cream. "Get the chocolate sauce."

"Why am I doing that?"

"Because we're going to bed where I'm going to do unspeakable things to you with that sauce, and then in the morning, after being fully satisfied, and having a good night's sleep, you'll talk."

"God, I love you."

"I know." She tapped the back of the spoon on his nose and took off toward the back staircase, leaving him standing in the kitchen, breathless.

He'd better not fuck this up, because his heart wouldn't recover.

Riley sat on the edge of Bryson's bed, toes curling into the plush rug, the faint thrum of her pulse filling her ears. The room was dimly lit except for the amber glow spilling from the lamp on the nightstand, casting long shadows on the walls. She watched Bryson cross the room, the bottle of chocolate syrup in his hand, the corner of his mouth curved in a way that was equal parts tease and promise.

"You were a wicked girl twelve years ago." He smiled that same boyish grin he had back in high school that made her insides turn to mush. "And now you're a wicked woman."

She laughed. "Do you remember our first time?"

Slowly, he inched forward. "Under the stars, in the vineyard, after the Fourth of July picnic. We'd figured out all the essential things by then. How to please each other. What we liked, didn't like… except I still always got caught with my hand up your shirt."

"You were the devil," she said.

"Where do you want it?" he asked, his voice low, almost a growl.

Her lips quirked. "Surprise me."

The first cool drizzle landed on her lower lip. She drew in a breath, his thumb swept it across, smearing sweetness before his mouth claimed hers. His kiss was warm and slow at first, tasting of chocolate and him, the mix dizzying and familiar all at once. When his tongue glided across hers, her grip on his T-shirt tightened, pulling him closer.

She desperately needed him. To feel him. To absorb all his love and strength. He'd always been so eager and willing to give her what she'd desired. He'd sensed her moods and shifted his to help her navigate her world. For so long, this man had been the root that held her to the earth.

Her hands slid beneath the cotton of his shirt, seeking the heat of his skin, the hard planes of muscle she'd memorized years ago and had never forgotten. He broke the kiss only to strip the shirt over his head. The lamplight caught on the ridges of his chest, the faint dusting of hair trailing downward, the flex of his shoulders when he leaned in again.

She lay back as he followed her down, his weight braced but still pressing into her enough to make her breath hitch. His mouth moved along her jaw, then lower to her neck, his breath warm as he found the sensitive place just beneath her ear. She shivered when his lips grazed over it.

He tugged her tank upward, masterfully wedging it between their bodies to reveal the curve of her breast. He kissed her there first, slow and reverent, before taking her nipple into his mouth, drawing a gasp from her. The scrape of his teeth was followed by the soft pull of his lips, sending heat pooling low in her belly.

"You're so beautiful," he murmured, lifting his gaze as he tossed her shirt to the side. "Everything about you is perfect." He placed a tender kiss on her belly, moving lower, until his fingers curled into her pajama bottoms.

When he peeled them down her legs, the cool air against her bare skin made her shiver again. His hands were firm on her thighs, easing them apart before his fingers stroked over her, slow and sure, until her hips arched toward him.

"Yes. Yes. Please."

His tongue sailed across her like a ship pulling into port, slow and steady, maneuvering in just the right spots to bring her close to the edge.

She clung to him, biting her lip, shaking her head wildly, as waves of pleasure crashed into her like a tidal wave.

Pausing for a moment, he shed his pants, lifted the syrup, and drizzled some on her thighs, licking it, before diving in with both mouth and fingers.

She tensed, digging her heels into the mattress. Blinking, she tried to suck in a deep breath, but all she could manage was a few panting moans before her climax broke like the crest of a wave smashing into the shoreline.

His lips danced up her stomach, across her breasts, until he found her mouth. He kissed her, hard, swallowing every sound she made.

And then, he slid into her in one long, steady stroke, his breath breaking against her lips. She held onto him, feeling the fullness of him inside her, the way his body seemed to fit against hers like they'd been made for only for each other. He moved slowly at first, each thrust deliberate, his gaze locked on hers as though he was memorizing every flicker of her expression.

Her second climax built gradually, each pass of his hips fanning the heat higher until it broke over her like a cork popping from a champagne bottle, pulling a soft cry from her as she tightened around him. He followed soon after, a low groan against her skin as his body shuddered, and then he stilled, holding her as if she might vanish if he relaxed his arms.

They stayed wrapped in the sheets, her head pillowed on his chest, the steady thump of his heart lulling her into a kind of calm she hadn't felt in years. Outside, a breeze rattled the branches, and the faint sound of crickets seeped through the open window.

Bryson's fingers moved idly in her hair, combing through the strands with a touch so absentminded it felt unconscious—like he couldn't not touch her.

"You used to always do that," she murmured against his chest.

"Do what?"

"Run your fingers through my hair after..." She shrugged. "Back then, I figured you were doing it because you thought you had to do something. Like it was the grown-up thing to do."

His lips curved faintly. "I've always loved your hair. The way it feels against my fingertips. But I never did it out of some weird male obligation after sex cuddle thing. I enjoy this part, too."

Something in her chest tightened at that—at the ease with which he said it and the fact that it was true.

"I used to lie awake after," she admitted, voice soft. "Not because I couldn't sleep. Because I didn't want to. I didn't want to miss any of it."

His hand stilled briefly, and then he tilted his head so he could meet her gaze. The amber light caught the edges of his eyes, making them burn just a little. "I didn't want to miss it either. But I was too damn young and too damn stubborn to admit that out loud."

She gave him a small, crooked smile. "Guess we were both stubborn."

"Still are," he said. "Difference is, I'm not interested in letting my stubbornness get in the way this time."

She shifted. "I want this. I want you. I want us." She swallowed, staring at him, unsure of what to say. Or how to say it. She let her palm rest over the slow rise and fall of his chest. She could feel every beat, every breath. She knew what he meant—what he wanted—but there was a weight pressing against her ribs. Not fear exactly. More like a fragile kind of hope she wasn't ready to drop in the middle of the floor, just yet.

"Bryson..."

"Hmm?" He traced the line of her jaw with his thumb.

"I do love you. I never really stopped." She swallowed, her voice catching slightly. "At first, I didn't think I'd last five minutes in Stone Bridge. But it's gotten easier, and I want to be here. I want to forge a relationship with my nieces and nephews. I don't want to miss out. But we've been apart for twelve years. But loving you now isn't the same. I've changed and so have you. We don't know each other the same way, and we can't simply be the couple we once were."

"I know that." He kissed her nose. "All I'm asking for is a shot at a second chance. I want to go for walks. Dinners. Spend time with you."

"I want that too." She pressed her lips against his chest. "And you should know, I asked Mateo to ship the rest of my things. I do plan on staying. I just can't promise you forever. I can only promise you that I want to see where this goes."

He held her gaze for a long time, then dipped his head, pressing a slow kiss to her forehead. "That's enough for me."

They lay like that for a while, listening to the low hum of the night and the faint creak of the old house settling. Her breathing synced with his without her even trying, the rhythm grounding her in a way that made her chest ache.

And for the first time since she'd set foot back in Stone Bridge, she let herself imagine a future here—one with him in it.

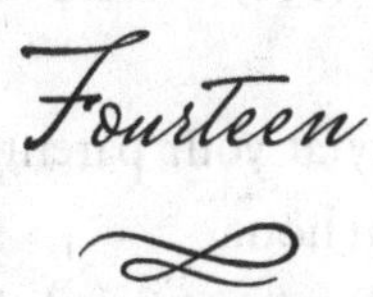

Fourteen

The Stone Bridge Cafe buzzed with the usual Friday afternoon energy, but the table by the front window felt like an island of tension in the midst of cheerful chaos. Bryson nursed his third cup of coffee, watching the police station across the street through the large plate-glass windows, waiting for some sign that Grant's questioning was finished.

Riley sat beside him, her arms folded tight, gaze fixed on the building across Main Street as though sheer focus might make her brother emerge faster. The set of her jaw told him she was one heartbeat away from marching over there and demanding to know every detail of this case.

"Just breathe," he murmured, resting his hand on her knee.

"I hate this waiting," she said, not taking her eyes off the station. "Not knowing what they're asking him, what he's saying."

"Harlan's with him. Grant's smart enough to follow his lawyer's advice."

Erin sat across from them, picking at the slice of pie she'd ordered but barely touched, while Kelly twisted the strap of her purse until the leather creaked. Her eyes kept darting toward the clock, toward the window, toward nothing at all.

"The kids are okay at your parents' place?" Kelly asked for the third time in an hour.

"They're having the time of their lives," Bryson assured her. "Mom's probably spoiling them rotten, and Dad's letting them 'help' with the afternoon chores. They're better off than any of us right now."

A slight movement across the street caught his attention. "There's Grant," he said, pointing as two figures emerged from the police station—Grant in his dark suit and Harlan with his distinctive silver hair and briefcase.

They were heading toward the crosswalk when a familiar SUV pulled into the station parking lot.

"Unbelievable," Erin muttered, her fork clattering against her plate.

Chad's vehicle came to a stop, and through the cafe window, they could all see the blonde woman in the passenger seat duck her head low, trying to hide despite being in plain view of half of Main Street.

"That's her. His mistress." Erin's voice was tight with barely leashed fury. "He didn't even bother parking somewhere else. She's sitting right there."

"Classy," Riley said dryly.

Chad got out of the driver's side, straightening his tie with the arrogance of a man who thought he was untouchable. But before he could make it to the station entrance, another car pulled up—Monica's pristine white Mercedes.

Bryson frowned. "What the hell is Monica doing here?"

They watched as Monica climbed out of her car, looking uncharacteristically rattled. Her usually perfect hair seemed slightly disheveled, and even from across the street, he could see the tension in her posture.

"Think she's here about the Main Street Beautification Project?" Kelly asked.

"Has to be," Erin said. "She was always working with Mom on budget approvals and funding requests. Makes sense they'd want to question her about the committee finances."

Grant and Harlan had reached other side of the street, but instead of heading to the cafe, they paused on the sidewalk, Grant's attention fixed on something behind them. Following his gaze, Bryson saw a third car pulling into the station lot.

Elizabeth stepped out with the regal bearing of someone who considered herself above such mundane concerns as police investigations. A deputy met her at the entrance, and she disappeared inside with the kind of practiced composure that had come from years of maintaining appearances.

"Oh my God," Erin breathed. "This is really serious, isn't it? They're questioning everyone connected to those committees."

The cafe had gone quiet around their table, other patrons stealing glances their way. Small towns thrived on gossip, and the Callahan family situation was quickly becoming the biggest story Stone Bridge had seen in years.

Grant and Harlan finally pushed through the cafe door,

the little bell above it chiming cheerfully in stark contrast to their grim expressions.

"How'd it go?" Riley asked as they approached the table.

"About as well as you'd expect," Grant said, slumping into the chair beside Kelly. "They're asking very detailed questions about committee finances, about who asked for what and when. What I signed off on. What I didn't. You name it, they asked me. Including stuff about the morning Dad died."

Harlan set his briefcase on the floor and signaled the waitress for coffee. "I'd prefer not to discuss specifics in public," he said quietly, glancing around at the other tables. "But the scope of their investigation is... broader than we initially thought."

"We saw Monica go in," Bryson said. "And Chad's here with his—" He gestured toward the window where the blonde woman was still trying to make herself invisible in the passenger seat.

"And now Mom," Erin added, her voice hollow.

"Monica makes sense," Grant said. "She worked closely the beautification committee. If there are questions about how those funds were managed, Monica would have had access to the records."

"What about Dad's death?" Kelly asked in a whisper. "Are they still—"

"Kelly," Harlan interrupted gently but firmly. "Let's not speculate about ongoing investigations in a public place."

The next twenty minutes crawled by with stilted conversation and coffee refills. Bryson found himself watching the station entrance, noting every person who went in or came out. When Monica finally emerged, she looked worse than when she'd arrived—pale beneath her flawless makeup, her usually confident stride replaced by something that looked almost like panic.

"I'm going to talk to her," Bryson said, standing.

"Don't—" Riley started, but he was already heading for the door.

He caught up with Monica in the parking lot, her heels clicking rapidly against the asphalt as she hurried toward her car.

"Monica," he called. "Are you okay?"

She froze for half a second, spine stiff, but didn't turn around. "Yeah. Fine. Don't have time to make small talk." She waved a hand over her shoulder dismissively.

"You don't look fine."

This time she did turn, and he was struck by how genuinely shaken she appeared. Gone was the polished, predatory confidence he'd come to expect from his ex-wife. In its place was something that looked almost like fear.

"Just leave it alone," she said, fumbling with her car keys. "Just leave me alone."

Before he could respond, she was in her car and pulling out of the lot with more speed than necessary.

When he returned to the cafe, Riley raised an eyebrow. "Well?"

"She's rattled. More than I've ever seen her. Even more than when I handed her a check and told her to go back to her maiden name." Bryson retook his seat, troubled by the interaction. "Monica's a lot of things, but she's not easily spooked. Whatever they asked her in there really got to her."

Another half hour passed before Elizabeth and Chad

emerged from the station. Neither looked pleased. Elizabeth's mouth was a thin, hard line, and Chad's expression was that of a man who'd just been told he wasn't as clever as he thought.

Bryson enjoyed that last part. Chad's arrogance had always grated on him, and the way he treated Erin was inexcusable.

They watched through the window as Elizabeth and Chad had what appeared to be a heated conversation in the parking lot. Then, to everyone's surprise, they both headed toward the cafe.

"Oh, great," Erin muttered. "Here comes the drama."

Elizabeth pushed through the cafe door first, her heels clicking sharply against the tile floor. The entire restaurant seemed to hold its breath as she surveyed the room, her gaze landing on their table with the kind of calculated precision that suggested she'd known exactly where to find them.

She walked straight to Grant, stopping in front of him with a slow, deliberate shake of her head. "I warned you that morning," she said, her voice quivering with the kind of fake emotion that might have fooled someone who didn't know her. "I raised you better than this."

Grant stared up at her, something bitter sparking in his eyes, but he didn't respond. He just sat there, holding his mother's gaze without flinching.

Impressive, Bryson thought.

But Kelly, on the other hand, had clenched her fists, looking like she might explode. "You have some nerve, Elizabeth. My mother warned me about you. Told me what kind of woman you are and always reminded me to watch my back. If she didn't think my husband was the kindest, most loving man... well, she would have told me to run."

"Watch your tongue, young lady," Elizabeth said, taking a step back. "Are you threatening me in a room full of witnesses? In front of my lawyer? Tsk, tsk. Not a good idea."

Kelly jumped to her feet, but Grant was already up, curling his fingers around his wife's forearm. "Sweetheart, not the time or place. Ignore her."

Kelly eased back into her seat, holding onto Grant like he was a flotation device, and she was drowning.

Chad had been hanging back near the door, but now he stepped forward. "Elizabeth, maybe you should wait outside. I need to talk to Erin about representation."

"Leave," Erin said, her voice tight with controlled anger. "Your girlfriend is waiting in the car. I'm sure she needs your attention."

Chad's jaw tightened. "I'm here as your lawyer. You should be thanking me for—"

"For what?" Her voice rose, drawing stares from other tables. "For coming home whenever it's convenient? For pretending to care about your family when you have other priorities? Do you even know where the kids and I spent last night?"

Chad moved toward her, reaching for her arm, but Grant was on his feet again in a flash. "Get your hands off my sister."

Bryson stood too, stepping closer. "Not my sister, but what he said."

"What are you two? Best friends all of a sudden?" With

a scowl twisting his features, Chad glanced between them with what looked like fear behind his eyes.

"Maybe we are," Grant said. "Now leave, before we make you."

Harlan cleared his throat. "Gentlemen, perhaps we could lower our voices. We're in a public place."

For a long moment, Chad's gaze darted between Erin and the others, clearly calculating how much more humiliation he was willing to risk. Without another word, he strode toward the door, muttering something under his breath.

Elizabeth followed without so much as a glance over her shoulder.

Erin crumpled, tears streaming down her face. "I can't believe I stood up to him. I can't believe I told him off."

"You did great," Grant said, reaching across to squeeze her hand.

"You know," Bryson said, "I'm sure my parents would let you stay at the house until you get on your feet. And if you need a job, we've got an opening at the tasting room. I can't keep working double shifts."

"I can babysit until you figure out what you want to do next," Riley offered.

"You're staying?" Erin turned, blinking out tears.

"My boyfriend wants me to. My sister needs me. And I think my brother wants me to stick around too."

"I do." Grant smiled. "But really?" He jerked his thumb toward Bryson. "This guy?"

Riley snorted.

Despite everything, the air in the room lightened slightly.

Through the window, they watched as Sandy emerged

from the station and looked around the street before heading directly toward the cafe.

"Riley," Sandy said as she pushed through the door, her expression unreadable. "I need you to come with me."

"Me? Why?"

"I just need to ask you a few questions. That's all." Sandy offered a slight, polite smile.

"Then I'm coming with her." Harlan eased from the table with his briefcase in hand.

Riley rose, her chin tilting in that stubborn way Bryson knew meant she'd face whatever came next on her own terms.

"I'll be right here," Bryson said.

"I know." She managed a smile as she and Harlan headed back across the street, disappearing into the police station.

And Bryson was left to wait again, watching through the window and hoping this nightmare would end soon.

Riley sucked in a deep breath and stepped across the threshold into Sandy's office. It had the kind of forced warmth that came from trying to make a small, official space feel less like an integral part of a police station. A framed Napa Valley harvest print hung crookedly on one wall, flanked by two mismatched diplomas. A jar of wrapped peppermints sat on the edge of her desk, beside a low vase of fading hydrangeas—blue gone brittle at the edges. The scent in the air wasn't coffee and paper, but lemon cleaner mixed with the faint metallic tang of the radiator knocking in the corner.

"I thought we'd do this here, instead of the interrogation room. No reason to make you any more uncomfortable than you already are." Sandy gestured to the chairs opposite her desk. "Have a seat, Riley. Harlan."

Harlan set his papers on the corner of the desk and eased back, taking a folder and opening it.

"Is this where you questioned my brother?" Riley asked.

"It is." Sandy smiled.

Feeling a tad better, Riley sat, crossing one leg over the other, her slow pulse pounded stubbornly in her ears. "How can I help?"

Sandy settled into her own chair. "I need to ask a few questions so I can eliminate you from anything that might come up later."

Riley frowned. "Eliminate me?"

"Standard procedure," Sandy replied, flipping open a thin manila folder.

"I keep hearing that term from you and everyone else."

"I'm sorry," Sandy said. "But there's no other way to say it, and this is official."

Riley shifted. She liked sarcastic, smiley Sandy better.

"Where were you when your father died?" Sandy asked.

"Patagonia," Riley said evenly. "I had just finished leading a hiking group when Bryson called with the news."

"Can anyone verify that?"

"The company I worked for. My best friend, Mateo. Half a dozen clients, the lodge staff, the park rangers," Riley said, ticking them off on her fingers. "Need me to send you their numbers?"

"Give them to Harlan, and he'll get them to me." Sandy's pen scratched across the page. "Have you traveled back to the U.S.—specifically Napa Valley—in the past year?"

"No." Riley glanced between Sandy and Harlan, who have her a reassuring smile as if this was all normal stuff.

Sandy clasped her hands, rested them on her desk, and leaned forward. "What can you tell me about Sean and Grant's relationship?"

"I haven't lived here in twelve years," Riley said with a tremor in her tone. "I was close to my dad, but not as close to Grant. They've had their issues over the years, but to my knowledge, they worked hard to maintain a decent relationship."

"What does that mean?" Sandy asked.

"I don't know." Riley raised her hands and slapped them against her legs. "Can you be more specific?"

"Sure." Sandy unclasped her hands and shuffled a few papers across her desk. "Was Grant harboring a grudge against your dad?"

"Not that I know of," Riley said.

"Did they fight a lot?"

"My dad said they'd been getting along, especially since Grant had kids. Grant softened a lot after that." Riley hesitated for a moment, afraid she might say something to hurt her brother. She glanced toward Harlan, who gave her a short nod. "I'm the one who had problems with my family. All of them, except my father. But I think he and Grant got along mostly well enough."

"Do you know anything about your brother's financial status?" Sandy asked.

"He's well-off. Not at the same level as the Boones or the Callaways, but I believe he's a millionaire."

"And how do you think he got that way?" Sandy asked.

"Hard work." Riley shifted her gaze once again to her attorney.

"How do you think he avoided Robert Wilkerson's Ponzi scheme?" Sandy asked.

"He's smart. He's good with numbers. And knew what kind of person Robert was. He even tried to warn people about him. At least that's what I've been told," Riley said.

"Okay. But what about that letter your dad sent you?" Sandy asked.

"I can't explain that. I just know what my brother had to say."

"You and your dad never talked about it?"

Tears welled in Riley's eyes. "I didn't know about the note until after my dad had died. My friend, Mateo, called me when it arrived."

"I'd like your friend's contact information so I can speak with him directly."

"I can give that to you," Riley said.

"Alright. What do you know about your mother's finances?"

"Not that much, truthfully," Riley admitted. "I mean, she married Parker because he was well off, but I don't know the first thing about how that worked. And I learned recently that she lost some money in that Ponzi scheme, but I don't think that put too much of a dent in their resources." Riley wanted to jump out of her seat and scream at her friend that she knew all this already.

"What do you know about Monica and your mother's friendship?"

"I didn't know they had become friendly until I got back to town."

"Are you aware that Monica's on the Main Street Beautification committee?" Sandy asked, leaning back and rubbing her temple. "And that your mother has a hand in that."

"I've become aware, but I don't know the logistics of it."

"Alright." Sandy waved her hand.

Harlan shifted his stance against the wall.

"I know you've been away a long time. But you know the people in this town. The history. Tell me what you know about the relationships between Monica, Kelly, and your mother."

"None of them are good," Riley said.

"And how does Grant play into that?" Sandy asked.

"Kelly doesn't like Monica, but that feeling is mutual. My mom doesn't respect Kelly and again, mutual. I really don't understand Monica and my mother having any kind of bond, except mutual hatred of the Boones." Riley sighed, frustrated.

Sandy picked up a pencil and tapped it against her temple. "One last question. Does your mom have any reason that you can think of to want your father dead?"

"I can't think of one," Riley said.

"What about pinning it on your brother?"

Harlan coughed.

"Is that what's happening?" Riley asked.

"I don't know, you tell me." Sandy's tone had just enough dryness to make it sound like a yes.

"I mean. My parents had a bad marriage. My mom constantly belittled my dad. It wasn't good. But if you're asking me for a motive—you know, like on TV—I just can't come up with one. Not one that makes sense." Riley sat back and pressed her palms into her eyes. "Can I ask you something?"

"Sure."

"Is it true? About the autopsy? About the poison? Is that my father's cause of death? Because we can't get an honest answer. All we've been told is there was 'something' in his labs that didn't make sense. A substance that could be considered a toxin, and his death is now suspicious."

Sandy's expression didn't shift. "I can't answer that."

"Can't," Riley echoed, "or won't?"

For a beat, the only sound was the radiator clanging twice before settling. Sandy set down her pen. "Riley, I need you to understand something—this is bigger than any one interview. The less you know right now, the less likely it is that someone can accuse you of interfering later. That's protection, not punishment," Sandy said. "And, it's both. We don't know exactly what killed your father. We just know it wasn't a heart attack."

Harlan closed his folder. "She's right. You're better off letting this play out through official channels," he said. "She's given us more than you think. Trust me."

Riley let out a humorless laugh. "For some reason, it doesn't feel that way."

Sandy's brow lifted a fraction, but she didn't comment. "We're done for now."

Sandy stood, and Riley followed her out into the waiting area, where Byson sat in one of the chairs.

He rose, and in seconds, was standing at her side, arm wrapped around her waist, as if to hold her up.

Harlan leaned against the counter.

"Thanks for coming in, Riley," Sandy said. "Harlan, can I have a word?" She turned and disappeared down the hallway, Harlan, one step behind.

Riley stared at the empty space, squeezing Bryson's hand.

"Are you okay?" he asked.

"I will be when I know what those two are talking about."

Bryson kissed her temple.

Two minutes later, Harlan emerged, his expression neutral. "Let's step outside."

"What did she say?" Riley asked.

"Things are moving quickly. Sandy didn't give me much, but she's doing her job. You've got a PI on board, and he's good. Let him dig. Let Sandy work. I'll be working, too. Go back to Bryson's. Try to have a day that's not all about this."

"That's it?" Riley blinked.

"For now," Harlan said. "Sometimes, the system works slowly. And this phase can be frustrating as hell. But Sandy knows what she's doing. I might not always like the way she questions someone. Or some of her tactics. And I know she doesn't like some of mine. But that's the dance. Right now, your job is to go home, spend time with your family, and try not to worry."

"That's no easy task." Riley glanced over her shoulder at the station, the closed door, the faint sound of a phone ringing inside. The knot in her chest tightened.

Fifteen

Riley looped her arm around Hasley's. "God, I so need this," Riley said as she and Hasley moved down Main Street. "I feel like everything is in limbo. Erin and I don't want to do a celebration of life until everything with Dad's death is cleared up and the suspicion around Grant is gone."

"Erin told me that Elizabeth was hounding her to schedule something while begging her to go home to her husband." Hasley smiled and waved to a couple walking in the opposite direction. Of all the Boone kids, Hasley was the most like their mother. Both in personality and in the way she carried herself.

"My sister cries herself to sleep." Riley took in a deep breath and let it out slowly. "She puts the kids to bed, makes sure they've drifted off, and then falls apart. Last night I stayed with her until she was completely out. And the unfortunate part is, she's not so broken up over her marriage. It's all the years of allowing herself to be a doormat. Of letting my mother and her husband wipe their feet on her like she doesn't matter." They paused at the corner, looking both directions. "She's so scared of being alone. She's got a college degree, but she's never worked, and she signed a pre-nup. About the only thing she's certain of is that Chad won't fight her on custody, but I don't trust that. The guy's a snake."

"Erin's not alone." Hasley hip-checked Riley. "Have you met my mom? She might not be a meddler, but once she's wormed her way into your life, she doesn't let go easily, and she's going to be there for Erin. We all will. Besides, her kids are too cute. This morning, Willa told me I was her new favorite auntie." Hasley stuck her chin up in the air. "Ashley was practically steaming with envy."

Riley laughed as she pulled open the door to the Stone Ridge Tasting Room. The room hummed with a late-summer ease. The air was rich with oak and blackberry, the chatter of tourists softened by a low pulse of jazz. Bryson stood behind the bar, sleeves rolled to his forearms, pouring a deep cabernet into waiting glasses. He was in his element, telling the kind of story that made people lean in, wallets halfway open.

Hasley nudged Riley with a grin. "Watch this—he's about to hit them with the 'three generations of Boone pride' bit. He learned that one from your dad."

Sure enough, Bryson's voice dipped lower, warm as the wine in his hand. The couple across from him all but melted.

Riley smiled, and her heart filled with a sense of pride she wasn't sure she had the right to. "He could sell sunscreen in a snowstorm."

"Or sand to someone already buried in it," Hasley

murmured. "He's the enigma of the family. The one that loves every aspect of the business, from growing, to distribution to marketing, to being right here with the customers. Not even my father can do that. Daddy has always enjoyed growing and the art of the deal. Devon, he's the PR and management guru. He can handle any nightmare tossed at this winery."

"And you and your sister?"

"We like the marketing aspect and the books. We're both really good with numbers." Hasley pointed her finger at Bryson. "If that one over there wasn't always breathing down our necks." Her breezy laugh reminded Riley of lazy summers.

Bryson caught Riley's eye mid-pour, that faint half-smile tugging at his mouth.

She and Hasley inched closer to the bar.

"Isn't this a nice surprise?" he said as he stepped around the counter to greet them, first kissing his sister's cheek. Then, he leaned in and planted a bigger kiss on Riley's lips. "Hmmm, that's nice."

Her cheeks flushed as she glanced around.

"Have a seat. Want a glass?" He glanced at his watch. "I mean, it is approaching that ladies who lunch time of day," he mused.

"We're heading to Oscar's," Hasley said, leaning on the bar. "Some sister-in-law bonding."

"Interesting choice of words, little sister." Bryson's gaze lingered on Riley. "Behave yourselves."

"She's safer with me than she is with you," Hasley shot back.

Before Riley could respond, the door opened and the

scent of gardenia swept in, followed by the staccato click of heels on wood. Monica.

"Wonderful," Bryson said with a tight jaw. "I swear, I can't get through a day without seeing my ex-wife. Makes me want to stick an icepick in my eyeballs."

"You should file a restraining order," Hasley said with some venom. "We certainly don't need her business. It's like she's just giving back the money from a settlement she—"

"Let's not go there, shall we?" Bryson lowered his chin.

Riley eased onto a barstool. No way was she leaving *her* boyfriend alone with this viper.

Monica's hair fell in perfect waves, sunglasses perched just so, her clothing that effortless style of casual that cost more than most people's rent. "Bryson," she greeted, voice smooth, eyes sliding over him like he was an accessory to complete her outfit. She shifted her gaze, landing on Riley, and all of a sudden, she looked like she'd swallowed a bag of sour balls. "Riley," she said, her smile curving with practiced precision. "I didn't realize you were still in town. I assumed you'd be halfway back to... wherever it is you run off to these days. Because, you know, you're good at that."

Riley gritted her teeth. "My father's funeral hasn't happened yet. I wouldn't leave before that." She cocked her head. "Not that I plan on leaving anytime soon."

A flicker of disdain passed over Monica's face—quick, but there. "Of course. Well, I'm just here to pick up my wine order. I should've known I wouldn't have any left over from the garden party. Everyone just loves the Stone Bridge Wine and expects that I, Bryson's wife, would only serve the finest."

"Ex-wife," Bryson corrected.

"Without the privilege of carrying the name anymore." Hasley hopped up on a stool and smiled a big, toothy grin. "Or did you forget that part?"

"Hmm." Monica tilted her head at Bryson. "Thought I'd come straight to the source." She rested her hand on the counter, ignoring the jab. "I was hoping to catch you here. We haven't—"

"Let me get your order," he said. As he turned toward the back room, Monica bit down on her lower lip. "I've always thought that color looked fabulous on him, and I'm glad he took me up on my advice about wearing jeans in the tasting room. They hang so well on his hips." She turned to Riley. "It's nice you've found time to visit. Must be hard, catching up on everything you've... missed."

"Some things," Riley replied evenly, "are exactly as I remember them, like Bryson's jeans. Which's he's always worn... in the tasting room. Might have even been at the urging of my father and the blessing of his."

Hasley covered her mouth, stifling a giggle.

"I doubt that." Monica's lips pressed into a polite smile. "Small towns never change, do they? Same families, same names, same... dramas."

"Some of us grow out of them," Riley said lightly. "And some of us hang on to them like we don't know the meaning of fresh laundry."

"And what is that supposed to mean?" Monica asked.

Riley leaned closer. "I'm not the one stirring the pot here. I simply came in to say hello to my *boyfriend*."

"Boyfriend?" Monica tipped her head back and laughed. "You're still the same delusional girl you've always been," Monica said as Bryson returned with the black Stone Ridge Winery bag, setting it on the counter. "Here you go."

Monica leaned in, lowering her voice in that faux-private way that wasn't meant to be private at all. "We should catch up sometime. Just the two of us. For old time's sake."

Riley's grip tightened on her purse strap. The nerve of this woman. But Bryson didn't hesitate. "Never gonna happen."

"Oh, I believe it will. It always does," Monica said, straightening. "Always nice to revisit the classics."

Hasley smiled bright enough to cut glass. "I hear the classics are overrated."

Bryson leaned across the counter, taking Riley's hand. "I prefer classy." He kissed her palm.

Monica's eyes narrowed, but she simply took the bag, pivoted, and clicked toward the door. "Enjoy your lunch." The latch shut behind her, leaving a faint trace of perfume in her wake.

"Well, that felt like I was back in high school, but it was the only way to drive the point home," Riley said.

Bryson let out a breath. "She's... consistent."

"Like a rash," Hasley muttered.

Riley smirked. "A chronic one."

"Now that we've saved you from disaster," Hasley said. "We need to get going." She glanced at her watch. "Our reservation is in five. We'll see you at home, big brother."

"Don't enjoy yourselves too much." Bryson smiled. "Especially at my expense."

"Oh, that's the entire point." Hasley laughed as they stepped out into the late-afternoon sun, warmth spilling across the quiet street. After a beat, Hasley nudged her. "So... you and my brother. What's the *real* deal?"

Riley blinked. "What do you mean?"

"I mean," Hasley said, sidestepping a planter, "he looks at you like he's just been sucker-punched and doesn't mind bleeding a little. And you... Well, you don't look at him like someone who's leaving anytime soon." Hasley leaned a little closer as she continued down the sidewalk. "Not to mention you tossed that nugget in Monica's face? Or was that just talk?"

Riley glanced at the brick sidewalk, chewing the inside of her cheek. "Bryson and I—we're figuring things out. Taking it—slowish."

"That's vague," Hasley said. "And vague is usually code for 'complicated and maybe worth it'."

"It's... both." Riley huffed a quiet laugh. "I will tell you that I'm still madly head over heels in love with your brother. That hasn't changed. But we have, and that means we need to be honest." She sighed. "Our lives are vastly different. But right now, my focus is on Grant and his problems." She took a steadying breath. "And burying my father. After that, it's one day at a time. However, I have decided to... come home."

Hasley grinned. "Good. I like you for him. I always have. Even if it took years for him to figure that out."

"Years." Riley lifted a brow. "And a Monica."

"We all make mistakes," Hasley said. "No idea what he was thinking, but she wasn't always that gross. She started off being somewhat normal. Until she wasn't. Honestly, all we wanted was for him to be happy. We didn't think she was it, but you weren't here for us to remind him about the right girl for him."

Riley's lips curved despite herself. "You really believe that, don't you?"

"Not believe. Know," Hasley said simply.

They turned a corner into a narrower side street toward Oscar's—and stopped short.

Riley stood beside a brick boutique, partially hidden, facing her mother and Monica. No practiced smiles now—both women's expressions were sharp, their postures taut. Monica's sunglasses were off, eyes narrowed. Her mother's lips were pressed thin, her hand wrapped tight around a small envelope, bulging in the middle.

Monica said something low, her voice just loud enough for Riley to hear her frustrated tone, but not enough to make out the words. Her chin jutted toward the package. Her mother shook her head sharply, muttering something that made Monica's mouth pinch tighter.

Riley instinctively slid her phone from her bag, thumb swiping to the camera. She raised it just as Monica extended her hand. The exchange was quick—a flick of fingers, the white envelope sliding from Monica to her mom. Riley had no idea if she caught the shot or not. She wasn't even sure why she'd taken it.

Her mother immediately tucked the envelope into her oversized tote, glancing around with the wary tension of someone who didn't want to be seen.

"Now that was interesting," Hasley said.

"I can't imagine those two being brunch buddies," Riley murmured. "No offense, but my mom hates all things Boone, and Monica once bore that last name."

Hasley's brow furrowed. "They've been... friendlier since the divorce—at least, when it comes to town business. I've never seen them like that, and let's face it, that exchange looked more like sparing than two women out for an afternoon of cocktails and shopping."

Monica's gaze flicked up the street, and Riley stepped back into the shadow of an awning, Hasley close behind her. Monica and Elizabeth exchanged a few last clipped words, then turned in opposite directions—Monica striding toward the main square, Elizabeth vanishing down a narrow alley toward a parking lot.

Riley stared at the screen in her hand, the image crisp and undeniable. "We're going back to the tasting room."

Hasley nodded, already moving. "Bryson's going to want to see this."

Sixteen

Bryson leaned back, wiped his mouth with his napkin before tossing it on his plate, and smiled as he stared at all the faces sitting at his parents' massive table.

The Boone dining room was built for mornings like this. It was built for the hum of voices, the scrape of chairs, the clink of forks against ceramic. Even with the breakfast rush winding down, the big walnut table still bore the evidence — half-drained mugs scattered between plates streaked with syrup, a platter of scrambled eggs long gone cold, a pitcher of orange juice sweating onto a folded linen napkin.

The scent of bacon hung in the air, woven through with the faint perfume of the lilies his mother had arranged in a vase on the sideboard. Every so often, a burst of laughter or a sharp call floated down the hallway from upstairs, where Ashley and Hasley were engaged in the school-morning ritual of chasing down missing shoes, lost homework, and the occasional child.

The house hadn't been filled with this kind of activity in years, and Bryson's mother was in her glory. All these people might not be her family—these children might not be her grandchildren—but his mom opened her home and her heart, giving them a safe harbor in the middle of a storm.

Bryson sat near the head of the table, elbows braced on the polished surface, coffee cupped in both hands. Across from him, Riley sat curled in her chair, one knee pulled up, her ankle hooked on the edge of the seat. By now, her tea was probably lukewarm, but she turned the mug slowly between her palms as if absorbing its lingering heat might anchor her here a little longer.

Devon sat next to her, phone in hand, his thumb flicking over the screen with deliberate slowness—which meant he wasn't engaged in the conversation of the room and more interested in what might appear on that damn cell.

Bryson had a good idea of what Devon was waiting for and it made Bryson want to reach across the table and snatch the damn thing right out of Devon's fingertips. Bryson was so tired of hearing about Emery Tate and her *situation*. The woman had created her own problems. There was no conspiracy theory. Nothing anyone could say would make Bryson change his mind on that.

Jessica, Grant's daughter, was twelve years old and stubborn as hell—like her father—hadn't moved since she finished her waffle. Arms crossed tight over her chest, she stared at the wood grain of the table like she could bore a hole through it with sheer will.

Kelly hovered beside her daughter, patient but stretched thin. "Alright, Jess. Time to get ready for school. Let's go."

Jessica didn't blink. "I'm not going."

"Oh, yes, you are," Kelly said sternly, but softly.

Bryson glanced over the rim of his mug.

Grant set his soda on the table and leaned forward, forearms on the table. "Young lady, your mother and I will not tolerate that tone. Not at home, and especially not when you're a guest at someone else's."

Jessica's chin lifted. "Then maybe you should tell me the truth about what's going on." She cocked her head.

The words landed like a dropped plate—sharp enough to cut through every other sound.

The room suddenly stilled, and all eyes were on Jessica.

"This is not the time or place." Grant kept his voice even.

Jessica's frown deepened. "It never is." She pushed her chair back and raced out of the room.

Kelly exhaled, hard. "Excuse me, please." She darted off after her daughter.

Bryson gripped his mug, staring into the dark liquid.

"Sorry about my daughter's outburst." Grant leaned back, ran a hand across his eyes, and then down his face. "Not only is she at *that* age. But she shouldn't have to deal with adult problems."

"No need to apologize," Walter said, leaning forward. "I've dealt with a few angsty teenagers myself."

"She's incredibly intelligent. A little bullish, like me, but she's really a good kid." Grant let out a long breath. "But lately, she's testing our patience. Sometimes I wonder if we're losing control."

"I, for one, think she's a lovely child," Bryson's mother said. "Reminds me of myself at that age."

"You're a good father." Riley smiled. "The way you handled her reminded me of the way Dad used to deal with me."

Grant blew out a puff of air. "You and Dad always did have a special bond."

Bryson pushed his coffee aside, staring at Riley, studying her expression, waiting for the tears to appear. But they didn't. Progress.

"Grant and I were always so jealous," Erin said.

"You know," Riley started. "I used to feel like the two of you had your own private little club. Like there was some super-secret handshake to get in, and I was never going to be able to crack it."

"We're all together now, and I'm sure Dad is looking down on us all, smiling. It's what he wanted. That's all that matters." Grant smiled.

Bryson had had his siblings. Their support had always been a given. They'd engaged in brutal verbal combat some-times, but when it mattered, they had each other's back. To see Riley and her siblings at the same table, after a decade, left Bryson's soul scraped raw.

Devon's phone buzzed against the table. He glanced at the screen, and his expression shone with constellation brightness. He lifted his gaze, catching Bryson's, then flipped the cell face down.

"Emery Tate? Again?" Bryson asked, jaw tightening.

"If it was, you should be glad I didn't take her call." Devon's face broke into his familiar smartass grin.

"Right. Because the second I'm out of earshot, you're

gonna tap that screen and return the call. Do you really think I'm that stupid? I know you're talking to her. The rumor mills are buzzing—saying Stone Bridge Winery plans on hiring a walking scandal." Bryson pushed his chair back and abruptly stood. God, this got under his skin. It wasn't so much that Emery was interested in working at Stone Bridge Winery. Or even the scandal, though that did make Bryson pause. However, Bryson knew when his brother got into his *feelings,* logic went out the window. It didn't happen often. Maybe twice in the last ten years. But when Devon fell, it was always for the wrong girl.

"You're being dramatic." Devon narrowed his eyes.

"And you're sleeping with her," Bryson said under his breath.

His mother rose, and she walked by, she gave Bryson a little love tap on the back of his head. "Enough of that. It's rude and not appropriate in front of our guests."

"Ouch." Bryson glared. "I'm only saying what we're all thinking."

"It would be unprofessional of me to sleep with a potential hire." Devon grinned.

"Sarah, Patrica, Quinn," Bryson said. "Shall I go on?"

"Stop it." His father's voice was deep, steady, impossible to ignore. "You boys are acting like toddlers. This wouldn't be the first time we considered someone with a questionable past. And might I remind you, that one is working out."

"Mommy! Mommy!" Willa's voice came from somewhere down the hall. "I can't find my favorite hair tie. I need my favorite hair tie."

"I know I should teach her that any hair tie will do, but

pick my battles, right?" Erin was gone before anyone could answer.

"I should go help Elsa in the kitchen." His mother kissed his dad's cheek. "There are leftovers in the fridge for lunch."

"Thanks, Ma." Devon snagged his cell and was out the door—to call Emery, no less. Freaking wonderful. But that was a problem for future Bryson.

"Let's take this to the study. Harlan and Declan, the private investigator, will be here any minute, and I'd rather not talk over cold eggs," his dad said. "This conversation deals with Grant's case, but if Harlan doesn't mind if Bryson and Riley are there, then neither do I."

"I doubt he will." Grant nodded. "I've discussed with him how I'd rather this family is in the know. Too many secrets, lies, and half-truths have torn us apart."

"All right then. Let's go." Walter waved his hand.

Bryson snagged a tray of mugs and the pot of fresh coffee that Elsa had brought in near the end of breakfast and followed the crowd down the hallway toward the study, glancing at the pictures on the wall, noting the mix of Boone-Callahan history.

Pictures of his great-grandparents with Riley's. And then there was his dad with Sean. But what struck him was how many there were of him, Grant, Riley, and even Erin. It was as if they were already part of the house. Their shared history had taken a weird detour, but now it had been righted.

Bryson set the tray on the coffee table and glanced around, watching the group slip into leather chairs, grateful

Riley had chosen one big enough for him to join her. He sat on the arm, and she curled up in the center.

Walter poured a cup of coffee and handed it to Grant.

He wrapped his fingers around the mug, stared at the surface like it might offer an escape, then pushed it back. "I haven't been able to drink this since Monday." The unspoken part hung heavy in the air.

No one rushed to fill the silence.

Bryson thought about that for a moment, letting his memory stretch over the last few days. It was odd that he hadn't noticed it. Though he did find it strange that Grant had chosen diet soda at breakfast. But one of Bryson's sisters drank diet soda like it was her lifeline to sanity.

Footsteps echoed in the hall, and Brea reappeared, ushering in Harlan and Declan West.

"Good morning, gentleman," Bryson's father said. "Please, help yourself to some coffee." He waved his hand.

"Walter. Everyone." Harlan looked as precise as always — suit pressed sharp enough to cut. A leather folio under one arm. "Some of you already know Declan, the private investigator I like to use. One of the best in the business."

Declan, lean and sharp-eyed, moved with quiet purpose, scanning the room like he was taking mental photographs before sitting down. "You must be Grant."

"That would be me." Grant waved his hand.

Declan opened a notebook, his tone calm, measured. "I like to get straight to the point. So, mind if we dig right in without all the formalities?"

"Please. I feel like I've been in limbo for years, not days." Grant sighed.

"All right. While I believe this is good news for Grant,

it's not necessarily good news for the family." Declan shuffled a few pieces of paper around.

"What the hell does that mean?" Riley asked.

"Let him talk," Harlan said, his tone soft.

"Parker and Elizabeth are asset-rich but cash-poor. Between Parker's cancer treatments, the trials, and Elizabeth's spending habits, they were in the red a year ago."

Bryson saw Riley's shoulders tense, her eyes narrowing just slightly—a reaction most people would miss, but Bryson knew her better than most. "What does that mean, exactly?"

"It means, they're struggling," his father said. "They have things, but not the means to pay for them, or live the way they are."

"My mother made it sound like the money she invested in the Ponzi scheme didn't affect them too badly," Grant added, his fists at his side. "I told her if she needed help, I was there, but she brushed it off as if it were nothing. Pocket change, she called it."

"Well, it wasn't. It was a sizable amount. Enough, that it cleaned out their savings and some of Parker's retirement fund. Your mother also re-mortgaged her house."

"Jesus," Grant muttered. "That's a lot of fucking money. Over a million."

"Shall I continue?" Delcan asked, glancing around the room.

Grant waved his hand.

"A few months back, small deposits started showing up in Elizabeth's account. Nothing overtly sizeable. Nothing that would make anyone question it. Cash or money orders. The amounts don't exactly match the missing revitalization fund withdrawals, but the timing's close enough to raise suspicion. Could be coincidence. Could be cover."

Grant shifted, tugging at his pant legs, his jaw flexing, face turning red as if someone had set the room on fire.

"Since I don't trust my ex-wife as far as I can spit, and Sandy had her in for an interview, Riley snapped this picture of her and Elizabeth yesterday." Bryson lifted his phone and showed the image he'd had Riley forward to him.

"What's this?" Declan asked.

"We don't know." Riley took Bryson's hand, but her gaze was on her brother. "Mom and Monica were near a boutique. The two were having a bit of an exchange. It looked a little heated. Mom was tense. Monica didn't look happy."

"Any idea what was in the package?" Grant held out his hand, and Declan passed the phone. "It's not very big. Just an oversized envelope that bulges in the middle."

"I couldn't even begin to guess," Riley said.

"Do these two women have a reason to have a secret meeting?" Declan asked.

"Monica has had Elizabeth do some work on the Main Street beautification project. So, I suppose anything is possible." Walter leaned against the desk. "But both women are all about appearances. They're the type who enjoy being seen. Being heard. Side streets are not their style."

Bryson pointed at the cell, then the stack of papers. "Sandy needs to see all of this."

"And she will, but it needs to be done the right way." Harlan lifted a hand. "Through proper channels. We can't have this coming back and making Grant look bad," Harlan said.

Declan flipped a page in his notebook. "One last thing —the fund's ledger shows edits under Grant's credentials. I had my IT specialist do a deep dive. Those edits originated from Elizabeth's home IP address."

The room went still, the mantel clock ticking in the corner like it was keeping score.

Grant's voice, when it came, was low and frayed. "This isn't happening. It doesn't make sense. Even with all this new information, I can't—or maybe I refuse—to piece it together."

"Sandy will find the missing threads, and when she pulls it, this thing will completely unravel," Bryson's father said in that deep, calm tone that made Bryson remember just how lucky he'd been to have been born into such a great family—wealth truly meant nothing without love.

Grant looked between Bryson and Riley. "I know I've said this a million times, but I didn't take that money. I didn't hurt my father. But I also can't believe my own mother would mastermind something like this. She's a little nutty, but she... she wouldn't do that to me. I'm her son."

"We're going to find the answers." Bryson held his gaze. "No matter what they are, just remember, no one in this room believes you're guilty of anything."

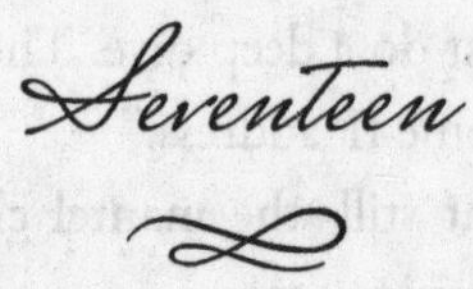

Seventeen

R iley sat on the back patio, book in her lap, gaze scanning the words on the page, but none of them reached her brain. Her mind filled with questions that she had no answers for, and her heart ached with a sadness that couldn't be comforted. She turned her head. Bryson sat next to her, legs stretched out, arms resting in his lap, eyes closed, as his chest gently rose and fell.

"How can you sleep like that?" she asked.

He chuckled. "I'm not. But if you thought I was, why would you wake me?" He opened an eye.

"Because I can't stand people who can doze sitting in a chair."

"Says the woman who told me she slept in a tent, in a sleeping bag, with no air mattress, for more than a month."

"Yeah, because I was horizontal, not partially vertical."

"Semantics." He shifted, sitting taller.

"Shouldn't you be working?" She glanced at her watch. "It's only four."

He sighed. "Trying to get rid of me?"

"No. It's not that." She closed the book, setting it on the table. "I just don't want you to get behind just because of what's been going on. I appreciate it, but your life shouldn't have to change."

"What's happening affects me, and not only because I care about you, or because my family opened up our home. Sean was my friend." Bryson tapped his chest. "There's a big hole here, and I need to know what happened." He took her hand, kissing the inside of her palm. "My mind keeps wandering to dark and dangerous places. I try to redirect, but it always lands on the same disturbing thought."

"I don't like believing the worst of my mother." She stared out into the bright blue sky. "It's one thing to know she lied and manipulated her way through life. I've seen that part of her for as long as I can remember. But to have a hand in my father's death? It's... it's... I struggle to accept that my mom could do such a thing."

"So do I." He reached out and pressed his palm against her cheek. "We're making assumptions, and that's dangerous. We need to let the ME and Sandy find the answers, while we try to focus on other things. Happier things. Like, having your siblings back in your life. Spending time with your nieces and nephews." He waved his hand. "All this."

"The view is spectacular. And it does calm me. Always has," she said softly. "Can I ask you a question?"

"Of course."

"Do you and your sisters plan on living in this house for the rest of your lives?"

He chuckled. "My sisters will eventually move out when they find the right man to share their lives with. But for now, they don't want to." Bryson jerked his thumb over his shoulder. "For me, living here makes my life easier. I wake up, walk out the back door, stroll through the vines, and have early meetings with my dad, other staff, and my siblings. I have an office here. The house is so massive, I could honestly go days without seeing my family if it weren't for the fact that we enjoy breakfast or a nightcap together." He leaned closer. "And if I'm being honest, it's kept women away. Who wants to date a thirty-one-year-old who lives with his parents?"

"I can't tell if that last part is a joke or not."

He shook his head. "My track record hasn't been very good, and I've learned that it's a bit of a turn off. The last few years, I've enjoyed being single. As in not dating at all. Because most women only see my last name and dollar signs."

"That's sad."

"It's reality. And you know that's true. It always has been. It's no secret how well off my folks are, and my brother, my two sisters, and I stand to inherit it all."

"If you ever did get married again, would you want to continue to live here?"

"Are you propos—"

"Bryson. Stop teasing. It's a serious question."

"I'm sorry," he said, shifting his chair. "When I divorced Monica, I swore I'd never get married again. That marriage was horrible. But since your return, my attitude about things might have shifted. Once this situation with Grant and your mom is resolved, I want to spend more time getting to know you again." He tapped his finger on her knee. "Where is this coming from?"

"I don't know. I was just sitting here, thinking about

the way your family is and how it's not the norm, yet perfectly normal," she said. "And wondering what the future holds. Wondering what was next for me when things settled, knowing you and I need to… date… not just \share a bed every night.

"I do like that last part, but there's so much we don't know about each other, even though we once knew everything," he said. "I've seen the subtle differences. Changes in the way you do things. How you handle yourself. Even the foods you eat."

"Wow," she said softly. "That's quite observant of you."

"I don't want to make the same mistake twice." He winked.

She smiled, easing back in the chair, holding his hand, allowing her mind to drift off into a half-dream state of what the future might look like. Picnics. Long walks between the vines. Sitting in the tasting room, listening to Bryson tell stories. Dinners with both families.

The door to the house screeching across the wood planks jerked her from happier thoughts as Grant stepped onto the back porch. His normally styled, curly hair looked like he'd been driving with the top down for days. Dark circles looped under his eyes. New lines appeared on his face. It was as if he'd aged ten years in the last twenty-four hours.

He reached the edge of the porch, planted his hands on his hips, and stared off at the rows of grapes that stretched on forever. "I just got a call from Harlan. He's on his way over with Sandy. He said she has news. Didn't know what it was, but said that she needed to speak with me, Erin, and…" he turned, catching Riley's gaze. "You. Privately. Sandy wanted the kids out of the house, so Kelly, Ashley, and Hasley are taking them into town for shopping and dinner as a special treat." He rubbed the back of his neck. "Jessica's already pitching a fit. I had to tell her that someone would call her with the... truth. That child is going to be the death of me. She's growing up too fast."

Riley pushed to a standing position, making her way toward her brother. Grant wrapped his arm around her, tugging her close, kissing the top of her head. She couldn't remember a time he'd ever done that.

"I'll go tell my dad what's going on." Bryson was on his feet. "I'm sure he won't mind giving up his office for a few hours. Or you can have mine. Anywhere in this house is fine."

"Actually, the kitchen would be nice." Grant released her, turning and leaning his hands on the railing. "It might feel... normal. Although getting arrested would be anything but."

Bryson paused at the door and glanced over his shoulder. "Not that I have firsthand knowledge of these things, but I doubt Sandy would be contacting your lawyer first if that were the case."

Grant shifted, giving Bryson a weak smile. "I appreciate the attempt to make me feel better. But she sent my kids away."

Riley stared at Bryson for a second, tilting her head toward the door. He took the hint and slipped inside without another word.

She ran her hand up Grant's arm. He didn't flinch. Progress. "Let's not jump to conclusions," she said. "Come on. I'll make some tea."

"Can't even drink that. It's like anything hot and in a mug reminds me of—" Grant lowered his head.

"We don't even know if that's what..." Riley swallowed.

"Killed him?" Grant swiveled. "The ME said with certainty, Dad did not die of a heart attack. That there were things in his system that didn't belong there. Doesn't matter that we don't know what they were, but I handed him a cup of coffee that mother made him, and she's lying, saying I wasn't even in her house that morning. Why would she do that, Ry? Why? This whole thing doesn't make sense." He turned, slamming his fist on the railing. "I'm sorry," he whispered. "I shouldn't be yelling at you."

Riley's world tilted sickeningly off its axis. Murder. The word hit her like a physical blow, stealing the breath from her lungs. Her father hadn't just died—someone had deliberately, intentionally taken his life. All this time she'd been grieving a tragic loss, but this was something else entirely. This was evil. Senseless. And now Grant was saying their mother was lying about him being there? Protecting herself while throwing Grant under the bus? The woman who'd raised them was capable of that level of betrayal?

"It's okay. It's not me you're mad at." The implications crashed over her in waves. If their mother was lying about Grant being there, what else was she lying about? And if their father had been murdered, if someone had poisoned him... Riley's stomach churned as she thought about all the people who'd had access to him, all the cups of coffee, all the meals, all the seemingly innocent moments that could have been his last.

Grant let out a sarcastic chuckle that sounded more like a grunting cow. "For a change."

She curled her fingers around Grant's biceps and tugged him inside the house. Her heart fluttered with an array of contradictions. Loving her brother had never been in question. Liking him had sometimes been a problem. But she'd always wanted a relationship with him and his family. It's why she called, texted, and wrote. But she'd never given it her all. If she had, she wouldn't have stayed away so long.

It sucked that it had taken something like this to bring them together.

The door screeched closed behind them, and Grant perched himself on a stool. "Erin should be down any minute. Told me she wanted to take a shower. I think that's code for a good cry before forcing herself to put on a brave face. I want to beat the shit out of Chad. I have for years."

"Have you ever confronted him?" Riley opened the fridge and placed a diet soda in front of her brother and opened one for herself before taking a seat.

The Boone kitchen table had seen its share of hard conversations, but she doubted this kind of devastating weight had ever settled within these walls.

Late afternoon sunlight streamed through the wide windows, landing warm on the wood, but it didn't reach Grant. His face carried too many shadows.

"Erin has always asked me not to." Grant shook his head. "It's always been about what Mom would say. And the optics. And the money. Not that Erin cared much about that, but she needed it because she was trapped. And she's been trying to please Mom for years, and failing miserably at it." He lifted the bottle, twisted off the cap, then took a big swig. "I've always been the golden boy in Mom's eyes, but she's always placed conditions on that position. Living up to mom's standards is a rough place to be. But when I married Kelly, my entire world changed. The only reason Mom still treated me like the favorite child was that she loved bragging to everyone about how I was a self-made man. She so enjoyed going on endlessly about me and my successful business." He laughed dryly. "She'd bulldoze over Kelly, as if she had nothing to do with it. It makes me crazy how Mom idolizes Chad and treats Kelly like she's not worthy of her time simply because her family doesn't have money."

"Can I ask you a stupid question?"

"Like I tell my children, there are no stupid questions." He lowered his chin. "Shoot."

"When we were kids, couldn't you see how manipulative Mom could be?"

He tossed his head back and laughed. Hard.

"I don't think that's funny."

"I'm sorry. I'm not laughing at you. Or even the question. That's about me, and how utterly self-centered and starved I was for our mother's conditional love. Now, it's about balancing relationships and doing what's right for my kids," Grant said, swiveling in his chair, taking her hands. "Yeah. I saw it. But I didn't know how to deal with it. Erin found ways to please Mom. She was all unicorns and rainbows. Dressed like Mom and did whatever Mom wanted. You..." Grant squeezed her hands. "Were Daddy's little girl and a free spirit. Mom looked at you and had no idea what to do. But me? I was sandwiched between two different types of perfection. And Mom would waffle between utter disappointment and building me up into something I wasn't." He leaned closer. "And then, she'd do some really crazy things."

"Like what?"

"Remember when I accused you of breaking my bike?"

"Yeah, but what does that have to do with anything?"

"Erin recently told me that Mom did it. That she actually saw Mom go into the garage and break the damn thing." Grant held up his hand. "And then there was the time that I thought you stole that game of mine. Well, Mom's the one who found it in your room. Not me. But I went along with it because I wanted so desperately to make her proud. And boy was she beaming."

Riley recoiled. "Jesus, Grant." "That's just twisted. It's sick."

"I know." Grant fiddled with his beverage. "Kelly has always believed Mom suffers from a personality disorder. I tend to agree with my wife. Her major was psychology, and she did work in the field before we had kids. I don't leave my children alone with Mom anymore. But Erin does, and that's always worried me."

He took another drink of his soda before continuing. "Thing is, I've enabled Mother all these years, and this is where we've landed." He sighed, rubbing a hand over his eyes, down across his nose, then his mouth. "But I do struggle to believe that she'd resort to harming anyone. Being conniving, lying, manipulating? Sure. She's all those things. He sighed. "There was a time Kelly and I were going to move. But I couldn't leave Erin in this town alone with that asshole husband of hers with nothing but Mom for support."

Riley leaned forward, palming Grant's cheek. "You're a

good man. A great father. And a wonderful brother. I'm so sorry I've been so hard on you."

"That's a two-way street, little sis. I held on to so much of her crazy bullshit because I didn't want to admit that she was controlling me—even to myself." He blinked, letting out a long breath. "I've picked up some traits from our mom. I examine my behavior, and more often than not, it reminds me of her. I'm ashamed of those parts of me."

"You're nothing—"

He pressed a finger over her lips.

"You're kind. But let's be real. I've held a grudge against a man for twelve years when I had no right to. Whatever happened with the two of you is between you. I've treated both of you badly because I couldn't let go of the past. That's our mother's influence. And I'm fucking done. I'm just done. She's carried whatever bullshit game she's playing too far. I don't know how she did it. But Walter, Mason, Bryson, and I have been comparing her deposits with the missing money, and deep in my bones, I know she stole it."

Riley gasped. "That means she set up her own son to go to prison." The betrayal was so profound it made her physically sick. Their mother—the woman who'd lectured them about family loyalty their entire lives—was willing to let Grant be destroyed for a crime he didn't commit. She'd looked Sandy in the eye and lied, knowing those lies could send her son away for decades. Riley had always known Elizabeth was selfish, but this? This was evil.

"Look at what she did to you." He arched a brow. "All because she didn't want anyone to know she had an affair."

Riley slumped backward as tears welled in her eyes. Her

entire existence crumbling in her lap. "She can't get away with this."

"I don't plan on rolling over and waving the white flag. However, I'm scared. Not just for me, but for my kids. I don't want this to touch them. I don't want them to go through life with this hanging over their heads. But no matter how it plays out. They lose either a father or a grandmother. And that just fucking sucks."

The sound of tires against pavement caught Riley's attention. "I think they're here."

"Maybe we should crack open some of that Stone Bridge wine," Grant said. "I could certainly use a drink."

She tapped her fingers on the counter. "Better stick with soda." She stood and went to the back door, stared out at the vines, and waited to learn her brother's fate.

Riley sat across from her brother and sister and the big island in the kitchen, her hands folded in her lap so no one would see her twisting her fingers. Memories of her childhood flickered in and out like an old black and white movie, all grainy with a faint tick and hum laced over the sound as it rattled through a projector.

Visions of her mother sitting on the sofa, book in hand, reading her story. It should have been a lovely image, filled with all the things a child would want at that time in her life. Only, the memory of that moment was of a mother hurrying to get through the chore of reading to her child. It wasn't the way that Kelly and Erin read to their kids— bringing to life every word, every detail in the story.

Longing filled her heart. She'd wanted her mom's love, affection, and attention. She'd never had any of it.

Grant sat forward, elbows on his knees, hands clasped so tightly his knuckles had gone white. Erin was beside him, arms locked across her chest like she was holding herself together by sheer force of will.

Harlan, perched at the head of the island, his legal pad open and pen idle between his fingers. Sandy stood at the opposite end, boots planted, shoulders squared, the kind of posture that said she was here to deliver truth, not comfort.

"I can't stand the silence," Grant said. "Can we get on with whatever you're here for?

"This is a tricky situation, and I'm between a rock and a hard place." Sandy shifted, showing a level of discomfort she hadn't before. "Some of what I'm about to tell you, I shouldn't as an officer of the law. As a cop, I rely on facts. That's generally the only thing that matters to me. But over the years, I've also learned to trust my instincts, especially when dealing with people I've known my entire life."

Riley braced herself, nails pressing into her palms.

Grant narrowed his stare. "I'd rather you not beat around the bush."

"You're going to have to let me do this my way." Sandy arched a brow. "I pulled Monica in again this morning."

Grant stiffened. "Because of that picture my sister took?"

"I'm not going to get into all the details of why I did that, because some of them would compromise my position, or the district attorney's. But a few things during this investigation regarding Monica and Elizabeth have... troubled me," Sandy said. "Before we get into that, Grant, I need to know something."

"What?" Grant asked.

Sandy pressed her palms on the counter, holding Grant's stare. "Do you use a signature stamp for any aspect of your business or for the revitalization committee?"

"No. Never. It would be kind of stupid to have my signature on something like that." Grant's voice was eerily calm and a little too steady. "Anyone could forge my name on a document or a check..."

Sandy glanced toward the ceiling, as if the answer to what she could or couldn't reveal might be hidden in the recessed lighting. "Monica's a tricky one. It took a lot to get this out of her, and honestly, I'm not sure how much I believe of what she's told me." Sandy lowered her gaze. "According to Monica, that's what was in that envelope."

"Why the hell would Monica have a stamp of Grant's signature?" Riley asked.

Grant reached for his soda, took a big gulp, then aggressively set it back on the counter. "So, now you're thinking Monica took the money? She doesn't have access to anything except one project, and we've made sure she has to jump through hoops to get approval for larger sums. If we left it up to her, Main Street would look like a tacky handbag on steroids."

"Monica claims Elizabeth gave it to her after Monica complained about all those hoops you just referenced." Sandy leaned her hip against the counter. "And then Monica mentioned that Elizabeth asked Monica to use the stamp to access and copy certain files for Parker. That even though he'd left the committee when he'd been diagnosed with cancer, he was still acting as a consultant, and it would just be easier than to bother anyone else with it."

"That's bullshit." Grant slammed his hand on the counter. "Parker walked away and never looked back. He was too busy fighting for his life."

"Relax, Grant. I know that." Sandy tilted her head. "Don't forget my husband is also on that committee, and I spoke with the mayor and called Walter before coming over here."

"What does any of this mean?" Riley asked, frustration seeping from every pore of her skin. She glanced at her sister, who wiped a tear from her eye. Turning her attention to Harlan, she said, "You've been awfully quiet. Shouldn't you be advising my brother as to what he should and shouldn't be saying?"

Harlan put down his pen, resting his hand on a stack of papers. "I'll stop him, or Sandy, if I think the conversation is derailing, but so far, this is all favorable for Grant. Not so much for Elizabeth or Monica. Let's hear the rest of what Sandy has to say."

"Before I break this down, I need to say something." Sandy's gaze swept the table. "The autopsy isn't finalized yet, but I'll be blunt—it's leaning toward homicide."

The word registered with cold clarity..

Homicide.

A half-forgotten memory bubbled up from somewhere deep in her subconscious—her father in the vineyard at sunset, shoulders relaxed, wine glass in hand, smiling like nothing in the world could hurt them. She could still hear his gravelly chuckle when he teased her about always wanting to "fly away somewhere new." Having it confirmed

—actually hearing Sandy say the word homicide—made the abstract possibility suddenly, terribly real. Someone had deliberately taken that from her, from him. The finality of it settled into her chest like a weight she'd have to carry forever.

She reached out with both hands, one curling around Erin's fingers, the other landing on Grant's.

Grant's voice came out low. "I didn't—"

"This is where I say, stop talking, Grant." Harlan lowered his chin.

"Thing is, I'm inclined to believe Grant above anyone else," Sandy said. "But this is where some facts get blurred with my instincts." She pulled up a stool, sat down, and clasped her hands together. "Grant swears he stopped by his mom's the morning of his dad's death. Once there, she begged him to quietly return the money. No one would be the wiser since she thought the only people who knew were her, Sean, and now Grant."

"That's exactly what happened," Grant said behind gritted teeth.

"That and you say she gave you two cups of coffee. One labeled—"

Grant slammed his hand on the table. "I'm not lying."

"I think it's your mother who's not being forthright," Sandy cut in. "She denies seeing you that morning. Denies giving you coffee." She leaned forward slightly. "It's your word against hers, but we questioned Parker about it."

"Oh, my god," Erin gasped. "And?"

"Parker admits Grant was at the house that morning. Went on about that damn leaky faucet," Sandy said. "But we don't have the mug. Without it, I can't prove who poured the coffee or what was in it."

"Also, a husband can't be forced to testify against his wife," Harlan piped in.

"You're not much help today," Riley muttered. "Can you tell us what was found in the toxicology report?"

"I can't answer that," Sandy said.

Harlan leaned back, folding his arms. "Where do you stand on motive?"

"That's an interesting question." Sandy drummed her fingers on the countertop. "Now, no yelling. No name-calling. Just listen."

"Alright." Grant gave a bitter laugh.

"Grant's name is all over this mess. It's hard not to look at him for embezzlement. But I can't find a motive for it," Sandy said. "However, we can find one for homicide if he did steal the money, though."

Riley closed her eyes and tried to pretend she didn't just hear those words come from her friend's mouth.

"Elizabeth has motives for both," Sandy said flatly. "She's broke, and she needs to cover her tracks. But if I'm going to prove it, I need your help."

"Help how?" Harlan asked.

"I've spoken to the local FBI office about all this, and we're in agreement. We want Grant to wear a wire. Talk to her. Get her to confess." Sandy leaned back, glancing around the room.

Erin's hand flew to her mouth, tears dribbling down her cheek.

Riley sat there with her mouth gaping open.

Grant leaned back, arms folded across his massive chest.

"You want me to waltz into my mother's house, with something strapped to my chest, sweating bullets, and get her to cop to one, stealing half a million dollars over the course of a couple of months? And two, killing our father? Her ex-husband?"

"Yeah." Sandy nodded. "I do."

"Well, that's a twist I didn't see coming." Harlan picked up his pencil and scribbled a few things on his pad.

"That's insane," Riley whispered.

"Actually, it's not a bad idea." Harlan glanced up. "However, my client is going to need a few things in writing from both your office and the feds. Standard stuff. He's not going to do it without legal protection."

Grant rubbed his jaw. "I'll do it, but I have a condition of my own."

Sandy lifted a brow. "That's not how this works."

"I can show you case studies where witnesses wearing wires—"

"Jesus, Harlan," Sandy muttered. "What is it that you want?" Sandy turned her attention to Grant.

"My sisters come with me," Grant said.

"She might feel ganged up on." Sandy twisted her lower back, stretching. "We can't have her feeling ambushed. I don't believe we'll have more than one shot at this."

Riley's stomach flipped. "Besides, Mom won't talk when I'm present."

"Same for me," Erin said. "Maybe if I hadn't left Chad, but that's not the case."

"Can they listen in?" Grant asked. "This may seem like an odd request. But I need to know they're on the other end. I can't have any more secrets with my sisters. They need to hear every word. Not just from my mother but also from me."

Sandy's lips pressed into a thin line. "That's not protocol and not necessarily my call."

"I hate to break it to you," Harlan said. "Nothing about this is standard. It's not like he's asking you for the moon. Just for his sisters to be in the van. I believe you and the feds can make that work."

"It's also the only way I'll agree to it," Grant said. "Knowing my sisters are with me will give me the strength I need to make my mother face the truth."

Silence stretched, thick as molasses.

Finally, Sandy exhaled. "I'll talk to the Feds. But don't go near her until I say so."

"You don't have to worry about that," Grant said.

"And keep the Boones away from Monica," Sandy said.

"As long as we stay around here, that's an easy one." Riley couldn't imagine anyone in Bryson's family wanting to spend time with Monica willingly.

Sandy's gaze swept them all. "Keep this quiet. No tipping off Monica or Elizabeth. You do, and this whole thing blows up." Sandy glanced at her watch. "Harlan, I assume you want to speak with your client. When you're done, please make your way to the station so we can hammer this out."

When she left, the silence didn't break right away.

Erin was the first to speak. "Grant? Are you sure about this? Mom can be... well, you know."

Grant's voice softened. "I'm not sure about anything. But I don't see another way."

"I agree," Harlan said. "And while this is shitty because

this is your mom, it's good news for Grant. I've known Sandy a long time. I watched her work with the feds on the arrest of Robert Wilkerson, and she dated him in high school. She doesn't do anything on a whim." He stood, tucking his pad into his briefcase. "Sandy showed her hand here today. I need to draft some legal documents, talk to the feds, and Sandy again. I need you protected because you'll end up saying some uncomfortable things to your mom. But we'll chat about that when I've had a chance to hammer out all these details." He moved toward the back door. "I know it doesn't feel like it, but we're nearing the end of this. Stay strong and stick together." He slipped out of the house and headed for his vehicle

Riley looked at her brother—the exhaustion etched into his features eased into something that looked similar to hope.

"This is going to be one of the hardest things I've ever had to do," Grant said softly. "But, at least, I'll have my sisters. Two people I love dearly."

Eighteen

Bryson stood at the edge of the backyard, his mind lingering on the day he'd found Sean. This morning wasn't much different. It came dressed in a haze of early light, draping the vineyard in soft layers. Dew clung to the grass along the gravel path, soaking the toes of Bryson's boots as he shifted his weight from one foot to the other. He'd been out here for twenty minutes, watching the fog retreat down the valley, letting the quiet steady him before the day started throwing punches.

Everything had felt out of whack since the second he'd rolled out of bed, much like that fateful day. But there was something different in the air. Something he couldn't quite put his finger on. Hope? The resilience of family? The willingness to do whatever it took? Whatever it was, it was there, strong and proud, and heavily rooted in the ground.

He glanced over his shoulder at the sound of measured footsteps behind him. Grant's silhouette emerged from between the shadow of the old oak and the side of the barn, hands buried deep in the pockets of a jacket that looked slept in.

"I remember, even as a kid, you always liked coming out here," Grant said when he reached him, voice low as if he didn't want to wake the day. "Riley would race out of the house in her Wonder Woman pajamas, hoping you and your dad hadn't walked the rows yet. My dad would just chuckle, standing on our back porch, watching her little legs take her as fast as she could run."

"I think I loved her even at ten," Bryson said.

Grant stopped beside him, close enough that Bryson caught the faint scent of soap overlaid with the stale tang of worry. For a while, they just stood there, staring at the undulating rows of vines that rolled out like green stitching across the earth. Somewhere down the slope, a tractor coughed awake. "My father always thought the two of you would marry, and that made my mother go into a tailspin. Erin and I would find things to do so we didn't have to hear my mom while she tried to school yours."

"The good old days." Bryson noticed the moment Grant's gaze shifted from him to the rolling hills stretching out before them, the weight of their conversation momentarily forgotten.

"God, this view." Grant let out a low whistle. "I can't imagine you ever tire of it."

"Nope," Bryson replied.

Grant didn't take his eyes off the horizon. His jaw worked like he was chewing on something stubborn. "I wanted to talk to you before I head down to the station."

Bryson tilted his head, studying him. "About what?"

Grant rubbed the back of his neck, still staring forward.

"This wire thing Sandy's got me doing... I've been turning it over in my head. I'm not naïve—I know how my mother operates. I can't predict how she'll react, and I'm not so sure I can get her to say anything useful."

"You'll handle it," Bryson said, keeping his tone steady.

Grant's mouth tightened. "Yeah, well... there's the chance it blows up in my face, instead. If she catches on? If she turns it around on me?" He laughed humorlessly. "Hell, she's capable of making people admit things they didn't do. And I say that from experience."

Bryson's brows pulled together. "But you didn't do anything wrong."

"Doesn't always matter," Grant said quietly. "Truth's one thing. Perception's another. And she's damn good at shaping perception."

"Not so much anymore," Bryson said. "She lost her touch a few years ago."

"But she can still do it, and that scares me." Grant turned to face Bryson then, eyes hard with something deeper than just anxiety—it was resignation, too. "That's why I wanted to see you out here. If this goes sideways—if I end up looking guiltier than I already do—I need your word on something."

"You're going to get through this. Everything's going to be okay."

"We don't know that." Grant's expression didn't change. "Promise me. If I'm out of the picture in any capacity, you'll look after Riley. Keep her steady. She's tough, but she's got blind spots when it comes to family. She'll try to carry things she shouldn't. And Erin—she's hanging on for the kids, but if I'm not here, she's going to need someone. Kelly, too. She'll put on a brave face, but the kids..."

The weight of Grant's request settled over Bryson like a heavy blanket. This wasn't just conversation anymore—Grant was genuinely terrified he might be arrested, convicted, torn away from everything he'd built. The man was asking Bryson to be responsible for the people he loved most, to step into a role that should never need filling by anyone else. The irony wasn't lost on him either—Grant, who'd spent years resenting Bryson's place in their lives, was now entrusting him with their care. It was both an honor and a crushing responsibility that Bryson wasn't sure he was ready for.

"Grant," Bryson said quietly, his voice buckling under the gravity of what was being asked. "You're not going anywhere. But if something does happen—and I mean *if*—you have my word. I'll take care of them. All of them."

"Thanks." Some of the tightness in Grant's shoulders loosened, but not much. "You're not so bad, Boone."

Bryson's lips curved faintly. "Careful. People might start thinking we're... friends."

Grant huffed a short laugh. "Don't push your luck."

They stood in the quiet, the kind that pressed in and made every distant sound sharper—the chirp of a bird in the hedgerow, the faint metallic creak of the barn roof warming under the sun.

"I'd better get going." When Grant turned and headed back toward the house, Bryson stayed where he was, watching the light creep across the land, feeling the promise settle like a weight across his shoulders—heavy, but one he knew he'd willingly carry.

"There's Grant's SUV." Riley pointed from her perch in the back of what appeared to be a van for Stone Bridge Water Authority. Her heart thumped in her throat like a jackrabbit.

The van hummed softly, parked two houses down beneath the dappled shade of a jacaranda. Inside, the air was warm with dust and a faint bite of citrus from a hand sanitizer bottle rolling around the cup holder. Riley sat forward, elbows on knees, eyes glued to the pale stucco of her mother's house. Erin's thigh pressed warm against hers.

Grant's vehicle rolled to a stop in the driveway. He slipped from the driver's side and walked up the path like a man out for a Sunday stroll, a study in casual. Hands in pockets, shoulders loose, pace unhurried.

Erin grabbed Riley's hand and squeezed.

Grant raised his fist, knocked on the door, and didn't once glance over his shoulder. That had to be a good thing.

The front door opened.

"Grant. I'm so glad you called. Things have been so tense since Riley, came back to town, and this other business about... well, you know. I've been wanting to chat." Elizabeth's voice, sweet and lacquered, slid through the wire.

"Me too," he said lightly.

"Come in." A little laugh. *"I just brewed a fresh pot of coffee."*

Erin stiffened. "Oh, god. No. She wouldn't? Would she?"

"That would be insane," Sandy muttered.

"No coffee for me," Grant said. *"Already had some."*

"Thank God," Riley whispered, her voice shaky with relief.

"*I baked this morning. Blueberry muffins. Your favorite,*" Riley's mother said, her voice artificially warm—the tone she used when she wanted something.

Riley caught Erin's sharp intake of breath and placed a reassuring hand on her sister's knee.

A chair scuffed inside. A door clicked. A soft hush fell over the kitchen.

"Don't eat the muffins, Grant," Sandy said.

"Seriously. Don't eat them." Riley gripped her sister's knee tighter.

"*I already ate. Thanks.*" Grant's voice stretched through the static.

"*You look tired,*" Elizabeth said. "*All this... unpleasantness. How is Kelly? The children? I've missed them so these last few days.*"

"*They're fine.*" A pause. "*We're all fine.*"

"*That's good to hear.*" A ceramic clink. "*Black, just how you like it.*"

"Oh, no. Don't do it," Riley whispered.

"*Seriously, no. I'm trying to cut back,*" Grant said sternly. "*Kelly says I'm too jacked up lately.*"

"*Suit yourself. But I wouldn't do it because your wife says so,*" Riley's mother said. "*She's too into all the weird herbal stuff. It's not good for you.*"

A long pause.

"*So—tell me everything. What have the kids been up to? How's Erin doing? I so wish she'd stop with this nonsense. Chad's a perfectly decent man. A good provider. I don't know why she's behaving this way, except for maybe Riley having*" some influence over her. *Riley certainly does know how to create a stir.*"

"I can't believe her." Erin shook her head.

"Keep the commentary to a minimum." The FBI agent adjusted his headset, eyes narrowed.

"*I'm not here to discuss any of that,*" Grant said, matching her ease. "*I'm more interested in what the town's been buzzing about.*"

"*Oh, Lord. The gossip in Stone Bridge.*" A brittle tinkle of laughter. "*They're already twisting your father's death into a melodrama. It's grotesque. Everyone should mind their own business and let us bury your father in peace. That includes your little sister. This is all her fault. She had no business calling the ME.*"

"*Uh-huh,*" was all that Grant seemed to want to say about that. "*For now, I'd rather talk about the funds missing from the revitalization committee.*"

The sound of china hitting china clanked in Riley's ear. "*We've had that talk, and now you're in a pickle.*"

"*Not exactly. My name's on approvals I didn't sign,*" Grant said. "*I wonder how that happened.*"

A delicate silence.

"Here we go," Sandy said. "Come on, Grant. You've got this."

"*You approve so many things. It's easy to forget. Easy to hope others do too, I suppose,*" Riley's mother said.

"*Ink doesn't forget, but funny thing is, I didn't do it. I didn't approve them, and yet, my name's all over it. Money's still missing. How did that happen, Ma? Can you explain that one? Because I didn't do it, and when I left Dad that morning, he was inclined to believe me.*"

"Grant, you can deny all you want. I understand why you're doing it, but it's a little late." Mild scold now. *"I'm disappointed in you. I raised you better than that, and unfortunately, the time to pay it back without consequences has passed."*

Erin's jaw tightened. Riley could see the old pain resurface in her sister's expression. In the front seat, Sandy shifted, raising her hands to the headset covering her ears as she leaned forward.

"You know, I've thought a lot about that morning," Grant said. *"You whispering in my ear, telling me I could just pay the money back, and no one would be the wiser. And Dad telling me I needed to do the right thing. But what really stuck out to me from that morning was how you mentioned that you and Dad were on the same page. I hadn't given it a second thought until recent events, but that doesn't sound like you and Dad wanted me to play by the same rules."*

"I believe your memory might be mixed up." More clanking noises filtered through the static. As if it were a spoon hitting the sides of a cup.

"Are you suggesting you didn't want me to quietly pay the money back?"

The pause this time wasn't delicate. It was heavy.

"No." A louder clank. *"I'm pointing out that you misunderstood your father. No way would he have wanted his only son to go to prison."*

"This guy is good." The FBI agent nodded.

"I heard Dad loud and clear. Especially the parts about Mayor Jessip, Mason, even Walter, already... investigating the missing money."

"I wondered how people in this town found out. I guess

your father got a good case of conscience and tossed his own son under the bus." Her voice sharpened. *"I've spent years cleaning up messes men have made in this town. Your father included. How do you expect me to clean up yours?"*

"Oh, come on. This is pathetic. How did I let this woman rule my life for decades?" Erin's whisper scraped across Riley's jangled nerves.

Grant chuckled. No humor in it. *"Oh, Mother. That's an interesting twist and makes absolutely no sense. All it does is deflect from the real culprit."*

"Who? Do you think it's someone from the Revitalization Committee?" Her mother's tone sounded breathy—almost childlike, and Riley could easily picture her mother's eyes widening as she attempted to project innocence—Riley had seen it so often when the affair with Parker surfaced.

Grant snorted. *"Not unless you've joined the committee recently."*

"Watch yourself," Elizabeth snapped.

Riley was done calling that woman, her mother.

"I won't be spoken to in that tone."

"We could trade barbs all day," he said. *"But let's trade facts instead."* Paper rustled faintly. *"Checks with my name. Ledger entries re-keyed after hours from your home IP. Vendor accounts routed and rerouted to accounts that... eventually can be traced back to you."*

"Are you accusing your own mother of stealing?" Her outrage was perfectly pitched, ripe for the audience she didn't know she had.

"You accused me. I'm just asking why your fingerprints are on my noose."

"You're being melodramatic."

"Maybe. Or maybe I'm being a son who's tired of you using your children for whatever games you're playing." Grant spoke the words slowly, letting them land. *"Do you remember the summer fundraiser right after Riley found out about you and Parker? When the silent auction 'mysteriously' came up short?"*

"Chaotic night," she said smoothly. *"Cash handling was sloppy, and I covered for that young lady. And you're very mistaken about what your sister saw."*

Riley closed her eyes for a long moment, refusing to let those two memories form in her mind.

"No. I don't think I am. I know what Riley saw. So does Erin. That missing money—it was all deflection to take the heat off you and your affair. And Riley wouldn't steal a dime from anyone. But you wouldn't know a thing about your youngest child because you haven't taken the time to get to know her." Silence. Then a soft clink—perhaps her mug set down a touch too hard.

"If you're here to sling mud and be cruel, then you can leave," Elizabeth said.

"Shit," Sandy said.

"It's all good." The FBI man grinned. "This guy knows his mother. He's taking her to places that will rattle her until she cracks. Trust him."

Riley didn't quite have that same confidence right about now.

"I only wanted you to know that I see you," Grant said. *"Before we get to why I'm really here."*

"I don't have time for childish games," Elizabeth snapped.

"My goodness, he's got her so riled up, she's going to

blow," Erin whispered. "And when that happens, she admits all sorts of weird things. She did that when she told me she bribed Chad to take me out."

"She did what?" The revelation hit Riley like a cold slap. Their mother hadn't just been controlling and manipulative—she'd actually paid someone to date Erin. Riley felt sick thinking about how many of their life choices might have been influenced by Elizabeth's hidden machinations.

"Shush." Sandy waved her hand.

"*Alright, Mother. Let's talk specifics. You ran into some... financial difficulties. First with medical bills. Then, with that Ponzi scheme that I told you not to invest in but was willing to help you recover from.*"

A cool exhale. "*So, Parker's medical bills are now my moral failure? Is that it? I kept this family's head above water for years while your father was nowhere to be found and your little sister was off galivanting—*"

"*Leave her out of this,*" Grant snapped, the first real crack in his calm.

Riley sucked in a deep breath and let it out slowly.

"*Don't take that tone with me,*" Elizabeth said. "*You think I don't know what it costs to be married to a man who checked out emotionally? A man who preferred the company of people who looked down on me and then took my child from me? I made sacrifices. You should be grateful.*"

"*Grateful for the way you turned Erin and me against Dad? Against Ry?*" Grant asked. "*I allowed you to poison me against Bryson for years, letting me believe I was better than him and even thinking he was the sole reason Ry left town. But that's not even half as bad as what you've done to Erin.*

Taking her husband's side. A cheater. A man who treats her like she's not even worth his breath."

"That's enough," Elizabeth said. "I think you should leave now. I will not be spoken to like this in my own home."

"Oh, no, Mom. I'm not leaving yet." Grant let the words breathe like a fine bottle of wine. *"Here's the truth I need. Tell me you did it. Tell me you forged my name and took the money. Just me. No one else. I don't care if anyone else ever finds out the truth. This is between a mother and her son."*

"I can't tell you that because I didn't do it," she said flatly. "You did."

"Listen. It's real simple, Mom. I want to hear the truth. Then I'll go and pay the money back. We both know I've got the funds. I'll do my best to make excuses. It was a mistake. I'll come up with something that hopefully doesn't land me in prison. I'll do that for you, but only if you tell me the truth."

A whisper of a movement. A rustle of fabric. Riley pictured Elizabeth standing, hand to throat, every gesture calculated for maximum effect.

"I will not be threatened in my own home," she said. *"Not by my son."*

"I'm not threatening you, Mom." He lowered his voice. *"I'm offering you a way out."*

"A way out?" Elizabeth echoed, wary despite herself.

In the van, Sandy's eyes flicked to the FBI agent. "I can't believe he took that approach, and she's potentially caving."

"It's a win-win for you. Parker's name never has to make a headline," Grant said. *"Your spending never has to be tallied in court filings. You tell me what happened. I'll pay back the shortfall. I'll say I was sloppy. I'll take the profes-*

sional hit. You keep your garden club. Your charities. Your dinners. I carry it, no matter the consequences."

Erin's drew in a sharp breath. In the front of the van, the FBI agent murmured, "Jesus, what a fucking lifeboat."

"You'd wreck your reputation to spare me? Why?" Elizabeth asked.

"Because I still love you," he said simply. *"And because I can survive this. The kids can survive it. I figure I can cut a deal. I'm respected. It can't be that bad. But I need the truth to protect you and the rest of my family."*

"And if I say there is nothing to tell?" she asked. *"Because why would I, after all those hurtful things you just launched at me like a grenade?"*

"Because you need to know that I'm the one holding the cards here," Grant said. *"I'm the one with the power, not you."*

"You've never been very good at poker, because my truth isn't going to change," Elizabeth said.

"Come on, Grant. Go for the jugular," Sandy whispered.

"Okay. Then you need to know that when I walk out this door, I go to Sandy with everything I have." A measured beat. *"IP logs. Access times. The signature stamp you used."*

"You have no proof of that," Elizabeth snapped.

Grant didn't answer. He let the silence linger, patient as a tide. But seconds turned to minutes, and Elizabeth didn't bend.

"What's it going to be?" Grant asked.

Elizabeth's breath steadied. *"Why should I trust you?"*

"Because I'm your son, and I'm here offering you myself as the sacrificial lamb just like you trained me to do." His

tone gentled, the way someone would talk to the wounded. *"Tell me it was you. Tell me you panicked. Tell me you were scared. Tell me you didn't mean for any of this to happen."*

Something clinked—a ring against ceramic, maybe. *"If I say those words,"* she murmured, *"what happens to me?"*

"I do what I said. I cover what I can. I keep the kids out of the line of fire."

"You can't keep them out," she said, almost tender. *"Not anymore. You've let too many people in. You've always been soft that way."*

Sandy's jaw flexed, and Erin whispered, "She's spiraling."

Grant sighed. *"Last chance, Mom. Or I start talking to people you don't want me to, and this unravels in ways you can't recover from—ever. My kids? Gone to you. Erin's kids? You'll never see them again."*

"Fine," Elizabeth said, voice void of any emotion. There was nothing there. No mother. Not even a human. *"I signed your name. I moved pennies to cover dollars. And your damn father couldn't mind his own goddamn business for one day. That's all I asked of that man. Just one day to talk you into doing exactly this, but no, he had to go and meddle."* A sharp scrape—her chair, turning, maybe. Then heels clicking on the tile floor. *"He was always so righteous, always sure he knew best. I'm the one who built a life. I'm the one who kept our name clean. I am not going to let all of that crumble because a man with dirt under his nails decided to play auditor."*

Riley's throat closed. Erin's grip on her hand became a vise.

Grant's voice thinned with hurt. *"He raised us. He loved us."*

"He loved the idea of you," Elizabeth said. *"The version he could show those Boones over coffee. He loved his myths."*

"That was you, not Dad," Grant said, so softly Riley barely heard. *"And what about Dad?"*

"Not sure what you're asking," Elizabeth said.

"You killed him."

"How dare you."

"Guess what, Ma. I kept the mug you handed me that morning. Labeled 'Sean'—in your handwriting. I can walk it straight to Chief Sandy. She can have it tested for whatever you put in it."

In the van, Sandy didn't move. Erin's breath hitched. Riley's nails bit into her palm.

Inside the house, the quiet turned glacial.

"Are you playing with me? Are you planning on holding that over my head for the rest of my life?"

"Holy shit." Sandy shifted her gaze between Riley, Erin, and the FBI agent. "Did she just confess to killing Sean?"

"Not quite. Give him a little more time," the FBI agent said.

Grant coughed. *"No. I'm not messing with you. And you should know, Dad's death is being ruled a homicide. That one, I'm not taking the blame for."*

"You ungrateful little shit." Another breath. The brittle clatter of a spoon. *"Do you know what it is to carry a family on your back and be told your spine is unseemly? Do you know what it is to smile at people whose checks have more zeros than morals? Your father never understood what it cost—to be*

respectable." Her voice hardened to glass. *"So what if I asked you to deliver coffee? I did what was needed, and you're the one with the mug, not me. You handed your father a death sentence, not me."*

Erin slapped a hand over her mouth as a guttural groan escaped her lips.

Stunned, Riley sat there. Unable to move. Unable to say a word. She couldn't even breathe.

The FBI agent was already speaking into his mic, low and fast. Sandy's eyes had gone flint-hard.

Grant's exhale shuddered. *"I thank you for that honesty, Elizabeth."*

"You better hold up your end of this bargain," Elizabeth said.

"I think killing my father—my children's grandfather—has changed my perspective on that," Grant said, gentle as a benediction.

"You can't prove I did anything, so good luck with that."

"Get out of that house, Grant." No sooner did Sandy utter those words than Grant appeared in the walkway. He ran a hand through his curly hair as he jogged down the path, past his truck, and toward the van.

"Grant," Riley exclaimed as she bolted out of the side of the van, arms stretched wide, Erin one step behind.

"Get behind the vehicle," the FBI agent ordered.

Grant wrapped his strong arms around both women, ducking around the side of the van.

Riley peeked her head from the side and watched uniformed officers hurry up the path. Two detectives followed. The door opened, and Elizabeth emerged, hands behind her back, her face arranged into a portrait of wounded dignity that cracked when she saw the van.

Grant was the first to step into sight, followed by Erin. Riley pressed closer to her sister, squeezing her hand.

"You ungrateful monsters," Elizabeth spat, voice carrying, veneer gone. "Ingrates, every last one. Filthy traitors who don't deserve the name I gave you."

Grant looped his arms around his sisters, tugging them close. "As much as I feel vindicated, I still feel guilty. It doesn't change the fact that I was—"

"Stop it, Grant," Erin said sharply. "She said it. She admitted it. She fucking planned it, and it could've been you that day, too. One sip, and you could've died. So, I don't want to ever hear you say that again."

Grant took a step back. "Erin?"

"What?"

"You said the word, fuck."

"I know." Erin briefly covered her mouth then dropped her hand. "It felt good."

"Unfortunately, this isn't completely over," Grant sighed. "Our kids are going to have to deal with the fallout. And knowing Mom, she'll fight this. She'll do the whole trial thing. It will be a spectacle."

Riley swallowed and slid her fingers into his. He squeezed hard enough to hurt, as the cruiser turned the corner and disappeared.

"Maybe she won't. She can't stand being embarrassed," Riley whispered. The silence that followed felt different somehow—not the tense, walking-on-eggshells quiet they'd grown up with, but something safer. For the first time in her adult life, Riley felt like she was sitting with her actual siblings instead of the carefully molded versions their mother had shaped them into. Grant had found his back-bone, Erin had found her voice, and somehow, in the wreckage of their mother's lies, they'd found each other. The family she'd always wanted had been there all along—buried under layers of Elizabeth's manipulation. "But for now, we breathe. We love. We live."

Riley looked at her brother. The wire under his collar was just visible, a thin dark line against the shirt he'd ironed in the Boone kitchen that morning, because it had felt like a thing he could control.

Sandy came toward them from the other direction at a measured clip, talking low into her radio, the FBI agent a pace behind.

"You okay?" Sandy asked.

"Not exactly," Grant said. "But I will be."

They stood there together until the jacaranda shook loose a violet blossom that landed on the toe of Grant's shoe. He stared at it a long moment, then kicked it off gently into the gutter, like setting down a weight he couldn't carry anymore.

"Let's go home," Erin said, voice steadying. "Although, I guess home for me is the Boones until I can find a place."

Grant squeezed Riley's hand, and they walked toward Grant's SUV, her mother's house taunting her in the background.

"Poor Parker," Riley whispered. "I wonder if he knew."

"I wish I knew the answer to that," Grant said. "Sandy didn't want him in the house, so she called Parker's son, who picked him up for breakfast. If Parker did know, I can't have him in my life anymore. If he didn't, well, I'm not going to walk away from someone simply because he made a poor choice in life partners."

Riley slid into the backseat of her brother's SUV. So many things in her life were still uncertain. But she had Bryson—and she had her siblings—that was what mattered most.

Nineteen

Bryson paced on the front porch, pausing to stare down the stretch of road heading away from town, searching for Grant's SUV.

"Relax, son," his father said. "It's over."

Bryson shook his head. "We might have the answers we needed to clear Grant, but for them? This is far from over. They lost their father and now, their mother. It's going to take a long time for them to heal from this." Bryson pressed his hands on the railing and stared at the sky. "If ever."

His father stood next to him, resting a firm hand on his shoulder. "What those three brave souls did wasn't just about making sure Grant didn't go to prison for a crime he didn't commit. It was about rebuilding a family."

Bryson swallowed the bile that bubbled up his throat. He shifted his gaze, staring at his dad. His hero. The man he aspired to be like his entire life. "Maybe, but it doesn't make this any easier."

"No one can be prepared for something like what those three are going through, or the fallout it's created," his dad said. "However, what you need to remember is they went into this believing Elizabeth was not only capable of setting up her son... but also killing Sean. Given time, support, and the bond they're creating with each other, they will survive this."

Bryson ran his fingers through his hair and blew out a long breath. His chest tightened. "Old fears are resurfacing," he said softly.

"You're afraid Riley will run."

"A little," Bryson admitted. "Maybe not race off to parts unknown, but from me."

"She's just returned home, and a lot has happened." His father took him by the shoulders. "I understand you have regrets. That you look back to those years and think of all the things you could've done differently. Thing is, all that matters is that you're there for her now. Be the roots she can ground herself to. The love the two of you have for one another has always been... enough. But like grapes, the time has to be right. This is the right vintage for you and Riley."

In the distance, Grant's vehicle came into view. "I hope your interesting metaphor is accurate."

"I'll leave you alone." His dad slipped into the house as Bryson stood there with his heart beating like a caged animal.

Grant's shiny SUV rolled up the long drive, the sound cutting through the quiet that had settled over the Boone property. Bryson leaned against the porch rail, arms folded, waiting as patiently as possible. This wasn't about him.

The sun had started its climb toward the center of the sky, casting the yard in a wash of gold that felt almost too good for the emotions swirling in his gut.

The rear passenger door opened first—Riley stepping out, shoulders squared like she'd had to brace them into place. Erin followed, exhaustion carved into her expression. Grant rounded the hood, his jaw tight, eyes shadowed. For a moment, Bryson wasn't sure which of them was holding the others up.

"I'm not sure I even know what to say," Bryson said when they reached the steps.

Grant met his gaze, stretching out his hand. "Probably the hardest thing I've ever done," he said quietly.

Bryson pushed his arm aside and pulled him in for a hug. It lasted only a few seconds. Strong. Stoic. Two men, letting go of years of... he had no idea. And forging a new brotherhood that couldn't ever be broken.

"Thank you." Grant took a step back. "Not sure any of us could've gotten through this without you and your family."

"As your dad would say... It's what the family we choose does."

Grant chuckled. "When Kelly and I got married, he told me that the most important family is often the ones we pick and that I picked a good one with her." Grant swiped his hands across his face. "He was right. I think he was always right, I was just too damn..." He blew out a puff of air.

"Don't do that to yourself." Erin eased closer to Grant, resting her hand on his back. "Through all the ups and downs. The fights. The craziness. He loved us. All of us. And he was proud of you."

Grant looped an arm around each sister. "He'd be most

proud of this. Of us. We're good now. You know that, right?"

Erin nodded first, quick and certain.

He pulled her in for a hug—brief, almost fierce—before turning to Riley. She hesitated for half a beat, then stepped into his arms. Her chin trembled against his shoulder, but she held it together until he let her go. "I love you, big brother."

"Right back at you, baby sis," Grant said. "I've got to get to the station. Sandy needs my statement. I'll call when I'm done."

Erin touched his arm. "We'll be here."

Grant flicked his gaze back to Bryson—one more silent acknowledgment—and then turned away. The SUV rolled out of the drive, tires kicking up dust as it disappeared around the bend.

Erin exhaled a breath that seemed to take the last of her strength with it. "The kids?" she questioned."

"Walking the vines with Devon," Bryson said. "Kelly couldn't send them off to school."

"I'm glad. I just want to go hug them. No idea how or what to tell them, but for now, I just need to see my babies." She raced down the steps and around the side of the house without another word.

That left Riley standing on the porch, hands hanging at her sides. Her gaze tracked the empty stretch of road where Grant had gone, and for a moment, she didn't seem to notice Bryson was still there.

"Ry," he said softly.

Her head turned, and the raw, unguarded truth of the day shown in her eyes. The strain of holding in too much for too long. The sorrow of losing both parents. The deep grief etched in her dark blue irises.

He opened his arms. She hesitated for only a breath before crossing the space between them. When she stepped into him, it wasn't a graceful fall but a gradual surrender—her forehead pressing against his collarbone, her fingers curling lightly into the back of his shirt.

At first, she held herself rigid, like she could still keep some of it in. Then her knees softened, her weight leaning into him, and the first shaky exhale feathered against his chest.

He lifted her into his arms. "I've got you," he murmured, carrying her all the way to the back of the house, where his mother quickly opened the porch door for them before quietly retreating inside.

The ceiling fan swirled warm air around them. He settled onto the loveseat, its new green cushions cradling them both. She curled into him, knees tucked, her cheek pressed over his heart.

He didn't speak right away, just traced slow circles along her arm with his thumb, the rhythm matching the steady beat of his breath. As she cried, the tension bled out of her, leaving only the tremors of release.

"It's okay now," he said, his voice low.

Her answer was a quiet, humorless laugh mixed with a sob. "Nothing about this is okay."

"No," he agreed. "But you've got Grant. You've got Erin. And you've got me." He tipped his head, brushing his lips over her hair. "That's not changing."

Her fingers gently twisted in the fabric of his shirt. "It

feels different now. Knowing they're... mine again. That we're us again."

"You deserve that. You all do."

They sat there in the hush of the fading morning, listening to the birds' chorus in the vineyard beyond. She shifted just enough to tip her head back and meet his gaze. "I don't know what comes next."

"You don't have to," he said. "All you need to know is you're not facing it alone."

Her throat moved as she swallowed. "I've lived my entire adult life from a distance. As if I were living it in the shadows of home. Not really letting myself be part of it, but never really letting go."

"Now you can have it. You can reach out and touch it. Be part of all that you've wanted."

"But my dad... he's gone. And that's left a hole so deep. And my mom, she took that. Stole it from all of us."

"I know." He kissed her temple. "But you never have to go through anything in the shadows again. It's not going to be easy. It's going to hurt. It's going to take time to heal, and it will leave a scar. The difference is, you won't have to face any of this without the love and support you've craved for the last twelve years."

For a long beat, neither of them moved. Then she lowered her forehead to his jaw, closing her eyes. He held her tighter, letting that promise rest between them without needing to be spoken again.

Whatever storms were still ahead, they'd face them together. And for now, that was enough.

Twenty

TWO WEEKS LATER

The late-afternoon sun spilled gold across the Boone lawn, the light rich and warm as honey. It turned the glasses of wine into glowing rubies, the laughter of children into something that felt almost sacred. From her place on the back porch, Riley could see everyone—Grant crouching in the grass to listen to Willa's animated story about a "butterfly that chased her." Kelly tackled Randy as he raced with a football tucked under his arm. Erin kneeled to tie Nathan's shoelace while he tried to dart off to catch Bryson.

Erin's hair caught the sunlight. The light brown shade shimmered warmly. It was stunning. It suited her far better than the blonde she'd been sporting. And with the new look came confidence. Riley couldn't be prouder of her sister.

"Hey, squirt. Watch where you're going." Jessica barely looked up from her cell as Willa bumped into her, spilling her soda. So far, today, Jessica had rolled her eyes in preteen boredom at least ten times.

But that boredom was about to turn into either a shriek of laughter or something dangerous as Devon and Mateo snuck up on her with two nearly bursting water balloons in their hands.

Riley covered her mouth, holding her breath in anticipation.

First, Mateo went in for the kill.

Splat.

Jessica stood frozen, mouth gaping open, eyes wide with shock as Devon crept up behind her.

Another splat.

For a second, everyone stilled, gazing at her, waiting for teenage angst to explode. Finally, she turned. "O.M.G., Mateo. You're toast. And Uncle Devon, payback is you know what." She took off running, and somehow the world had simply righted itself.

Riley sighed, wrapping one arm around her middle as she waved to Mateo. She hadn't expected him to show up to her father's funeral, but she shouldn't have been surprised. That man had turned out to be the best thing she'd collected from her travels. If someone could collect people.

And Bryson had the biggest man crush on him—it was pathetic.

He glanced her direction as he leaned forward, resting the football on the ground, getting ready to take a snap.

Chuckling, she covered her mouth as Mateo and Jessica slinked across the yard with more water balloons at the ready.

Hasley snapped pictures from the sidelines, trying to get the best candid shots. Brea and Ashley stood off to the side, sipping wine and chatting while Willa occasionally darted between them, calling to her father to watch, and to Hasley to make sure she got the shot.

The air smelled faintly of grilled food from the caterers, the bite of red wine, and the sweetness of whatever dessert the kitchen had tucked away for later.

It was loud, messy, and alive. And for the first time since she'd stepped foot back in Stone Bridge, Riley thought—this was home.

She let her gaze drift beyond the yard, over the gentle swell of the vineyard as it rolled toward the horizon. The vines shimmered in the light breeze, the leaves flickering between sun and shadow. She could almost see her father there, moving down the rows with his careful, unhurried gait, running his fingertips along the leaves as though memorizing their shape. She could almost hear the tune he whistled when he thought no one was listening.

Memories of Walter and her dad crashed into her mind. They'd discuss their fantasy football picks with enthusiastic voices, while she and Bryson followed them around in the early mornings because there was nothing better than a stroll in the vines with her favorite people.

The ache rose swift and hot, but it wasn't the sharp pain of loss anymore—it was something rounder, deeper. The feeling of being rooted, of belonging. Of knowing there were no longer ghosts lingering between the grapes.

The sliding door behind her whispered open. Walter stepped out, his frame casting a long shadow in the gold light. In his hands, he carried a framed photograph, the kind of old wood-and-glass frame that had weight in both heft and meaning.

"That scene out there looks like trouble." He waved his free hand. "And aching knees."

She chuckled. "Bryson has so much dirt on his *white* shirt, it will never come out."

"And it looks like his brother is covered with grass stains. Not much has changed over the years with those two. Same squabbles. Same brotherly love."

"Same razor-sharp tongues and dirty jokes."

Walter shook his head. "They get their sense of humor from their mother." He raised a finger to his lips. "Don't tell Brea I said that."

"Never." She smiled. "I'm glad for this moment," Riley said quietly. "Your eulogy..." Her voice caught for a second. "It was perfect. My dad would've loved it."

Walter's eyes softened, his voice deep and sure. "It was an honor. Your dad was a good man. And one of my oldest and dearest friends. Much like you and Bryson used to get under our feet sometimes, we did that to our fathers." He let out a long breath, rubbing his temple. "You should know that Harlan has agreed to be Parker's attorney."

"Why does he need one?"

"Legally, he can't be forced to testify against his wife," Walter said. "And from the two conversations I've had with Parker, all he knew was that they were in financial ruin and that his wife was working on a strategy with her son to fix it."

"That sounds shady."

"I think my good friend Harlan is keeping things from me." Walter lowered his chin. "But he can't break client-attorney privilege, so this one is gonna have to play out in the courts since your mother is still screaming her innocence."

"I'm worried about bail," Riley said.

"It'll be a hefty sum. Unless Chad decides to cover the bond, I'm not sure she'll be out anytime soon." Walter squeezed her shoulder with his free hand. "Let the court system work while you enjoy a little reprieve from it all." He extended the frame toward her. "This has been hanging in my office for years. I thought you might want it."

She took it, careful not to smudge the glass, and the sight inside stole her breath. Two men—her grandfather and Bryson's—stood side by side in a stretch of vineyard, the earth around them still raw and newly turned. A single vine separated them, fragile and defiant, near a wine barrel with a bottle balanced on top like a crown jewel. Each man had an arm slung around the other's shoulders, their free hands raising glasses in mid-toast.

Her throat tightened. "This is... amazing. They look so young. When was it taken?"

"I was a small child. And that bottle," Walter said, leaning in, "was from the very first vintage Stone Bridge Winery ever produced."

Riley stared at the photograph as though she could hear the murmur of those long-ago voices, the creak of the barrel, the wind slipping between young vines.

"The Boones have always been tied to this land," Walter continued. "And so has your family. Your grandfather helped plant those vines. You're as much a part of this as we are."

She swallowed against the ache rising in her chest. It was

one thing to know her family's history. It was another to see it—proof captured in a single, sunlit frame.

The children's laughter drifted toward them, and she glanced back over the yard. Willa and Jessica had roped Randy into some game involving long loops around the tables, squealing whenever Bryson got close enough to "tag" them.

"I spoke to the family who owns your old house next door," Walter said casually.

Her head snapped toward him. "What? Why would you do that?"

"I believe I told you, if it went on the market, I'd buy it. But I wanted to find out if they had any plans. Turns out, they'd decided to sell in a few months." He smiled faintly. "I made them an offer they couldn't refuse."

She blinked at him. "Walter—"

"I thought Erin might want to rent it," he said simply, as though it were the most natural thing in the world.

Her lips parted, but no words came out. Emotion swelled like a gathering storm, and she had to blink against it. "That's... incredibly generous."

He shook his head. "It's not generosity. It's right. You're family. Always have been."

The truth in his voice was almost her undoing. She wanted to thank him in a way that would matter, but before she could, he squeezed her shoulder and disappeared back into the kitchen, leaving her with the photograph clutched in her hands like it was a message from beyond.

The screen door banged open, and Bryson jogged up the steps, a sheen of sweat across his brow, half-dried dirt covering his skin—and clothing. "Hey," he said, catching her around the waist. "You okay?"

She pressed the frame to her chest as she leaned into him. "Nothing's wrong. Absolutely nothing."

His lips brushed her temple, the kiss grounding her. "Good. Because I love you."

Her smile was wide and certain. "I love you, too."

He pulled back, a mischievous glint in his eyes. "So... I've got an idea."

She gave him a mock-groan. "I'm not moving in with you. Now that the funeral is over, I'm going to find a small apartment in town. Once I find a job, that is."

"I have a solution to the employment situation. Something flexible, since you'll be helping Erin with the kids when she's working in the tasting room."

She tilted her head. "I'm almost scared to ask."

"You," he said, grinning now, "are going to be the new social media manager for Stone Bridge Winery."

She laughed, the sound catching even herself off guard. "I don't know the first thing about social media. I've never used it before."

"Then you'll learn. Jessica even offered to help you. You've got the personality for it, and God knows we could use one."

She shook her head, still laughing. "You're ridiculous."

"Maybe." His grin softened into something more tender. "Now, it might be easier if you'd continue living here with me."

"Not happening," she said, though her voice was more fond than firm.

"I'm not going to stop asking." He leaned in and kissed

her, slow and sure. "But we've got time." He pressed his lips against her mouth in a passionate kiss that caught the attention of half the backyard. Whistles. Shouts. A clank of a wine glass.

"Mommy! Look! Are Uncle Bryson and Auntie Ry gonna get married?" Willa asked.

Bryson pulled back and winked. "Now that's—"

She covered his mouth. "Like you said—time."

As Bryson's kiss faded, and the sounds of family drifted back in,Riley looked down at the photograph again. Her grandfather's hand rested on Bryson's grandfather's shoulder, two men bound by soil, sun, and hope. Everything rooted here—the vines, the memories, the messy beautiful tangle of family—had grown strong. Looking out at the people she loved against the backdrop of rolling vineyards, Riley felt the truth of it in her bones. They'd done more than just make it through. They'd found their way home.

In that moment, she knew that someday, she and Bryson would make their promises permanent. All those years of regret had transformed into something precious. Love had ripened in the shadows of sorrow, and this vintage —their vintage—was worth the wait.

Acknowledgments

Writing is often a solitary process. I spend countless hours in my office, alone, crafting stories and creating people who don't exist. However, nothing happens in a vacuum, and one of my favorite things to do is research. This is where I often find myself going down strange rabbit holes, and search engines often become confused by my odd patterns.

Anyone who knows me well knows that I enjoy a good glass of wine. My husband and I visited Napa Valley, and I immediately fell in love with the small-town vibes, the rich history, and, of course, the wine. I knew I wanted to write another series set on a Vineyard. So, I set out doing some recon, looking into all the places I could set my story: Washington, Oregon, the Finger Lakes, and even Vermont.

A funny thing happened when I searched for small, family-owned vineyards in Vermont. A name from my hometown appeared. But I thought, nah, that can't be him. So, I continued my search, moving it to California. Once again, his name appeared, this time in the Santa Cruz area, so I clicked on the link. Sure enough, it was the same Bradley Brown I knew from my little town outside of Rochester, New York, where we both grew up.

I reached out, not even sure if Bradley would remember

me. It had been about forty years. But that same day, I heard back, and we began a series of email exchanges and a few phone calls, during which Bradley was kind enough to answer all my questions about owning a vineyard, making wine, and even some bizarre questions that had more to do with fiction than reality.

I learned so much from Bradley and I can't thank him enough for his time. While this book is complete fiction, the information I gathered from those interviews helped make the story and the characters come to life.

The wines from Big Basin Vineyard have become some of our favorites. I highly recommend them. You can order from their shop online, and if you are in the Santa Cruz area you can visit their Estate Vineyard as well as their Tasting Room & Tapas Bar.

About Jen Talty

Jen Talty is the *USA Today* Bestselling Author of Contemporary Romance, Romantic Suspense, and Paranormal Romance. In the fall of 2020, her short story was selected and featured in a 1001 Dark Nights Anthology.

Regardless of the genre, her goal is to take you on a ride that will leave you floating under the sun with warmth in your heart. She writes stories about broken heroes and heroines who aren't necessarily looking for romance, but in the end, they find the kind of love books are written about :).

She first started writing while carting her kids to one hockey rink after the other, averaging 170 games per year between 3 kids in 2 countries and 5 states. Her first book, IN TWO WEEKS was originally published in 2007. In 2010 she helped form a publishing company (Cool Gus Publishing) with *NY Times* Bestselling Author Bob Mayer where she ran the technical side of the business through 2016.

Jen is currently enjoying the next phase of her life...the empty nester! She and her husband reside in Jupiter, Florida.

Grab a glass of vino, kick back, relax, and let the romance roll in...

Sign up for my Newsletter (https://dl.bookfunnel.com/82gm8b9k4y) where I often give away free books before publication.

Join my private Facebook group (https://www.facebook.com/groups/191706547909047/) where I post exclusive excerpts and discuss all things murder and love!

Never miss a new release. Follow me on Amazon:amazon.com/author/jentalty

And on Bookbub: bookbub.com/authors/jen-talty

Shattered Dreams
An Inconvenient Flame
The Wedding Driver
Clear Blue Sky
Blue Moon
Before the Storm

NY STATE TROOPER SERIES (also set in the Adirondacks!)

In Two Weeks
Dark Water
Deadly Secrets
Murder in Paradise Bay
To Protect His own
Deadly Seduction
When A Stranger Calls
His Deadly Past
The Corkscrew Killer

First Responders: A spin-off from the NY State Troopers series
Playing With Fire
Private Conversation
The Right Groom
After The Fire
Caught In The Flames
Chasing The Fire

Legacy Series
Dark Legacy
Legacy of Lies

Secret Legacy

Emerald City
  Investigate Away
  Sail Away
  Fly Away
  Flirt Away
  Anchor Away

Hawaii Brotherhood Protectors
  Waylen Unleashed
  Bowie's Battle

Colorado Brotherhood Protectors
  Fighting For Esme
  Defending Raven
  Fay's Six
  Darius' Promise

Yellowstone Brotherhood Protectors
  Guarding Payton
  Wyatt's Mission
  Corbin's Mission

Candlewood Falls
  Rivers Edge
  The Buried Secret
  Its In His Kiss
  Lips Of An Angel
  Kisses Sweeter than Wine
  A Little Bit Whiskey

Shielding Jolene
Shielding Aalyiah
Shielding Laine
Shielding Talullah
Shielding Maribel
Shielding Daisy

The Men of Thief Lake
Rekindled
Destiny's Dream

Federal Investigators
Jane Doe's Return
The Butterfly Murders

THE AEGIS NETWORK
The Sarich Brother
The Lighthouse
Her Last Hope
The Last Flight
The Return Home
The Matriarch

Aegis Network: Jacksonville Division
A SEAL's Honor
Talon's Honor
Arthur's Honor
Rex's Honor
Kent's Honor
Buddy's Honor
Duncan's Honor

Garth's Honor
Hawke's Honor

Aegis Network Short Stories
Max & Milian
A Christmas Miracle
Spinning Wheels
Holiday's Vacation

The Brotherhood Protectors
Out of the Wild
Rough Justice
Rough Around The Edges
Rough Ride
Rough Edge
Rough Beauty

The Brotherhood Protectors
The Saving Series
Saving Love
Saving Magnolia
Saving Leather

Hot Hunks
Cove's Blind Date Blows Up
My Everyday Hero – Ledger
Tempting Tavor
Malachi's Mystic Assignment
Needing Neor

Holiday Romances

A Christmas Getaway
Alaskan Christmas
Whispers
Christmas In The Sand

Heroes & Heroines on the Field
Taking A Risk
Tee Time

A New Dawn
The Blind Date
Spring Fling
Summers Gone
Winter Wedding
The Awakening
Fated Moons

The Collective Order
The Lost Sister
The Lost Soldier
The Lost Soul
The Lost Connection
The New Order

www.ingramcontent.com/pod-product-compliance
Lightning Source LLC
Chambersburg PA
CBHW011114100726
47898CB00011B/3079